THE DOOM OF QADIRRA

The Last Shadow Epic, Book Seven

by

AJ Cooper

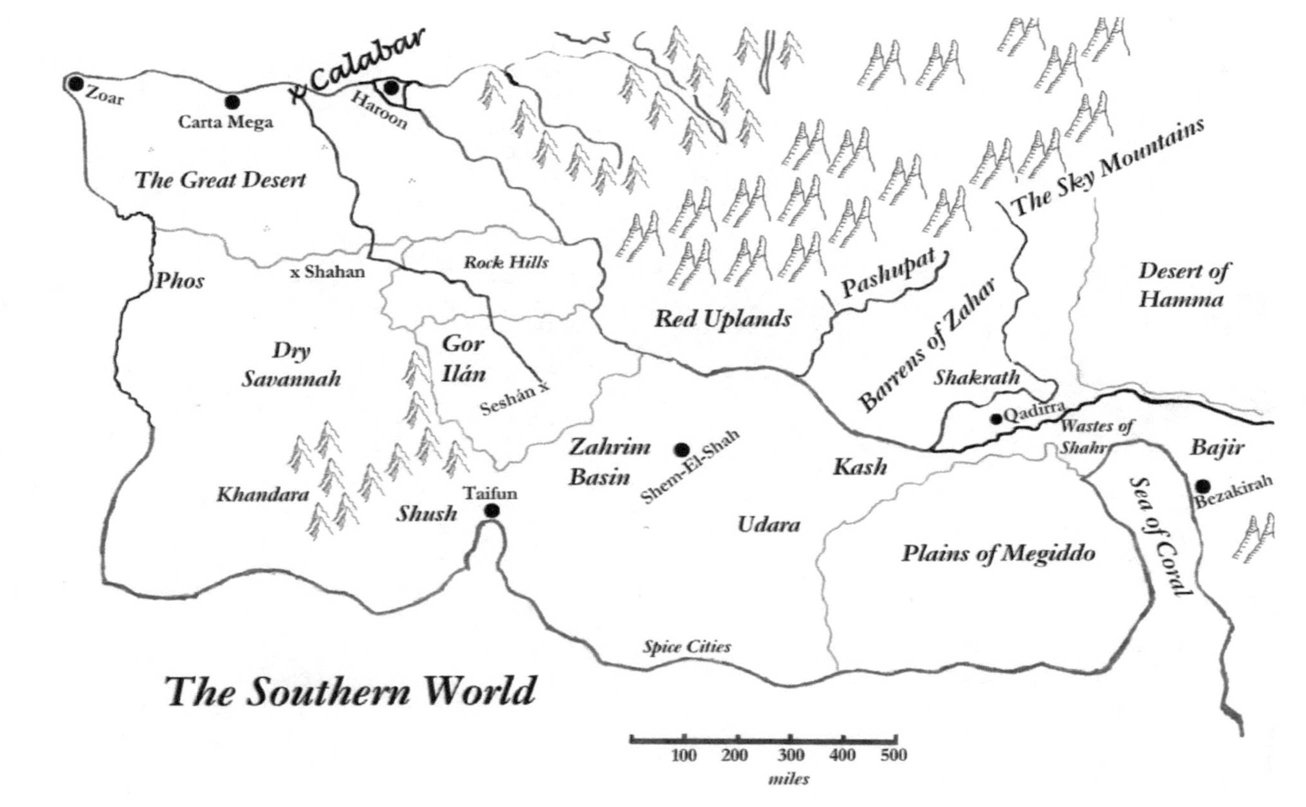
Zoar
Carta Mega
Calabar
Haroon
The Great Desert
Phos
x Shahan
Rock Hills
The Sky Mountains
Desert of Hamma
Pashupat
Red Uplands
Barrens of Zahar
Shakrath
Qadirra
Wastes of Shahr
Bajir
Bezakirah
Dry Savannah
Gor Ilán
Seshán x
Zahrim Basin
Shem-El-Shah
Kash
Khandara
Shush
Taifun
Udara
Plains of Megiddo
Sea of Coral
Spice Cities
The Southern World
100 200 300 400 500
miles

Chapter One: A Port Called Calabar

When *The Storm Skipper* broached shore, Reev Nax couldn't believe his eyes.

Ivan Xandrast had called their next stop a "port" on the Empire's southern coast, but all Reev could see was a desert valley between two mesas, a lonely dock that had seen better days, a well, and a building far in the distance.

This was the "port called Calabar" that Xan had told them about, the stopping off point where the party could resume their journey to *Naron Da*. Despite Reev's disappointment, it was one step closer to their goal, to reaching the Dark Land, called *Naron Da*, where, prophecies said, he would tread Seymus under his feet.

As the sailors tied *The Storm Skipper* to the dock, the party began to filter out. The four of them — Reev Nax, Fortunato, and Xan, all humans, and Wrinn, an elf — quickly gathered their packs and luggage and hurried onto the dock, amid the burning desert sun.

Next came their two Elvish horses, Cobalt — belonging to Reev — his tan coat glistening in the sun, his bony horns protruding from the fur on his head, then Asté, belonging to Wrinn, silver with a white mane. She shook her head as she trotted into the scorching heat.

Last of all came Tyra Jade, Fortunato's black wolf, her tail wagging, her red eyes gleaming with excitement.

They made an account of their belongings. Reev looked to the west, into the endless desert horizon of scrub and dust and dry rock, and saw that the sun was dipping low in the horizon. Dressed in a loin cloth, his chest bare to the sun's scorching rays, he was less protected, but it was about night.

"You said there was an inn here," Fortunato said to Xan. "We won't travel the road by night."

In the waning light, Xan nodded his head. A dark figure he looked, with black hair and a thick black beard. He was dressed in a kirtle far too thick for the desert, and yet he was their guide. Behind his back was his double-sided sword, called a butterfly blade, a pole with two sabers fixed to either end.

"There is an inn," Xan said. "I cannot vouch for it, however. I never stayed there."

~

They ventured beyond the well, down a road leading through the sand and scrub. Reev realized the building he had seen in the distance was the inn that Xan had spoken of.

As they walked, a black cloud of bats buzzed by in the twilight. It was hot, so hot — hot enough to sap one's strength and soul. But Reev would carry on.

As they pushed on ahead, through the scorching twilight, Reev could see that the inn was vast, comprised of many sections along a central courtyard. It was faced with plaster that the desert sands had painted yellow. At its fore was a sign:

The Twisted Tree Roadhouse

Behind him, Reev could see, the sailors from *The Storm Skipper* were approaching the inn as well, from the distance.

~

The inn had a cantina facing the courtyard. As Fortunato, Wrinn, Xan and Reev sat quietly, nibbling at a spicy mushroom-and-chicken dish and sipping wine, the sailors walked in and began to eat and drink as well.

"You know," Wrinn said softly, "they're drug runners."

Reev looked at him askance.

"I looked underneath the crates of cloth they were supposedly carrying," Wrinn continued. "I saw a few packets of Haroon spice peeking out of them."

Fortunato made a motion to speak quietly. His eyes then inclined to the sky.

In the dying throes of sunlight, the firmament had changed, and no longer was it red and gold, but clouds had moved in, dark clouds.

"Can it rain in the desert?" said Reev.

"It rains, once or twice every year," Fortunato said, "but when it does, it's a deluge. Quick! Let's get to our rooms."

~

And as the sun set, and the deluge began, and lightning flashed, and thunder rolled, the four retired to their rooms. Reev and Wrinn boarded together, Fortunato slept alone, and Xan took a room at the end of the row. As they shut and locked their doors, they did not see six dark shapes on six dark beasts approach the inn from the desert sands.

~

When the dark figure knocked on Reev and Wrinn's door, the two had not yet gone to bed. They had busied themselves with a game of backgammon, between wondering at the height of the room's ceiling and the fine furnishings. The dark figure knocked again, and waited, then moved on with a hiss.

When the dark figure moved to Fortunato's room, Fortunato was sound asleep — and that was quite unlike him — exhausted from the journey, and from what the sailors had slipped into his drink with intent to rob him.

When the dark figure moved to Xan's room, Xan sat up, and felt a frozen hand of fear clutch his heart, for he had sensed this figure before, and not long ago, he had been its thrall. The dark figure knocked, and Xan stood up to his feet, alongside his bed. He drew near.

"Room service," the dark figure said.

"No — no," Xan said. "You're not room service. You're — "

"Xan," the dark figure's voice was like a whisper that carried at the volume of a shout. "Is that you?"

"No, no," Xan said, "Ivan Xandrast is staying in room —" He struggled to remember where the captain of *The Storm Skipper* had been staying. "Room 18."

The dark figure passed him by then, and five other dark figures followed him.

Lightning flashed outside Xan's windows, and he shut them. He said prayers under his breath that the dark figures would not return.

~

The next day, a sandstorm raged over Calabar, blocking out all sight. But news reached them even then, as they waited out the storm — a massacre in room 18, blood everywhere, and cuts it seemed no human was capable of.

Fortunato, Reev, Xan and Wrinn knew then they were being hunted.

Chapter Two: Eastward

Ambrass watched as her cousins Julian and Anton slashed with their machetes through the jungle brush. They had been traveling days down a little-used road amid the rainforests of Kash.

Ambrass had seen what the natives called "an old man of the forest," an orange ape hanging from tree branches. She had spotted more snakes than she ever wished to see in her life.

Her fellow gypsies called her their queen, and she was their leader, now that her husband Gaius had passed away. Before Gaius died, he had told her where he was taking him. He had remembered a tale his grandfather told him, that Vharat, the homeland of the gypsies, was directly south of the Land of Sur. And so, if they survived the jungle trail, and made it so far, Ambrass thought they had a good chance of finding their home, and at last reaching a permanent refuge.

It seemed so long ago, the day the gypsies departed their former refuge, the city of Galiope in the far north. It seemed so long ago, she had left the life she loved behind, and with her people traveled south in colorful wagons. Here they were — in the far southern parts of the world, now close — if Gaius could be believed — to their homeland.

Gaius's word, a tale from their grandfather, was all they had. They had that, and the Empire's tacit permission to traverse the Southern World, for Ambrass had made her case to the emperor, and he had consented.

Julian and Anton were sweating heavily, but as they made progress on their wagons, it was becoming clearer that the rainforests were beginning to diminish, as the ground ascended. The air was sweltering, but it was growing less humid. They had traversed many miles, and passed through many dangers, yet they had remained alive, and they were pressing on.

~

The thick greenness was gone behind them as they ascended a high ridge, to what appeared to be a plateau. Far in the distance was a river, and beyond the river black silty ground. The ground was now flat, as the wagons one by one broke free of the jungle terrain. Ambrass saw in the distance what looked like a road, or what had once been a road. This road she began to follow, whipping at her horses, and the other wagons, following her lead, began to speed on.

Where were they? Ambrass knew they were headed due east, and if the continued east, they would reach the Land of Sur — and from there, Vharat.

So a tale from Gaius's grandfather had said.

"Ambrass!" called out Julian in the wagon behind her. "This doesn't look right. Past Kash is Megiddo… This isn't Megiddo."

But they were headed due east, and Ambrass was their queen. How could they go wrong, if they were headed due east?

"Just follow me!" Ambrass said, feeling confident, and having a strange sense her confidence was not misplaced.

More or less, Ambrass had begun following the remnants of the road as it took twists and turns and at last followed the waters of the large black river. Eastwards, eastwards they traveled, and Ambrass felt she could taste Vharat on the wind, on the water, the stories of the wine on the leaves like dew, honey dripping down trees like sap.

At last, they had come to another bend in the road, across a bridge it seemed had been recently built or repaired.

"Ambrass!" Anton called out two wagons behind. "I don't think this is the right route… we're supposed to be in Megiddo."

But the sound of the wheels grating on the road soothed

Ambrass, and they were headed east. They had not strayed far north or south. How could she have been led wrong?

"Trust me, Anton!" Ambrass shouted.

And she flicked the reins, and the horses stormed over the bridge, into a black-soiled plain.

~

There were irrigation canals stretching beyond the river, and along the canals, plots of wheat now gold for the harvest. There were workers amid the fields, wearing straw hats, but Ambrass recalled the word of consent she had received from Emperor Verrus, and that she did not have to fear the hand of the Empire intervening.

The workers in the fields paused and took note of them as the train of gypsy wagons crossed over the bridge, and entered the plain, headed along the road as it took them east.

The plain was vast, and the canals penetrated deep. Underneath a scorching Sextil sun, the gypsies continued to make progress.

Ambrass noted that in places there were bubbling pools of tar, and in places stone ruins. Ambrass had no idea where they were, but she was certain they were near Sur, that their happy ending in Vharat had never been closer. At the thought, she smiled, and it was the first time she had smiled since Gaius passed on.

In the thick heat, the air wavered. Midges and mosquitoes bit at her constantly. The sun had arisen, and fixed high in the sky, when down the road came the sound of thunder.

No — hooves.

When Ambrass saw the warhorses, dressed head to hoof in scale-mail armor, and the riders on the horses, completely covered in glittering chainmail, ins helmets with chainmail coifs, heaving spears in their hands, Ambrass felt for the first time a pang of fear, a pang of worry she had made the wrong choice.

That inkling only grew as the chief of the riders babbled, at first in a foreign tongue, and then trying something new, the common Imperial tongue — "Who intrudes upon the domain of the God Manifest, King of Kings Artabanas?"

Ambrass was bewildered, baffled. "The Emperor Verrus has allowed us safe passage through his lands," she said. "We do not intend to linger. We are going to our homeland, south of Sur."

"Madness!" shouted the chief rider. "The *lugal* empire holds no sway here. Here the King of Kings, God Manifest, Beloved-of-His-Father, rules from his eternal throne. The penalty for trespass is death, but I think the King of Kings may profit more in keeping you alive. The Sea Raiders will pay a high price for a face so comely."

"We will go back the way we came," said Ambrass.

Beneath the helmet, Ambrass was sure the chief rider was smiling a sadistic smile.

"No," said the chief rider. "You will fetch a nice weight in silver and gold in the markets of Karthoon… You will add to our coffers, as we defeat the *lugal* empire."

"An audience with your king!" Ambrass said. "I beg of you!"

"Be careful what you wish for," said the chief rider. "Nonetheless, it is a custom of the Fharese people to not deliver justice without the King of Kings' assent… you and you alone may visit before the God Manifest, and plead your case. Your people, however, will be held in captivity until such time as justice is dispensed."

Chapter Three: One in a Billion

The morning after the sandstorm, Xan led Fortunato, Wrinn and Reev to the trailhead. They began their journey, then, the journey they hoped would take them to *Naron Da*, and the Dark One's defeat.

~

Bran was one in a million.

Or was it one in a hundred million, or three thousand times a million?

That was what his mother insisted to him, the miracle of his birth. A miracle — that was what the town preacher had called it, that a rokahn having fallen upon his mother, had not produced a stillborn child.

A miracle? For Bran, and others from his hometown in Redman Territory, there was enough room to doubt.

Bran knew, because of the rokahn blood flowing through his veins, the gods could never love him, that he could never see Heaven. As for his life in the mortal realm, he could easily go between the rokahn world and the human world, and not miss a beat. Part of him wished to live among the dark-holds and shifting war-bands of his half-siblings. The other part of him was happy to be here, amid the stone towers and the grand bazaar of Shahan. But here, he would never be quite accepted.

He was far taller than any human, and more muscular. The beginnings of horns emerged from his forehead. As for his skill with the blade, the fusion of the two bloodlines had made him better than anyone he knew, rokahn or human.

At his side was his trusty kukri-knife he had taken from a Pashupat mountain guide. It had not yet failed him.

He was here at Shahan to find a new job, a new war to participate in, a new target to kill. War or killing was his trade, and many would pay a pretty denara to have someone extinguished at the end of Bran's kukri-knife.

And so he lingered at the outskirts of the bazaar, waiting for someone to come up to him, and for a notice to catch his eye at the end of the stone posts. But as he stood in the blazing afternoon sun, the raging desert heat that his half-rokahn body could handle but which humans could not bear except dressed up in white clothing, something else beckoned him.

Or someone.

There were six figures approaching Bran, garbed all in black. At their sides were an assortment of blades, colored blackish-gray. In the hands of the chief of them was a sword. As the chief of them stepped near to Bran, he saw he was almost as tall as Bran, and that beyond a black hood was what seemed to be an iron mask.

Beyond that mask, Bran could not make out eyes. It was just an iron mask, and infinite darkness behind.

"Bran," the man's voice was an icy winter wind in the Pashupat Plateau, enough to make a less cold-hearted man's heart freeze. "We have a task for you."

"I demand a high price for my work," Bran told the masked man, as he drew out his kukri-knife, "but I do good work, and I do it to completion."

"We are men of power," said the man in black, "but we have limitations. Doors and gates we cannot enter without invitation. But to those who invite us, we can lay them waste.

"Doors and gates are open to you, though, Bran. We wish for the deaths of three men, and the capture of another. Four *lugals* travel down the Great Taifun Road. One you will find, wearing a loin cloth and having draped a coin necklace over his chest. Bind him and bring him here.

"We can offer you gold enough to purchase a kingdom for yourself, if you do it well."

And Bran did not trust the man in black, nor did he like him, but could he resist such a price? He had a feeling, if he said no, the man would reach into Bran's chest with an icy hand and rip out his heart.

~

Days had passed through the desert, and the road, winding through scrub in view of dry mesas, followed the path of springs and pools, along which small towns had grown up. Reev fought thirst all day, passing down the road, draped now in a white shawl to ward off the worst of the sun.

He had not expected the road to *Naron Da* to be easy. And it had not been.

In the day, it was so hot that the stones along the road were like white hot coals, but at night, it was cold enough that blankets were required, whenever Fortunato set up their tent. Yet as Sextil passed into Harona, they had made serious progress, and there were signs the desert was waning — stretches of tall grass rather than scrub.

And Xan at last said, "We are leaving the Empire de facto and de jure, and entering the Empire de facto only."

"What do you mean?" Reev said.

Wrinn behind him was panting in the heat.

"The Empire does not technically control this land," said Xan, "but all the satraps and kings are puppets on the emperor's string. So it is, throughout all the Southern World."

"You mean there is no land that the Empire does not control?" Wrinn said.

But Reev had a strange feeling there was a pocket of resistance somewhere. Somewhere far away, there was a land not under

Emperor Verrus's thumb.

Chapter Four: The Most Beloved

On the back of a horse, her hands bound, Ambrass saw amid the flatness and the bubbling pools of tar, a break in the monotony. Under an ochre sky were the towering walls of a city.

The walls seemed recently built, with no sign of weathering. The gatehouse was painted blue, and all along its breadth were the gold forms of aurochs and dragons. The paint was fresh and vibrant, with no sign of fading.

"Qadirra," said the chief of the armored horsemen, called cataphracts. His name, Ambrass had learned, was Kavadh.

"Lie prostrate, kiss the ground," said Kavadh. "Shout seven times, 'Athra, restore Fharas and strike dead the *lugal* emperor!' "

Ambrass would obey. Her people had been captured at the borders of this land, called by its inhabitants Great Fharas and formerly called Potam. Ambrass's people depended on her, and she would obey.

She dismounted from her horse and joined in with the cataphracts, "Athra, restore Fharas and strike dead the *lugal* emperor!"

But Ambrass had said it at a whisper.

"You shall not meet the emperor unclothed," said Kavadh.

"Unclothed?" Ambrass said. She wore a red shirt and a leather skirt, gypsy attire. Her stockings covered every part of her legs, even amid the scorching heat.

"You will dress with respect, when you meet the King of Kings," Kavadh said.

~

One of Kavadh's lackeys entered into Qadirra, and returned from the gates bearing a green lace veil. She draped it over her head, and her face was covered, not to be seen.

She recalled that before the Empire had assumed control of vast swathes of the Southern World, it was illegal for a woman to walk about with her face uncovered.

Yet Ambrass held her people's life in her hands. She would do whatever the so-called King of Kings wished, so that they could be on their way, and resume their journey to Vharat.

She entered into Qadirra, attired in the manner that the so-called King of Kings, ruler of so-called Great Fharas, demanded.

The city was being rebuilt, but entire city blocks, Ambrass saw, were composed of ancient ruins.

Where the city was being rebuilt, the buildings were of mudbrick or of mudbrick faced with plaster. And the people walking in the streets, the men in headwraps or turbans, the women in veils, seemed far too few for a city so vast in area.

Yet Ambrass was here to beg, to plead, and make her people's case. For their fate rested in her hands. She found herself uttering prayers to Kama quietly as she rode, as the street became a thoroughfare, and then a plaza of half-finished blue tile.

Part tile and part dirt, the plaza overlooked a palace also under construction. There, men in chainmail like Kavadh stood by with scimitars in their hand.

"His Worship, God Manifest, will see you at dawn," said Kavadh. "There you may make your case. Until then, you will have a room in the women's apartments. Choose your words carefully, Ambrass."

~

The women's apartments were a separate wing of the palace. There, women were free to take off their veils and walk about in comfortable clothes. There were hundreds of women, it seemed, and Ambrass did not know which ones were the King of Kings' wives. Southrons, Ambrass recalled, had a custom of having many wives, and any rich man had several.

At the gate was a eunuch, swarthy, with a scimitar at his side. As Ambrass was led to her room, she continued to utter her prayers, for her people, for the terrible situation she had brought them into.

And as she entered the room, she saw a carpet made from a tiger skin, a plush bed, and a laver filled with water.

When she turned, it was not the eunuch standing there, but someone else.

It was a woman.

Her hair was black like the space between the stars. She was fresh-faced, young, beautiful, and couldn't be much older than Ambrass. Her eyes, the color of caramel, lighted in view of the window. She wore a green shirt that revealed a hint of belly, and billowing green pants. Around her neck was a necklace, fixed with a red gem that seemed to have an inner fire glowing within it. Ambrass looked at the gemstone necklace, and couldn't look away.

"My name's Samira," said the woman in the Imperial tongue. "And yours — ?"

"Ambrass," she replied.

"I am the King of Kings' chief wife," Samira said. "Artabanas's most beloved. I know you are not here for such happy reasons. Usually, when an emissary comes to my husband, he leaves without a head. But I will tell you a secret, Ambrass, that my husband will tolerate much, and endure much grief, if he is rewarded with the sight of a dance."

It was something to keep in mind.

"Thank you, Samira," Ambrass said, and she realized, she couldn't stop looking at Samira's gemstone necklace and the hidden fire it contained.

Chapter Five: Hunted

The road continued through the desert, between mesas and clefts of rock, as a terrible feeling settled into Reev's gut, one he couldn't shake.

As they passed by an Imperial man walking north, Fortunato called out with the desert greeting, "*Namsita!*" and the Imperial stood by, and took stock of him.

He seemed to be pondering something in his head. At last he spoke.

"*Namsita,*" the Imperial said, with less enthusiasm. "You should know, I was passing through Shahan. A monster was asking people questions, about four *lugals* traveling down this road."

Lugal, Reev learned, was the term southrons used for Imperials.

"How do you mean," Xan said, "a monster."

"A monster," the Imperial said. "I know a monster when I see one."

The Imperial continued on his way north, and Fortunato, the captain of the effort, stopped and pondered.

Xan said, "We're being followed. But a path branches off in a mile. If we take another route, we may avoid notice. If we can make our way to Seshán, I will know how to recover."

"Yes, yes," Fortunato said, "I think you're right. Another path — and maybe we shouldn't use the roads at all."

Down another path they turned, and the path began rapidly ascending. There were rocks, and rocks in the grass. There were chimney stones. And Reev prayed they would not lose their way, that Xan knew where they were going.

~

Bran marched down the desert road, spinning his kukri-knife about his hand.

He could see the scrub brush and the mesas, the sand and the rocks. The sky was clear and cloudless.

He had seen, in his journey, a *lugal,* two *lugals,* five *lugals,* three *lugals* and a southron, but never four *lugals* walking side by side. Nor had he seen what the man in black had described, something he'd remember, a *lugal* in a loin cloth with a coin amulet about his neck.

He had a feeling there was something more to the men in black, and to the four *lugals,* than simple Bran had perceived.

Those men, dressed in black, seemed to radiate evil, and Bran in his more fanciful moments wondered whether they were men at all.

But they had promised him gold, "gold enough to purchase an entire kingdom."

Perhaps, if Bran had a kingdom to himself, he wouldn't have to worry about disquiet, about distasteful looks. Perhaps King Bran would attract a human wife, where ordinary Bran repelled them.

Yet could he trust those men, dressed in black?

Bran did not have high confidence in his intelligence, in his ability to comprehend difficult concepts. Back in the schoolhouse in Redman Territory, he had struggled to add up two and two. But he did have high confidence in his instincts.

His instincts, like that those men dressed in black weren't men at all.

And also, that the four *lugals* were long gone from the Great Taifun Road, and perhaps had caught wind of the fact he was searching for them.

He turned around and retraced his steps. He found himself, at last, at a fork in the road. One path led southeast into the Rock Hills.

He stuck his tongue out, to taste the wind. He tasted trouble coming from the Rock Hills.

He ventured down the road, toward them.

~

As Reev, Fortunato, Xan and Wrinn passed through the rocky terrain, there were pools of water, and trickling creeks, and they had ample opportunity to refill their waterskins.

Reev astride Cobalt, Wrinn astride Asté, and Fortunato astride Tyra Jade were making progress, even with Xan's slow walking gait.

The road that Xan was leading them on had a terminus in Seshán, and in Seshán they would be able to recalibrate the journey, and find their way back on the path they had intended.

The Imperial they had encountered on the road indicated that someone, or something was hunting them, and Reev, after the dangers they had faced on the long journey, was more inclined to heed the voice of paranoia rather than the voice of reason.

What was hunting them? The Imperial had said, "a monster."

The enemy they faced, Seymus, had many monsters at his beck and call. There were rokahn. There were kehrad. There were tribes of wicked men. And there were, of course, the Six Servants of Seymus that thankfully Reev had not seen in months.

The Six Servants of Seymus, garbed in black, had swords that wounded not just the body but also the soul. Fortunato of Ríva had been struck by such a weapon, of dark iron, but then had inexplicably recovered. Such a wound had killed everyone who received it, before, in all of Varda's history.

As the sun set amid the rocks and rock formations, Reev prayed quietly, with not a little bit of fear, that they'd be protected from this monster that the Imperial had warned about.

"Let's get a fire going," said Fortunato. "I have a feeling it's going to get cold, here at night."

It was not cold — it was freezing — despite the scorching heat just hours before. But they managed to find wood and driftwood, collected from the rock-stunted vegetation.

The fire, though, frightened Reev… the sight of it, that it might attract the attention of the monster that was hunting them.

The Imperial said the monster was looking for four *lugals*, and so Reev had a thought of finding some stranger to accompany them and throw him off the scent.

He wondered, he feared… but in the end, all he could do was sit around the fire and pray, and hope for the best, and the gods' protection.

The flame danced, and they told scary stories, one after another. They shared road-bread and water. Then, one by one, they fell asleep in the relative warmth of their bedrolls.

Chapter Six: The Rains of Tahrim

When the sun rose, Ambrass had already been up for two hours. She had dressed in her skirt and shirt, washed her hair and tied a ribbon in it, and laid over that ribbon her green veil. She had borrowed from Samira, Artabanas's chief wife, perfume and ointment, and smeared it over her shoulder and head, so that she would have a pleasant odor, and make her case — that her people should live.

She uttered prayers to Kama and to whatever god would hear her, that they would take her and her people where they belonged. She uttered prayed prayers that they would reach Vharat, and the wine on the leaves of the trees like dew, and the honey flowing like sap. She uttered prayers, and as the sun rose in the city of ruins and mudbrick outside her window, she turned, and saw the eunuch was standing at her door.

"His Worship, God Manifest, awaits you," said the eunuch.

Ambrass could not quench the trembling in her fingers or the pit in her stomach, the fear that was threatening to take control of her. The prayers only helped what they could. But when the eunuch led her through halls of majesty, draped in silken curtains of red and gold and yellow, past rooms full of plush cushions where women in veils drank tea, the bright colors and the majestic furnishing caused her to marvel, and forget for a moment the situation she had found herself in.

The eunuch pushed on, through a wooden door. There was the smell of incense.

And there was a stepped throne.

On the stone throne, which also looked recently built, was a man.

Despite the grandeur of the throne, dominating much of a spacious hall, despite the purple robe he wore, its train flowing down the steps, despite the gold sun circlet designed in the same manner of what they called the *lugal* emperor, Ambrass couldn't help but think the man had a weak look.

He had a thin build, and his fingers were long and wiry. His arms and legs were lanky, and Ambrass thought did not have the look of a warrior, or even one who was healthy.

His eyes were a dark brown, his black hair was thin and wiry and speckled with gray. Ambrass's first sense, as she beheld him, was one of deep insecurity, one which was confirmed by his words.

"The gypsy queen does not fall prostrate, as is our custom," Artabanas said. "Perhaps, not to the slave market we shall take them, but to the executioner's block."

"Your Worship," said Ambrass, "we did not wish to disturb you. We wish to be on our way."

"But you have disturbed us," Artabanas said. "And you are worth more to us sold, than gone."

Artabanas reached for his scepter, and Ambrass remembered what that meant — that he would send his Royal Guard — men now approaching, dressed in chainmail and bearing scimitars — to strike her dead.

Remembering Samira's suggestion, she said, "The strum of a lute, the tapping of a cymbal, the pounding of a timpani..."

And Artabanas smiled, and no longer reached for his scepter.

She looked back, and saw, as Samira had told her last night, that a lute player was in the corner, and a man with a cymbal, and a man standing before a timpani drum.

"What tune pleases the king?" Ambrass said.

"The *Rains of Tahrim*," said Artabanas.

And the lute immediately began to play to a foreign mode, the timpani to a striking beat, the cymbal adding excitement as the melody swirled and cascaded about the room.

Ambrass cascaded and swirled with it, spinning and dropping and sometimes ending in the splits. She steeled herself as the music played, tapping her feet and then twirling from one end of the room to another. At last, she ended, removing her veil, baring her face for Artabanas to see.

At the sight of Ambrass's face, Artabanas seemed to change, and to look upon her in a new way.

"Your dance has pleased me, gypsy queen," said Artabanas. "Another day, another night in my palace you shall stay…"

"And what of my people?" Ambrass said.

"Your people are quartered near the shores of the Black Khazan, amid the tar pits of Bogash. They shall not depart until this issue is settled between us."

And Ambrass had a horrible feeling as she saw Artabanas staring at her in a way she didn't like, gangly and sickly Artabanas. How many wives, she wondered, had this despot killed?

She hastily put on her veil, to stop the gaze of Artabanas's eyes.

~

Cataphracts had led Julian and his people to a shoal on the edge of the Black Khazan. Between the wagons and about them, liquid tar bubbled in pools. As Julian whipped the reins, and pulled his wagon to a stop, he could see the cataphracts in their glittering chainmail, their horses covered head-to-hoof in scale mail, eyeing them.

Julian's cousin, the gypsies' queen, Ambrass, had ventured to the capital of this region, Qadirra, to make her case before the one who called himself the King of Kings. Artabanas was his name, Julian recalled.

The cataphracts were chatting quietly among themselves. Julian could see all of them were armed with large scimitars and shields, and Julian would fear getting into a scrape with them.

The gypsies, on their journey home, had encountered many dangerous of varying kinds, from treacherous wilderness to raiders in the Zahrim Basin. But against a group of warriors so heavily armed and armored, Julian shuddered at the thought of the gypsies' odds.

A cataphract clucked and his horse trotted ahead. He overheard the cataphract demanding Julian's brother Anton unhand his sword.

Quietly, smoothly, Julian unhooked the sheath of his recurve dagger from his belt and shoed it under the wagons' seat. Then he drew his recurve dagger and hid it under his sleeve.

He had bought the recurve dagger at an exorbitant price in the bazaar of Shem-El-Shah. He would not unhand it. He would go about armed.

When the cataphracts got to Julian, and demanded he hand over all weapons, he said, "I am unarmed."

And the cataphract, giving him a thorough examination of the eye, believed him.

Chapter Seven: The Face

They passed through the Rock Hills, Wrinn and Reev, Xan and Fortunato, and made progress.

The Empire de facto but not de jure, Xan had called the political situation.

And though Reev heard that a satrap presided over the Rock Hills, he had little doubt that the satrap was a puppet on the emperor's strings.

A puppet on Verrus's string, Reev thought with a shudder.

The unworthy emperor was one Reev had seen up close and personal, after Reev's imprisonment in the Imperial Palace. The thought of Verrus's power extending to where they stood gave the four urgency, perhaps even more so than the thought of a monster following them.

Yet would the monster know they were now on a different road, taking a road that pierced the stone-covered hills and rock chimneys, through scorching days and freezing nights, over rapids and waterfalls?

Reev only knew one thing, that they were making swift progress as they traversed the Southern World. It was now Harona, past his birthday. He was nineteen years old, and he was no longer the simple boy whose life consisted of reading books in his room at the Buckhorn Inn and eating a meat pie whenever he got the chance. Now, he was striding through the far southern parts of Varda, bearing the garb of Telantis — a loin cloth — a necklace of his people's homeland about his neck, at his side his sword of *estirion*, Doomblade. Now, even his body bore Telantis's sigil, lightning marks tattooed on his neck.

Such attire made him stand out wherever he walked. But he walked boldly… boldly, to *Naron Da*.

Through the rock, gold grass was beginning to peek, and the boulders and chimney stones were lessening in number.

It was a warm day in Harona when Xan announced they had reached the High Plain, called in the southron tongue *Gor Ilán*, the homeland of the now-vanished Fharese Empire. Where there was no gold grass to be seen, there were wheat fields and walnut groves. The sun scorched down on them as they continued down a dirt path, through the midst of the High Plain, toward the great city of Seshán.

~

Bran watched the four *lugals* venture down the path, to the gold plain which the *lugals* ruled, but where *lugals* such as them would not be welcome. Bran also would not fit in amid the scattered farmland, the small villages and the ancient fortresses. He would have to travel by night, and night was when his vision was best.

Bran had almost caught them before they crossed into the High Plain. They would have been no match for his kukri-knife. For now, they slipped away, but Bran could see them now, blood dripping from the slits he had made. He could see it now, gold bars enough to purchase a kingdom. A kingdom... *King Bran, and his wife.*

~

As they pushed on through the roads, portions paved and portions dirt, the folk of the High Plain made their feelings about the four northerners known. Women in veils would spit in Fortunato or Xan's direction as they passed them by, and men in headwraps glared at them, making their hatred obvious. For Reev's part, he ignored the slights and pushed forth boldly ahead, more often than not leading the expedition, headed ever southwards toward Seshán.

Along the road were caravan-posts that did not welcome Imperials. But occasionally there were inns where they would be so lucky as to have a tall glass of ale or a red wine, and there Imperial faces could be seen, northerners like them, kindred faces in a foreign land. They, too, it seemed, were headed to the great city of Seshán.

Like in the Rock Hills, but less than the desert, the days were scorching and the nights were cold. Reev couldn't remember the last time it had rained.

It was almost the month of Brightleaf when the city appeared.

Not a city, it seemed to Reev, but a monument.

For there were buildings built along the road in an Imperial style, but these faced what looked like a titanic stepped pyramid. Under the scorching sun, they drew near the stepped pyramid, as Xan said, "It is not a pyramid, but a throne."

Reev marveled at the sight of it, so towering in its height.

"Here, the King of Kings ruled," said Xan, "back when there was a King of Kings of Fharas to speak of…"

But Fharas, and the King of Kings who ruled it, were apparently long gone.

As the road took a turn before the massive road, pushing past the town — a collection of shops, shrines and homes clearly not built by southrons — Reev could see massive crowds had gathered before the stepped throne.

Reev, leading the group, continued down the road Xan had indicated, and they found themselves amid the crowd.

They were amid bodies, then, men and women, all Imperials. There was noise, and there was the color of tunics and trousers. Amid it all, there was the sound of a guide — "This is the great Stepped Throne of Mirzanes, where in ancient times the Fharese King of Kings would give his edicts… As you can see, there is little historical development around the stepped throne, but here in historical times the assorted minor kingdoms and satrapies would gather, and bring him gifts, in addition to the taxes he was owed…"

The Imperials here were tourists, touring the remnants of a vanished kingdom, here to see a bit of history from a bygone era. As Reev pushed through the crowd, Reev could see a stall set up on the edge. A man stood behind the stall, and he was selling leaden miniatures of the stepped throne of Seshán.

The Imperials gathered were tourists, and they were listening to a tour guide. Reev wondered how much of his speech contained truth.

But Reev looked about him, and saw that Wrinn, Fortunato, and Xan, were nowhere in sight — lost amid the crowd.

~

In the crowds, amid the scorching heat, Fortunato had lost track of Reev and Wrinn.

He looked about him, and caught sight of Xan amid the confusion.

"You can see the steps stretch upwards almost three hundred and fifty feet," the tour guide was saying. "Each step was cut by slaves in quarries in the Gold Mountains thirty miles from here, and ferried by ox cart, and assembled," the tour guide was saying at a shout.

~

"The steps are crafted from a dark gray granite," the tour guide shouted. "The same material was used for the King of Kings' palace, ordered to be demolished during Claudio's invasion."

Wrinn searched about, scouring for any sight of Fortunato or Reev.

He saw only Imperials amid the crowds, Imperials he did not recognize.

"Claudio ordered the throne to be demolished brick by brick," the tour guide continued. "However, the Imperial Council intervened and the order was not carried out. However, after Claudio's invasion, the center of power for Fharas moved eastwards and southwards…"

Then Wrinn caught a glimpse of a face that was not Imperial, a face tawny and furry, with large horns growing from the forehead. The face was not rokahn, nor human, but both. A massive hand reached for Wrinn, but Wrinn slipped away.

~

Reev, Xan, and Fortunato had regrouped in the road beyond the crowds, on the outskirts of Seshán and its stepped throne.

Wrinn at last staggered out from the swarms, and shouted, "I saw the monster…"

To Reev, Wrinn appeared truly shaken.

"He is half-human, half-rokahn," Wrinn said.

"That's impossible," Fortunato said. "A rokahn and a human cannot have a child. They are stillborn, always."

"Well, I know what I saw," Wrinn said. "A monster…"

Reev thought stranger things had happened than a half-rokahn wandering the earth. And even if Wrinn was mistaken, he had seen a strange creature. What else could it be but the creature they had been warned about, the creature hunting them?

The one the Imperial on the road, and Wrinn had called, a monster?

After Fortunato's words, he seemed to be pondering what Wrinn had said in his mind.

Wrinn, after all, was not a liar.

"These roads," Fortunato said, "are well-traveled. We are being sighted and seen. The Empire has given us safe passage thus far, but dark forces are at work. They will try to hinder us from reaching

Naron Da. In fact, they will stop at nothing to do so."

There was a pause, a wind.

The monster, hidden in the crowds, dared not show his face to them, to confront them boldly.

Reev looked into the distance, and saw beyond the shops and homes built up around this tourist trap, the stone walls and turrets of an Imperial fort. Imperial soldiers were nearby, and as Fortunato had said, they had not hindered them thus far.

"Where does this road lead to, Xan?" said Fortunato.

"Down through the Zahrim Basin," said Xan, and he seemed to be in another time and place, lost in thought. "Through the Salt Lands. Then, the rainforest of Kash. Past the ruins of Qadirra. To Bezakirah and then another desert road."

"Perhaps, there is another way to Bezakirah," said Fortunato, "through the wilderness, not as well traveled."

"We could hire a guide," Xan said.

Perhaps, if the guide led them through a wilderness way, they'd not be sighted and seen, and the enemy would not know to look for them.

~

Bran was watching his quarry in the shadows of the pyramidal throne. He had locked eyes with one of the *lugals,* one he recognized as an elf. In the Southern World, all *lugals* were lumped together, elves and humans both.

He had been spotted. He would have to adapt.

Lurking, waiting, he knew no god could hear his prayers, because of his rokahn blood. But would a god wish to help him?

He had a feeling that the men in dark clothing had assigned him to an evil end.

As he crouched, there were footsteps. He turned, and saw men in shining breastplates, on their heads helmets with red horsehair crests.

Lugal soldiers.

"Signore — "

Bran looked at the *lugal* soldier who had spoke, not sure what to say.

"You are lurking in the shadows," he said. "Staring at four under our protection. Will you have a word with us in Fort Adamantus?"

He would have a word — and if they tried to stop him, there would be a trail of dead *lugals* stretching from Fort Adamantus to the pyramidal throne.

~

They passed a mile down the road and found themselves in a southron village, where there were no men clean-shaven with short hair, nor women walking about unveiled. There, Xan inquired in the market square, and found a guide.

"Yes, yes, signores," said the man, Farhad, cloaked in white and wearing a headwrap, "there is a way to Bezakirah that you can take, through the Red Uplands. It is rather treacherous in winter, but I will be your guide for two *libra*."

The party's coinpurse was fat. Wrinn had earned a great deal of coin as a gladiator, amid the arenas of Imperial City.

For two *libra*, Farhad joined the group, and they ventured down little known paths, headed due northeast, in view of the wilderness south of the Sky Mountains.

Chapter Eight: Dancer

Nights and days had passed since Ambrass's dance, and Artabanas granted her his mercy. She had spent her days in the women's apartments, and food and tea was taken to her in the morning, in the afternoon and the evening. She chatted with Samira and had learned more, how the Kingdom of Fharas had been vanquished by the *lugals*, or so the *lugals* thought. A descendant of the King of Kings remained, a royal line the *lugals* had thought extinguished, but endured.

Over a morning tea, Samira continued.

"The *lugals* thought our power was spent, that we were about gone," said Samira, "but my husband, praise his name, knew that the Imperials forgot the Plain of Potam in their conquests. It was there the great city of the Naamer lay in ruins, Qadirra…"

"The Naamer?" Ambrass said.

"Their kingdom once stretched from Qadirra to Baradon… back when the Desert of Hamma was much smaller, and rains were not so rare as to cause joy. Yet Qadirra, where we sit, was their chief city. It lay in ruins, but my husband and his family, and all that remained of the Fharese army, came here and rebuilt it."

It was still being rebuilt — parts of the city were stone ruins and nothing more.

"The *lugals* haven't bothered us," said Samira. "I think they're afraid, afraid to meet their match. For five years, we have begun reconstructing our kingdom here, where long ago the Naamer reigned, in their capital city of Qadirra. Fharas will rise again, and the King of Kings, God Manifest, will again rule over all the world."

Ambrass, though, had her doubts.

She sipped her tea, and thought of her people. She thought of her cousins Anton and Julian, stuck with the other gypsies in their wagons.

She had danced, and the King of Kings had spared her from death. But the King of Kings said nothing about her people.

~

In the afternoon, it was announced a feast was being held. Ambrass feared what was happening to her people. But she knew there was little to be done, that all she could do was beg Artabanas. She was not a guest, she had begun to realize. She was a prisoner.

The feasting chamber was lit with torches and oil lamps. Symmetrical, floral patterns painted a wall of plaster. The walls, too, were unfinished, with portions of mudbrick visible.

The feasting chamber was dull and dim, but the food was not. At tables were stews of lamb and leek and onion, seasoned with salt and pepper, cumin and curry. And Ambrass, though she was not hungry, that she only thought of her people, felt her stomach growl of its volition at the tantalizing scents.

Wine, though, was not served. In the Southern World, it was viewed with derision. Some even called it devil's water.

Yet Ambrass thirsted for such a drink, perhaps to ease her fears and nerves, at she sat down at a table with a golden tablecloth next to Samira, and took stock of her surroundings.

The table where Artabanas ate was surrounded by a gold curtain, and raised high above everyone else.

Samira and Ambrass had donned their veils, and no women ate uncovered.

Ambrass could see Kavadh and his soldiers in loose shirts and trousers. And there was someone else, seated at a table near the emperor's curtained dais.

A man sat there, or so it seemed at first. He had an arms, legs, and a humanoid body covered in a striped robe. But his arms, his legs, and his face was covered in fur, and his mouth protruded, as to form a muzzle. His eyes were black and beady.

Ambrass saw that around his arm was a gold bracelet with a dull red gem set into it.

Ambrass opened her mouth, and before she did, Samira began to explain.

"That is Fenris," Samira said. "Well, that is what Gordanas calls himself now. He was once a great magus, a member of the order of magi, and when we reached the ruins of Qadirra, he hoped to purify them.

"He entered into the temple of a jackal-headed god. As he stood before the jackal-headed god's statue, a ray of the moon covered him from a window, and he was changed. Sometimes he returns to his human form, but only when he is moonstruck."

"What do you mean, moonstruck?" Ambrass said.

Samira ignored her, and began to eat her stew greedily. Ambrass joined in halfheartedly, giving up on learning what the bracelet was that Fenris wore, with a dull red stone inset within it.

The more she looked at the bracelet, the more the color of the gold seemed unusually lustrous, unusually fine. Ambrass couldn't take her eyes off the bracelet that Fenris was wearing.

Leaning against the table where Fenris sat was a large wooden staff, shaped like a shepherd's crook.

As Samira shoveled stew down her throat, Ambrass sat in fear, thinking of her people, when there was the sound of a timbrel and a harp. To that was added the sound of drummers drumming, and the piercing notes of flutes.

Kavadh stood up and shouted, "Artabanas declares, let the gypsy queen dance for her supper, and for her life."

Samira looked up from her greedy eating. Her eyes said, "What are you waiting for?" and Ambrass rose, then retreated away far from the table, then toward the curtained dais where King Artabanas was sitting.

Ambrass realized in that moment that the curtains, whether by magic or by the craft of artisans, allowed Artabanas to see, but none could see him.

For an audience of one she cleared her throat. For an audience of one she danced.

She dropped to the floor to the cheers of the audience. She kicked her feet and Samira howled her approval. She did a pirouette that ended then splits, then shimmied from one corner of the dining chamber to the other. When she had skipped back to the dais, the music was reaching a crescendo. She spun about, a spin that ended on her knees, and to the drifting of her veil to the ground.

There was scattered applause.

"I have never seen a better dancer," said Kavadh.

And when Ambrass turned, and saw Samira, it seemed she wasn't pleased with Kavadh's comment.

~

Back in the women's apartments, as they retired to bed, Samira offered her criticism. "*Lugals* think we proud Fharese are prudes, covered as we are in veils… but when the King of Kings demands a dance, it should end with more than just a veil torn off."

Ambrass shuddered at the thought.

Chapter Nine: The Upland Lights

"You are aware of the four *lugals* traveling through the High Plain," Bran repeated the Imperial officer's words, before his desk in his chamber at Fort Adamantus.

"Two Imperial citizens, one northman, one elf," the officer said. "You are following them. Our emperor Verrus has instructed to keep an eye on them, to make sure we know where they've gone at all times. But we believe they have caught wind of our surveillance. They are entering into no man's land, the uplands northeast of here where few travel. Emperor Verrus will not tolerate this. But if Imperials follow them into the wilderness, they'll know.

"A creature such as you, though, is fit for mountain halls."

"So I'm not in trouble," Bran said.

The Imperial officer smiled. "No," he said. "And I know a creature such as yourself might follow these four for hunger, or blood feud, but I have a feeling you are under the employ of others. Allow Emperor Verrus to make you a better offer…"

~

Brightleaf arrived, and the party had reached the waters of a gushing river.

It babbled and roared over a series of rocks and boulders.

"The uplands are ahead," said their guide Farhad. "We must ford this river."

"What river is it?" said Fortunato.

"If it were not for the rapids in the Rock Hills, and the falls of Upper Khazidea, you could take a canoe, and arrive in Haroon. You could be back in the Empire, where you *lugals* belong," said Farhad.

"We must ford it," Xan mumbled.

Farhad strode out into the waters, followed by Fortunato and Tyra Jade, then Xan, then Wrinn, then Reev — leading both Cobalt and Asté by the reins.

The five of them sidestepped, and the animals swam, as the river's current threatened to sweep them away. But forceful step by forceful step, they crossed across the breadth of the river, a shallow part where humans could cross by foot.

At last, they had emerged on the other side, cold, shivering, and had regrouped amid the growing cold. Reev in his loin cloth had managed the waters the best. Wrinn had a dour look.

"Through the uplands, twenty days," said Farhad, "and we will make it through, Athra willing, before the worst of the snows."

By the time the day ended, they were in the uplands full and true, where stalwart cedars predominated as the land ascended toward the Sky Mountains far to the north. The ground had acquired an ochre reddish tint, and the soil was well watered. The night was freezing, but there was enough wood to start a raging fire.

In the days that followed, Reev at last succumbed, and wore a cloak over his loin cloth. They all had stuffed their desert gear into their packs, as they traversed the uplands that approached the roof of the world, headed due east along an ascent in the ground.

To Reev, it seemed the uplands were abandoned, that none lived here. But he had a terrible feeling, they weren't alone.

In the days ahead, as they ascended, the air grew colder and colder, and there was a frosty wind blowing from the north. Following Farhad's direction, they pressed eastward, along this region that was the rim of the Southern World, and the place — it seemed — people least wanted to live.

"No one lives here," Reev said.

"Not many, anymore," called out Farhad, "but in ancient times, when the summers were hot in Shush, the court would retreat here and form a summer capital, and from there, the King of Kings issued his decrees."

"There is no Fharese King of Kings ruling these lands," Xan mumbled.

"No," said Farhad. "The flower of Fharas is gone. The last of kingly blood killed. The *lugals* reign, and I know you are *lugals*, but curse the *lugals*."

Fharas, Reev understood, was the kingdom that ruled these southern parts of the world before the Empire had completed its conquest of Varda. Once, Fharas and its King of Kings outshone the Empire and the emperor itself in its glory, but now, its power was gone, and its memory was only recorded in history books.

But they were now in a land where no one lived, and therefore the Empire that ruled Varda, and the unworthy one who ruled it, Verrus, did not reign with all his strength. About them were cedars in a frosty wind, and rain.

"Others once lived here, too," said Farhad, "even before the King of Kings held his summer capital."

"Who?" said Reev.

"A people unknown," Farhad replied, "whom none recall. They left their mark though, and on cliffs they built their houses to protect from a nameless foe."

What foe were they fighting, Reev wondered?

But as the days progressed, and a week turned to two weeks, he saw rock cliffs, and on them the remains of houses that had endured for all these centuries.

What had hunted these people, these people that time forgot?

What had they been hiding from?

~

The Empire wished to be apprised of the four *lugals*, for Bran to be nothing more than a hostile escort. They had promised him a steady payment of ten silver denara per week.

The six men in black had promised Bran the world however, enough gold to purchase a kingdom.

Bran did not know what he would do when he caught up with his prey, whether he would accept the steady payment of the *lugal* empire or roll the die and see if the six men in black really could offer him the world.

He did not know, clutching his kukri-knife as he waded through the waters of the Khazan. Perhaps, the human side of him would caution him as he laid his eyes on the four *lugals*, and appreciate that steady modest payment. Perhaps the rokahn side of him would take over when he found his prey, and he'd leave a trail of bodies that would be the talk of Varda.

As he stepped past shore, into the high uplands, he looked about himself and sniffed the air. The *lugals* had a long head start. He would walk swiftly, into the night.

~

On the roof of the world, the feel of the wind was bitter. When it rained, and it rained often, coming in sprays an hour at a time, the feel of the rain was icy, colder — to Reev's feeling — than snow. The air was growing thinner as they pressed eastward, and the party, led by Farhad, saw no sign of civilization as they ventured through the wilderness.

Nothing, Reev noted, except the abandoned houses carved into the side of cliffs, a people that had disappeared but which had made their mark on the land.

"The *lugals* believe in many gods," said Farhad, "and in the rural villages of the Southern World, that too is our belief."

They had paused over a vista of the red soil, a valley between two interlocking ridges.

"But my father always told me that Athra the Fire-Lord is locked in a cosmic struggle with the prince of cold and darkness, and that there are no others in Heaven or Hell."

"And what is the name of the prince of cold and darkness?" said Xan.

"Samash," Farhad replied.

"We call him Seymus," said Wrinn.

But Athra the Fire-Lord was not worshiped north of the Rock Hills. No fire temples could be found in the Empire, in Gallia or in Zarubain.

The prince of cold and darkness, Reev remembered the man had said.

It was cold, and the sun was sinking beneath the western horizon.

They built a fire in the bitter cold, having softened their road-bread in water. The meager fare was all they had eaten since they left the High Plain, and it filled the stomach, but it had little taste.

The dancing flames illuminated the face of Farhad as he spoke.

"Athra the Fire-Lord is mighty," he said, "but he did not rescue his people from the *lugals*. He did not rescue his people from men such as yourselves.'"

He eyed Fortunato, then Reev.

"The fire temples are dwindling in number," said Farhad. "There are fewer magi than ever before, tending the sacred fires, now that the flower of Fharas has withered, and the four-pointed star no longer flies."

The four-pointed star… ancient Fharas's flag.

"Now," said Farhad, "the night. The bitter cold night. No fires to light our path. Samash is winning."

"Seymus will not win," Reev said. "His defeat is assured."

Amid the darkness of the landscape, beyond the fire, in the horizon, Reev saw something glimmering. Wrinn turned and gasped.

"Look!" Wrinn shouted.

Reev looked where Wrinn's eyes were fixed and saw what looked like a glowing white orb in the sky, suspended in the air. It was hovering above the landscape, perfectly still in the horizon. Then it darted away.

"Samash! Samash!" Farhad began to cry, but Reev didn't think this was Seymus's work.

He stood up from the fire and drew Doomblade, though swords could do no damage against such creatures.

Were they creatures?

Then more lights appeared in horizon, moving swiftly across the sky, brilliant white orbs arranged in the pattern of a carpenter's square. The carpenter's square pattern of lights was moving across the red earth, and painting the red earth in light, as the lights swiftly moved overhead, and then vanished into the inky-black horizon.

"Samash! Samash!" Farhad shouted.

But it wasn't Seymus, what Farhad called Samash.

Yet Reev wondered what the lights were, brilliant orbs shining in the night. He remembered the houses that had been carved from cliffs, and he wondered if the lights were what those ancient men had been protecting themselves from.

~

Bran watched lights move toward him, lights arranged in the pattern of a carpenter's square. As they drew near him, the lights' swift movement slowed down and then lingered over him. He looked up into the light, the brightness inestimable, peering to the white orbs now hovering above his head. He felt a presence all about him, and he thought — *I am not alone. I am not alone.*

Chapter Ten: Obeisance

Ambrass had been told her fellow gypsies were captured, and being held on the shore of the Black Khazan. She herself was in captivity, unable to leave the palace of Qadirra and the man who called himself the King of Kings.

The land they called Great Fharas was once known as Potam, a land between two rivers, the Black Khazan to the south and the Blue Khazan to the north. Yet Fharas, Ambrass knew, had little power, and the only reason this project endured was because the emperor did not know about it.

Tucked away in a pocket of the Southern World, far from Emperor Verrus's eye, this so-called reborn state was able to continue. It had been able to exist for five years.

But perhaps, the Empire would notice before the King of Kings sold she and her people into slavery. That was what Ambrass was banking on.

In her room in the women's apartments, Ambrass brushed her hair and puckered her lips in the mirror. She did not know what the day would entail, what opportunities the gods might place in her lap. She had dedicated, now, her life, to returning her people to their ancient homeland, Vharat.

"Wine on the leaves of the trees like dew," Ambrass said softly to the mirror. "Honey, flowing down the bark like sap."

Would it be so? Would they find their homeland? There, they would stake out a life for themselves, and the centuries of wandering would end. They would end happily.

As she sat brushing, looking from her mirror to her window, to the tar-pocked fields beyond Qadirra, she heard what sounded like mumbling.

Mumbling — and then a ghostly voice, like a voice from

beyond the grave.

Ambrass dropped her brush and left through her door, down the hallway.

The noise had come from Samira's room.

Ambrass opened the door, and she saw Samira standing there.

Samira didn't notice her.

She wasn't alone.

Samira's room, which she had never looked into, was crowded with gold lamps and gold rings and necklaces, and other objects of gold. She had been hoarding objects of gold, and they were piled from the floor to the edge of her bed.

Samira was standing before a table of silver. On the table was a gold candelabra, and from it a creature had emerged.

It had the torso of a human and the face of a man, but both were colored green, and where legs and feet should be, a tendril of green smoke was wafting up from one of the candelabra's fixtures. The creature's eyes glowed like yellow coals, as it leered at Samira.

"Samira," she said, "I have done all I can."

"Lies," snapped Samira. "Lies, lies — that is all I hear from your kind."

Ambrass inched back from the door, consumed by wonder and fear.

"I won't hear another word," said Samira, "tell me where *Mainyu* is, or I'll never release you."

"You'll never release me, anyhow," the creature said.

"Curses to you, in Artabanas's name," Samira said.

The creature's eyes seemed to roll into the back of his head, and his body shrunk, turning to vapor, seemingly sucked into the candelabra's fixture.

Samira opened a shelf of the silver desk, and tossed the candelabra angrily inside.

When she turned and saw Ambrass, a look of shock appeared on her face.

Samira hadn't noticed her.

"I apologize, Ambrass," Samira said. "I thought I closed the door."

Ambrass had opened the door.

"You've seen my work," Samira said. "My true work. For some call me a sorceress, but I do not have powers over earth and fire and wind and water on my own. All throughout the Southern World, invisible creatures cause mischief. One of a cunning tongue and mind, one crafty and resourceful, can trap them and cause them to do what one wills."

"It didn't look invisible to me," Ambrass said.

"Genies hate gold," said Samira, "yet they are attracted to it. With the right words said, and the right motions, you can trap them in a candelabra or a lamp. There, they shall do your will. And they shall appear to the naked eye.

"But they lie to me. They lie, yes! They lie, and it makes me so very angry."

"What's *Mainyu*?" Ambrass said.

Samira's expression darkened. She turned slightly. "Have you heard? The *lugals* have crossed the Black Khazan. I don't want to say it's over, now. But I suppose it is…"

A change of subject, Ambrass supposed, was best.

And the *lugals*, what these folk called Imperials, would perhaps rescue the gypsies from their plight.

~

The entire court strode out to meet the Imperial ambassador. Artabanas rode behind Kavadh and the other cataphracts surrounded them, perhaps to make a last stand, the last stand of the Fharese King of Kings.

They had thought they could recreate Fharas in the land of Potam, and it would escape the emperor's eye. But the Empire now controlled all of Varda. There was no place hidden from the emperor's eye.

Ambrass, provided a palfrey, was considered a part of the emperor's court though she was a captive. She would endure their treatment in hopes the King of Kings would let her people free. But now, it seemed, she wouldn't have to worry about it.

Hours after their journey began, as the dry tar-pocked dirt was beginning to turn to salt pans and pits in the ground, Ambrass caught sight of red-gold standards and knew the Imperials had arrived.

Kavadh drew his scimitar, perhaps a last stand against a foe that was sure to defeat them. But when they reached the Imperial lines, Kavadh slowed his gallop, and the entire party came to a halt.

The Imperials' faces were covered in sunlight. They looked so different from the inhabitants of so-called Great Fharas, being as they were clean-shaven with short cut hair. They were attired brilliantly in steel breastplates, with red half-capes over their shoulders, and on some of their heads helmets with red horsehair crests.

But the chief of them wore no helmet. His hair was gold, his eyes a piercing gray. He rode on a white warhorse, at the front of the Imperials.

Ambrass thought there were about a thousand of them behind the gold-haired man, who was presumably the legate.

Behind him was a large object covered in a red sheet.

Artabanas at last rode to the front.

"For millennia you have put the sole of your *caliga* over the neck of my people," Artabanas said. "You have demolished our fire temples, or otherwise caused by your conquests their powers to cease. You have driven us from Seshán and from Shush, and now to this holy place, but here the memory of Qadirra endures. So too does its power — and the people of Qadirra curse you."

The people of Qadirra were long dead.

"Signore Artabanas." The gold-haired legate did not bow, nor did he incline his head. He did not so much as dismount from his horse. "The Imperial Council passed a resolution of advice and consent last year, directing the emperor to drive you from this place. But you shall be glad to know, a new emperor has taken the throne, one who has acquiesced to the struggles of your people. The new emperor, Verrus, will allow this project to endure between the shores of the Black Khazan and the Blue Khazan. He will allow you to rebuild Qadirra, and reign over Great Fharas with his recognition, if you will cast your crown before his image."

The gold-haired legate made a signal, and one of the legionaries pulled the red sheet from the massive object.

In the light of the sun, it glittered: an image carved of wood and painted in the likeness of Verrus.

Ambrass shuddered at how lifelike it was. Perfectly, did it represent the man she had met in the council chambers, down to the flaming red hair, the sickly pallor of his skin, the terrible blue eyes with bottomless black pupils that threatened to steal the soul.

Artabanas seemed to wail at the sight of it, for fear. But with his wiry fingers he laid hold of the golden circlet he was wearing. He cast it before Verrus's image. He cried out, as if he had done a great wrong.

And Ambrass sensed, he had.

"The Emperor Verrus appreciates the gesture," the gold-haired legate said. "He wishes to add, he hopes Qadirra is rebuilt, for his own family lineage has a connection to it."

The Empire had no connection to the ancient city of Qadirra. It had been wiped away long before the Empire was a thought formed in its founders' heads.

Ambrass looked at disgust with Artabanas, at what he had done. And now she couldn't help but feel, as the gold-haired legate dismounted and took the circlet, then mounted and placed the circlet back on Artabanas's head, that the project to rebuild Qadirra was cursed.

Artabanas seemed stricken by something as he turned around, and began to gallop back in the direction of Qadirra.

Ambrass uttered prayers under her breath as she turned and galloped in his wake.

How long would they wait? What now would they endure?

The Imperials would not rescue her people from Artabanas because an unworthy man sat on the Imperial throne.

She prayed, silently, for Verrus's death. She prayed, silently, that somehow her people would be rescued.

~

The cataphracts continued to stand guard over the gathered wagons of the gypsies. The gypsies had continued to subsist on the food they had brought, and the people of so-called Great Fharas had not brought them any provisions.

Salt pork and jerky, road-bread and crackers were all they had with them. They had been disarmed, now, save for Julian, and though Julian learned that the Imperials had at last heard of this rebellious project between the shores of the Black Khazan and the Blue Khazan, the ancient land of Potam, that the wicked emperor Verrus would leave the reborn Fharas be.

What then, would they do? Julian supposed, for now, they would plot, and wonder, and wait.

A cold wind was blowing across the gathered wagons, a cold wind that had winter on its edge.

Chapter Eleven: Thievery

A gale was blowing through the Red Uplands, and snow was drifting down from the heavens. They were truly on the roof of the world.

It was the middle of Brightleaf, Reev recalled.

They had elected not to take roads, to traverse the wilderness, and though now their movements were unknown, traveling in such a manner had a cost. The bitter cold, the rough going, had no end in sight. And they were running perilously low on road-bread. Fortunato wished to hunt and add some meat to their diet, but Farhad insisted that they march as far as they could to put the Red Uplands behind them before winter.

"Even in summer, the Red Uplands are cold," Farhad said as the snow fell, and they pushed on through the night. "But in winter, none can survive."

Yet Reev suspected that Gallia, far north of here, had far harsher winters than the Red Uplands. Now, though, he had grown accustomed to the heat, and the thin shirts and light pants that the southrons wore were not sufficient in the cold. In a world not built for snow, a little snow was deadly.

Reev braced his cloak against his body.

He recalled the lights he had seen not long ago.

But after the freezing night ended, in the morning, the snow began to melt. The ground took a turn, and it was clear they were beginning to descend. The sun kissed them as they made their way down.

~

Bran watched the five figures from the cliff.

He saw that they had brought a guide, a southron, not a *lugal*. They were trying mightily to hide their movements, movements that the *lugal* empire wished to observe and to understand.

They were going east, due east across the Southern World. Past the Red Uplands and its frosty winds were the Barrens of Zahar. Past the Barrens of Zahar, if one traversed southeast, was the cursed land of Potam and the ruined city of Qadirra. Beyond that was Bezakirah.

Bran thought they were going to Bezakirah, but why would four *lugals* go to Bezakirah?

If the southrons the *lugals* had met thus far despised them, the zealous men and women Bezakirah would hate them with a murderous hate.

Bezakirah was also a stopping-off point for the great desert. Were they after something beyond the desert sands?

Perhaps, the six men in black would know.

~

It was still Brightleaf when the ground was near sea level, but the cold had evaporated. It was back to scorching days and cold nights, as the ground lost its red color, day by day, and they were out of the Red Uplands. Stretching into the distance was yellow grassland interspersed with green trees.

"We are about out of food," said Fortunato. "We need to restock."

"There is a Zahari village not far from here," said Farhad.

~

The folk of Zahar eyed them darkly as the four *lugals* and their guide entered the market square. The women of the Zahari wore silken headwraps on their heads and the men wore bandanas fashioned from wool. Hurriedly they went about their business, in this village built on the shores of an oasis, which seemed far from the Imperials, the *lugal* empire they hated.

Yet they refilled their stores of road-bread, and as the angry looks in the Zahari village built to heckling, the five quickly sped on their way.

Through the Barrens of Zahar they traveled, scorching in its heat even as Brightleaf passed into Anthanos.

They would travel to Bezakirah, Reev remembered, and from there, take another desert road.

~

As the Imperial officers had instructed Bran, he lit a fire signal as he entered the Barrens of Zahar. He waited an hour before an Imperial soldier came riding amid the dry grassland astride his horse.

"Your Honor," Bran deigned even to say to a *lugal*, "five men the Emperor Verrus wishes to keep apprised of are moving due east. I believe they are headed to Bezakirah and the great desert. Where they wish to go after that, I do not know."

He counted the coins as the Imperial dropped them into his coin purse. His coin purse now was fat.

He had allowed his human side to control him, the side of him that believed in law and the maintenance of peace. Yet now, his quarry were easy prey in these barrens, and perhaps his rokahn side would take over. Perhaps, he'd use his kukri-knife the way it was meant to be used, and take up the six men in black on their offer.

He rushed forward, through the blazing sun of the barrens.

~

As the party traveled from oasis to oasis underneath the

burning sun, refilling their waterskins whenever possible and allowing Cobalt, Asté and Tyra Jade to drink heavily, Reev felt the party's energy was being sapped collectively, day by day, under the oppressive sun. The grass and dry brush was interspersed with pockets of blowing sand. But Farhad insisted that if they pressed on further, they would reach the waters of the Blue Khazan, and the blowing sand and scorching sun would ease. From there, they'd have a straight shot to Bezakirah.

As they reached a village called Saanah, Fortunato shouted something indiscriminate. They collectively turned back to look. Men were approaching in woolen bandanas bearing scimitars.

"The sultan, Carabh, sees you are intruding through his lands," the chief of them spoke the Imperial tongue through the lens of a thick accent. "Four *lugals* travel through the Barrens of Zahar in the month of Anthanos. He asks, where are you going?"

"To Bezakirah," Farhad answered.

"Bezakirah," said the chief warrior. "And no other place?"

Farhad made no response.

"A monster has been following you," said the chief warrior. "Our sultan Carabh has had his mouth set with hooks, and dragged him to the dungeon for execution. Do not bring your evil to Zahar."

"We would not so much as think of it," Fortunato said.

~

When Bran stirred awake, he had little recollection of what had gone on, why he was in a mudbrick room faced with iron bars.

As he sat back in the dry cell, his mind swimming, bits of memory came to him. A band of warriors had approached him outside an oasis village — a band thirty strong. With his kukri-knife he had laid them low, slashing and cutting them apart… a bleeding massacre on the sand.

A band a hundred strong had come — a plume of smoke, the

smell of something foul, fighting unconsciousness… the sharp pain of metal hooks tearing against his cheeks.

Then — blackness — and he was here.

Bran stood up from his prison cell. He could see the guard standing in the corner, garbed in desert dress.

They had made a mistake. They had left them alive.

Perhaps, even in the Barrens of Zahar, executing someone for looking a bit funny required a few extra steps.

As the poison fog cleared from his mind, he strode up to the iron bars. He would show them what a half-rokahn, half-human was capable of.

He pushed, and then he pulled. He charged ahead, and flexed with all his might. As the prison guard began to shout, he shook and tore at the iron bars until the frame fell loose, crumbling against the mudbrick. The prison cell collapsed with a great crash, and the prison guard fled, but Bran was faster.

Before he had reached the door into the hall, Bran had laid hold of the guard's neck, and snapped it. He tossed the prison guard to the ground. "Where is my kukri-knife?" Bran howled.

He took the prison guard's shiv, and stormed past the hallway. There were guards rushing at him, guards bearing scimitars. He punched one and slammed another to the ground, then stabbed the shiv into his heart. He stormed ahead, down mudbrick corridors, tossing aside statues and paintings, punching holes in the plaster ceiling above.

"Where is it? Where is my kukri-knife?"

When he reached the sultan's throne room, dozens of warriors flung themselves at him, striking with their scimitars in vain. But even armed with a shiv, he was deadlier than they, stabbing a warrior in the heart and slashing another's throat in one swift motion, punching one to the ground and then — heaving another warrior in the arms — throwing him countless yards across the room, to a bone-crunching landing on the wall.

The warriors fled.

Bran saw the sultan on his throne, a look of hopeless terror on his face. On his head was a red turban with a blue aigrette, and at his side was Bran's kukri-knife.

"You!" Bran howled. "You thief!"

The sultan tried to flee, but Bran sprinted to him. In two lumbering steps, he was upon the sultan, and taking the sultan's neck in his hand, ripped so hard the sultan was decapitated with a loud pop.

Covered, now, in blood — dripping in fact — Bran took his prized kukri-knife from the sultan's side. He strode out of the fortress to the sight of fleeing warriors wailing in terror.

Beyond Bran were mudbrick houses in view of date palms.

The capital village of Zahar, Saanah, was now in his path, and he had his kukri-knife. Bran would lay it waste.

Chapter Twelve:
The Seven Bracelets

One morning, the eunuch who guarded the women's apartments appeared at Ambrass's door.

"Lady Ambrass," he said, "the King of Kings has witnessed your good behavior, and has decided to lessen some restrictions on your movements. You may exit the women's apartments, if you continue to wear a veil, between sunrise and sunset. He demands, however, that you eat dinner each night in the dining chamber, in view of him."

In view of him. A snakelike chill of disgust passed through Ambrass's spine. At the thought he wanted more from her than being a dutiful guest, she shuddered. But it was growing difficult to ignore.

She would bear these wounds, however, for her people. She wound endure every arrow for their hope that they would return where they belonged.

Wine on the leaves of trees like dew, honey flowing down the trees' bark.

She would avail herself of the lifted restrictions. She donned her veil. Then she followed the eunuch through the halls, and then pushed past him, beyond the door.

~

She passed then beyond the corridors, beyond the brightly painted rooms of plush pillows and colorful curtains, to where she knew the dining chamber was.

She wanted some fresh air.

The so-called King of Kings allowed her to wander the grounds of the palace. Was it such a stretch to venture outside, into the open air?

She would try her luck. She would tempt fate. She could no longer bear another moment in Artabanas's palace.

Outside, the air was hot, but it was no longer as scorching a feeling as before. Now, Ambrass thought she could sit outside for as much as a half hour without wishing to leap into an icy river.

The scorching weather in this hot plain made her miss a homeland she had never known, Vharat where wine was on the leaves of the trees like dew, where the sap was like honey.

She recalled — the gentle summer heat and the long days that never ended when the dog star arose. The nights were all too brief. That had been Gallia — would Vharat be like Gallia? Did Vharat have its own Dragonpaw Inn?

Perhaps, Ambrass would found Vharat's Dragonpaw Inn. She wouldn't need a cellar — just shake the dew off leaves into cups.

She felt her eyes water. She was beginning to weep. She worried she'd lose control.

So not heeding the danger, ignoring the armored guards now eyeing her, she pushed past the mirrored pools of the palace yard, into the half-ruined, and half-rebuilt, City of Qadirra.

~

Date palms were visible throughout the city, looming over the buildings of gloomy mudbrick. Date palms, she knew, provided a kind of honey.

But she hoped that the honey that oozed from the trees in Vharat was the kind of honey like bees made, the kind of honey that Glenda, innkeeper at the Dragonpaw Inn, would add to Ambrass's tea on crisp autumn days.

Ambrass found herself beyond the palace. The people of the rebuilt Qadirra were few. Its rebuilding had been a top-down engineering project, not natural. And Ambrass wondered what secrets Qadirra hid, and why it had attracted the attention of those who wanted to rebuild the Fharese Empire.

In the west of the city, most that Ambrass saw was ruins, the stone frames of ancient buildings, stretching toward the wall. But in the midst of the ruins there was a square set up, with stalls, and people gathered. Ambrass had no money, and was relying on the King of Kings Artabanas to feed herself. But perhaps, a bit of distraction would help ease her sorrow.

"What will happen to my people, Kama?" Ambrass said under her breath.

She wondered how Glenda, in her happy outpost at the Dragonpaw Inn, was doing. She wondered what Glenda would think of all that had befallen Ambrass and the gypsies.

And there was someone else in Galiope Ambrass missed, someone who now seemed a phantom, a memory she had tried now for years to suppress, a memory — a towering figure who threatened to take control of her life and her soul. Who was that figure? Who was that towering being in the back of her mind, whom she feared to allow herself to love?

In the market square, a man in a turban was selling monkeys in a cage. Another woman in a veil was selling canisters of various spices. Others had sheaves of barley for sale.

Yet the citizens of Qadirra were milling about, for there was little to do all day. In towns in the Empire, there were theaters and there were music halls. In Gallia, too, actors performed plays on stages throughout the city.

But here in Qadirra, they neither drank wine nor listened to music. What was there to do but look at what merchandise was available, and talk amongst themselves?

Yes, they talked, and as Ambrass pretended to examine a set of diamond rings, she heard two women chatting amongst themselves,

"The Imperials have sent away their armies, but there is another army approaching."

"The Cathayans?" said the other woman.

"No," the woman answered, "filthy *lugals*, but instead of red crests on their helmets, their crests are green…"

Ambrass moved from stall to stall, and as she did, she continued to eavesdrop. As she pretended to gawk at a pair of leather sandals, she heard two men speaking, "Fenris has possession of *Azar*. Kavadh is holding *Satar* in a lockbox. But as long as *Mainyu* is unaccounted for, this city will never be safe."

Ambrass turned around to face the men, bearded men dressed richly in red shirts and tan trousers.

"Pardon me," she said, and she knew she was breaking custom, but she remembered overhearing what Samira had asked the genie — where *Mainyu* was. "I am from the palace. I am wondering, my good sirs, what is this talk of *Azar*, and *Satar*, and *Mainyu*?"

The men eyed her. They stared for a few moments, stunned that a woman such as Ambrass had been so bold.

At last, one spoke. "You do not know, my lady, about the Seven Bracelets of Arstibara?"

Ambrass shook her head. Did shaking one's head mean "no" in the Southern World?

"An evil genie crafted seven magic bracelets to wage war on what he called the wicked people of Qadirra," the man said. "They give the wielder great power, but their purpose is to destroy all that remains of this city."

"The city is intact," Ambrass said.

"Yes," the man said, "because ancient Qadirran witchcraft prevents them from working within the bounds of the Black Khazan and the Blue Khazan. Seven were made: *Ab, Azar, Mainyu, Zam, Satar, Mah and Abrah*. But the greatest bracelet is *Mainyu*, for it has no opposition."

Ambrass pondered what he had said in her mind. "Thank you,

good sirs.”

Samira was desperately trying to find the bracelet called *Mainyu*. What special powers did *Mainyu* have?

Ambrass could only guess.

Chapter Thirteen: Zealots

Headed due southeast, speeding from one oasis to another, now feasting in villages where it was possible — stomachs now full of roast lamb and roast goat, vegetables and desserts fashioned from date honey — the party of four followed Farhad through the dry grassland. As they pushed southeast, bits of rumor escaped from the villagers — that the sultan Carabh had been killed, and that the chief village of Zahar, Saanah, had been put to the sword and burned to ash. And as they continued southeast, the dry grassland was dissipating, giving way to sand and dust between sparse tufts of grass.

The sand was stinging Reev's eyes, and getting into his throat. He was growing thirsty, and though his waterskin was filled to the bursting, he knew there was a limit to how far they could travel through dry desert without refilling. Cobalt, Asté and Tyra needed to drink more than any of them. In the desert, water was more precious than gold.

Amid the barren landscape, as the sun began to set, there was the sight of a stone well. "A well!" Reev shouted, and Fortunato began walking in its direction. Farhad opened his mouth to say something, and then stopped himself.

They reached the rim of the stone well, and Reev realized that the others in the party had been drinking more heavily, that their waterskins were not as full as his.

In the dry dust, in the stinging sand, Reev stood alone, garbed in a loin cloth, his shoulders wrapped in a white desert shawl. His amulet glistened as Fortunato, then Xan, then Wrinn, filled their waterskins to bursting.

Then, there was the sound of shouting, and the blast of a

trumpet.

Figures were approaching from the horizon of dry dust and yellow grass. They were garbed all in black.

They were waving scimitars and battle-axes, screaming in their language. And as trumpets blew, more were joining them.

"Let's run!" howled Wrinn.

But Reev hesitated.

The mob of warriors began to scream as they surrounded the five of them, at first in their own language, and then, one of them, in what they would call the *lugal* tongue.

"You have drunk the water of the holy prophet Kagan!" he screamed, a young man, his face turned red. As he shouted, he bared his brown teeth.

Reev had only seen the party fill their waterskins, but when he looked to Wrinn, he saw that Wrinn's mouth was dribbling.

"We are sorry!" Farhad said, and then began to speak in one tongue, and then another. But they seized Farhad, and then they seized Xan. They were about a hundred in number, and thousands more were approaching from the barren landscape.

The four warriors of the light were skilled at war, but they were not demigods. They could not handle all the mob at once. The mob seized their weapons, and then bound their hands in rope. They drove them through the landscape of dry dust and dry desert, to a village in view of a mudbrick fortress, amid cries of "Blasphemer!" and "*Adwanim!*"

In the fortress they were thrown into a prison of mudbrick and iron bars, beaten with a birch rod one after another, then stripped down to their undergarments and separated.

Outside the mudbrick walls of Reev's cell, he could hear the sound of fires starting and the shouting of the mob.

~

Bran had gone overboard. He knew he had, leaving the torched buildings of Saanah, seeing as he walked away the bloodied bodies of the countless villagers. Their sultan had taken his kukri-knife, and Bran had taken it out on them.

He had lost time, and he had lost track of his quarry. Yet he would do his best to recover, and locate their trail. The four *lugals* would fetch a pretty price, and yet Bran had allowed the rokahn part of him to take control.

If he were to catch up to the four *lugals*, and intercept them, he would have to redouble his efforts, and make haste.

~

In the dark of his cell, Fortunato caught sight of lamplight. A southron in a long white desert robe was standing beyond the iron bars, in his hand a brightly burning oil lamp.

"Sir," he said, "come with me." In his other hand, Fortunato saw, were keys, which he finessed into the lock, and opened the door.

He followed the southron through winding corridors, beyond a walkway, past unornamented corridors of mudbrick, and at last a mudbrick room partially faced with plaster. In a room, set with many oil lamps, was an Imperial soldier with brown hair and keen brown eyes.

"Signore," he said.

Fortunato bowed his head.

"Have a seat."

Fortunato sat down at the desk where the Imperial soldier was sitting.

"We do our best in Shakrath," said the Imperial, "but the people cling to old superstitions. The faith of Mazda has waned, but old habits — 'Do not drink! Do not venture there!' — do not die easy. And a mob's justice is difficult for a proconsul to quell. But you and your party have not broken the law. We will speed you on your way."

"I thank you, proconsul," Fortunato said.

"One question," said the proconsul, "you are going to Bezakirah, no?"

Bezakirah was the stopping off point before another long leg in the journey, another long period of traveling. Yet despite the Imperials' magnanimity, Fortunato would not tell anyone he did not have to that they intended to go to *Naron Da,* to the Dark Land, to tread Seymus underfoot.

"We are going to Bezakirah," Fortunato admitted. He would tell the proconsul no more.

"And what are you doing there?" said the proconsul. "If the Shakrathites hate Imperials, the men and women of Bezkakirah would murder them on sight — were it not for our restraining hand."

"I appreciate your restraining hand," Fortunato said.

He eyed the proconsul.

"As for why we go to Bezakirah, our business is our own," Fortunato said. "I'll leave it at that, if I can."

The proconsul eyed him.

"There is a tunnel underneath the fortress," the proconsul said. "I recommend not visiting any villages in Shakrath. You have water. Make haste, all the way, to the waters of the Blue Khazan. The road to Bezakirah goes through Qadirra…"

"The ruins of Qadirra," Fortunato corrected him.

But the proconsul pursed his lips, and his eyes glistened.

Chapter Fourteen: Consulary

In the dining chamber, Ambrass ate a stew of lentils and beef, sitting next to — as always, it seemed — Samira. Ambrass couldn't help but think that the so-called King of Kings Artabanas was staring at her as she ate the stew behind the gold curtained dais that hid him.

Yet amid the sound of chomping teeth and spoons in liquid, the idle sound of chatter, there was a noise, and movement — doors sweeping open, and then slamming shut. Kavadh was approaching in the dim lamplight.

"Your Worship," he said, "an army of *lugals* wishes to have an audience with you."

The diners looked about in stunned silence. Then, there was more motion, a hand dividing the gold curtain, and Artabanas in his golden circlet stepping out. "Another *lugal* army?" he said. "The Empire is so afraid of us, they leave us alone."

Ambrass knew those were delusions of grandeur. The Empire let Artabanas alone because they weren't threatened by a pet project in the land of Potam. And also something else, something that Emperor Verrus had declared, that his family lineage had some connection to the ancient city of Qadirra.

"An army, a vast army, is gathered outside the city," said Kavadh. "They are armed with swords and shields and giant crossbows, like the Imperials, but the crests of their helmets are green, not red. Their legate wishes to speak with you."

Artabanas mumbled curses under his breath.

His silence was assent.

~

The doors swept open and slammed shut again. Now Kavadh was followed by another.

The stranger's breastplate seemed an imitation of an Imperial breastplate, indeed everything seemed an inferior mimicry of the Imperial Army's glory, but the top of his helmet was hooked, and from it radiated a green, not a red, horsehair crest. His sword, too, was a short-sword in the Imperial style, clipped in a sheath at his side.

As for the one who bore the breastplate and the shield, he was an Imperial, but something about his features seemed strange to Ambrass. In the light of the lamps, his complexion had a sickly green pallor.

"What is this?" Artabanas said, overcome by fury. "I have signed a treaty — "

He had cast a crown.

" — with the *lugal* heathens, and now you come back, dressed now in green, and say the matter isn't settled."

"I do not serve on behalf of the Empire," said the soldier, "but am in fact a legate of the consulary armies of the Imperial Bay Company. His Worship the Emperor Verrus has granted us a monopoly on the trade of pepper, cumin, and tar south of the third parallel."

Artabanas had turned a shade of red.

"Our men have done a survey of the land of Great Fharas," he said, "and we have noted the rich deposits of tar between the banks of the Blue and the Black Khazan. The shareholders of the Imperial Bay Company would like a cut of any tar extracted from those fields. Start, say, at twenty-five gallons for every one hundred gallons you extract?"

"Get out," Artabanas howled. "Get out!"

"If you will not agree to these terms," said the soldier, "we will have no choice but to lay siege."

"Get out!" Artabanas said. "Get out! Draw swords, Kavadh, and strike him dead."

Kavadh drew his scimitar and the consulary legate fled through the double doors.

The Siege of Qadirra had begun.

~

Julian had watched an army in green half-capes and green horsehair crests march over the Bridge of the Black Khazan. They hadn't returned.

The army had the look of Imperials, but something off, something lesser in quality, like they were a pale imitation of the Imperial Army's glory. As Julian stirred, eating crackers amid the burning heat of the day, he wondered just what had happened to his cousin Ambrass. He supposed no news was good news. But was that true?

In the days that followed, rumors swirled that the armies of the Imperial Bay Company had besieged Qadirra. Qadirra did not have much food in its granary to spare. But one afternoon, Julian spied in the distance dark-featured men on horseback riding over the bridge, a band thousands strong — men Julian recognized as horsemen of Megiddo. The forces of Great Fharas, and the forces of the King of Kings, Artabanas, were preparing to make the counterattack.

Chapter Fifteen: Through Sand

Having left the fortress in Shakrath behind, now venturing through dry dust and stretches of open desert, no longer heeding the threat of empty waterskins and trusting solely in Farhad's navigation, the five sped across the landscape to their goal.

Reev was occasionally leading them, having foresworn his white desert shawl, now dressed in a loin cloth alone.

Farhad had warned of desert mirages, of seeing things that weren't there, as they raced with all they had in them toward the shores of the Blue Khazan. There, they'd find the road to Bezakirah, and then — where would Xan lead them? Xan knew the way to *Naron Da.*

Reev looked about him as a scorching wind blew, as through a veil of dust there was a dark shape. The dark shape was gaining on them.

~

As Bran sighted the four *lugals* and their guide, a contest was underway between his human and rokahn natures, for he knew deep down that the six men in black were not men at all, that they had intended to lead Bran to an evil end. Yet they had promised him gold enough for a kingdom, and they did not seem unable to grant their request, being as they were something other than common men.

With each stride, Bran was gaining on them, speeding after them amid the sand-blown wastes that were the border between Shakrath and the cursed land of Potam. He sped forward, and he was gaining on them.

~

Fortunato looked back and saw a visage he knew he'd never forget. Wrinn had been correct.

There was such a thing as a half-human, half-rokahn, for it was just behind them, and it was gaining on him.

Among humans he was a giant, taller even than a tall rokahn. His face had rokahn elements and human elements, but Fortunato thought he could see the human face that would have been, but for his rokahn father. His light eyes and his aquiline nose told of a human lineage, but the fangs jutting out of his lips like tusks told of something otherwise. In his hands was a curved knife, and he gripped it as if to murder.

"It's a mirage!" Farhad howled. "It can't be real!"

That was what Farhad wanted to believe.

"How far are we away?" Fortunato shouted. "Tyra Jade will bear you, Farhad…"

Xan mounted Asté behind Wrinn. Reev charged ahead.

Xan and Wrinn on Asté, Farhad and Fortunato on Tyra Jade, and Reev on Cobalt, and they began to speed away from the half-rokahn at a quicker pace.

But Cobalt and Asté were panting for lack of water, and Tyra Jade was whining. How long would their mounts be an asset, and when would they become an obstacle?

~

Bran saw the four *lugals* and their guide mount on beasts, but the beasts they rode were not fit for the heat and dryness of the desert. Bran would follow them, and he would wear them out. He would follow their scent, as his rokahn blood allowed, and Bran would have enough gold for a kingdom

King Bran, and his wife…

Chapter Sixteen: Her Eyes

The siege of Qadirra had gone on for days. Ambrass had kept quiet in her room, fearing not for Qadirra nor for Artabanas, but for her people, now captured and under threat by the shores of the Black Khazan.

The armies of the Imperial Bay Company intended to starve out the people of Qadirra, or rather rebuilt Qadirra, to extract from Artabanas some sieve of wealth. But Artabanas had refused to acquiesce.

Ambrass had a difficult time giving Artabanas any plaudits at all, but she supposed it was not ignoble to refuse to concede to the interlopers.

Interlopers — an army operating within Imperial borders, one did not have the interests of the people or those they ruled, now running free through the Southern World. Ambrass had nor respect for the Imperial Bay Company. She supposed she had no respect for the Imperial Bay Company, or the rebuilding project within the borders of Potam.

In her room, she thought of her people, and she prayed. The Imperial Bay Company had encamped around the city. The people of Qadirra were under threat. Ambrass didn't care. Her mind went elsewhere — and yet... and yet... there was noise, and motion. Footsteps.

The eunuch was standing at her door.

"Lady Ambrass," he said, "the King of Kings wishes to have an audience with you."

Ambrass would not dance for him. Of that she was certain. She no longer had it in her to try to please him.

~

Artabanas took Ambrass in her green veil by the hand, and as they broached the castle gate, and entered the yard with its mirrored pools, "I wish you to see, gypsy queen, that there is strength in Fharas yet. I wish you to see, I am truly the King of Kings of my people, and that Fharas will rule again over the whole of the world."

Ambrass demurred, wishing to be gone, wishing for this man to leave her people be, wishing for the Empire or even the Imperial Bay Company to drive him from the rebuilt Qadirra, and rescue the gypsies from his wiry hands.

But as they climbed the stairs to the battlements of the wall, she could already here the sound of battle begin — a horde thousands strong, rushing in from the north.

They were cataphracts in glittering mail, and auxiliaries — wild men riding on horses and carrying bows. They were all the strength of Fharas, sent against the forces of the Imperial Bay Company.

And though Ambrass made a silent prayer that the cataphracts and the horsemen would fail, when the battle began, it was clear from the outset that the armies of the Imperial Bay Company did not have the strength and bravery of the Empire in them. The cataphracts bowled over the Imperial Bay Company's lines, and in that moment, a few already began to flee. As the battle progressed, and the Imperial Bay Company fought back half-heartedly, it was clear the Imperial Bay Company only vanquished foes that showed no resistance.

By the time the sun had grown high in the sky, by the time the day was about done, the consulary armies of the Imperial Bay Company were fleeing into the desert sun, and the day was won.

They would not be getting their twenty five percent tax of tar in the rebuilt lands of Qadirra, in the rebuilt Great Fharas.

Yet when Artabanas turned to Ambrass, his eyes were a storm.

"Ambrass," said Artabanas. "I see the way your eyes look upon me. I see how little respect you have for me. Though you try to hide it, I know. I will sell your wagons to raise funds for the great war that is coming. I will sell your people in the slave markets of Karthoon. As for you, you may depart in the morning. Your people shall be in bondage, but a queen shall never be."

Chapter Seventeen: The Summons

As the stinging dust swirled about Reev and the others, the animals were beginning to slow their pace, their bodies to shut down in the wake of the heat and the lack of water. Reev dismounted from Cobalt, and as he did, he saw the dark form of the half-rokahn staggering ahead, veiled in dust.

They would all be dead, it seemed, for against such a creature, four humans and an elf did not seem an adequate match.

Yet as he stood, there was the sound of shouting — Farhad gazing into the horizon in horror. A wall of sand stretching to the clouds was approaching from the east.

"A sandstorm!" Farhad howled. "We are all done for!"

Reev twisted and looked about. He thought the animals would do better in a sandstorm.

The half-rokahn was eyeing the wall of sand, and had stopped his pursuit.

Reev looked to his right, and saw amid the stinging dust and poor visibility, the shape of a tower — a place to take shelter. And though they had been beaten and seized in Shakrath, though the tower could have a wicked tower keeper, it was better than dying in the wind and sand, or at the end of the half-rokahn's curved knife.

"Look!" Reev shouted, and before they had turned, made his way toward the tower's dark shape, an outline in the sand.

~

The tower was of a strange style, with plain columns and a jagged spiked roof. At the front of it was a massive iron door, with holes where gems should be, but the gems had been pilfered.

Xan, Fortunato, Wrinn and Farhad came rushing up to the door, as Reev laid his hands upon the handholds, and pulled.

It was locked.

And Reev saw there was a keyhole.

"It's locked," Reev said.

He saw in the distance, the half-rokahn was fleeing, sprinting away from the approaching wall of sand.

"It's locked," Reev repeated, "but Ivan Xandrast has the Skeleton Key."

Xan seemed to have forgotten he was in possession of what was a former warlock's tool, which once emitted heatless black smoke but now glowed with a faint white glow.

Xan took the Skeleton Key from his pocket, the magical key that could open any lock in Varda. Could it unlock this one?

He pressed it in, and there was a clicking sound, then the sound of humming, and the doors fell open, just as the cloud of sand rushed over them with a roar.

They fled into the darkness of the tower and shut the door behind them.

~

"We are alone," Xan said amid the pitch darkness. "We can wait out the storm."

There was a spark amid the darkness, then a chorus of sparks. Then there was a blazing fire. In Farhad's hand was a torch, and it illuminated a flagstone floor, and walls of black stone.

"What is this place?" Wrinn said.

"I do not know," Farhad replied, "I haven't been here before, but the architecture it looks… it looks…"

He paused.

"It looks like the work of Naamer," Farhad said.

"Naamer?" Wrinn said.

"The ancient ones who ruled what is now the Desert of Hamma left many wonders in their wake," Farhad said. "Yes, yes, let's explore, while we wait out the storm."

Farhad strode out amid the vastness of the tower.

To Reev's mind, the tower seemed bare, but its architectural features were perfectly preserved. Along the walls were serpentine reliefs and holes where gemstones should have been, but which had been pilfered. He drew Doomblade and thought he saw something — the flash of a green face, two pairs of yellow eyes, an angry hiss.

The party had spread out throughout the tower. Outside, the sandstorm howled. Reev prayed for Tyra Jade, for Cobalt and Asté.

Farhad was walking up to a panel in the wall. In the panel was what looked like wedge writing.

Fortunato strode up behind him.

"What does it say, Farhad?" Fortunato said.

"It's Naamer writing," Farhad replied.

~

Bran strode up to the doors of the tower, through the whirling sand and wind that would kill most any human. He laid his meaty hands inside the handholds, and pulled with all his rokahn might.

It was sealed so well, and so strongly, he might as well have been an ant, tugging with his black fingers.

He turned around and saw six figures in the sand. Six figures in black. They were approaching.

~

"*Ka a na ga,*" Farhad was reading the Naamer writing on the metal panel in the tower's wall. "It says, 'I summon.' "

"*Ka a na ga wa nachshli.* 'I summon the Sons of Nachash.' "

The air in the tower changed, and there was the sound of a

wind, though no wind blew on Reev's skin.

Farhad looked about in terror, as burning fires appeared where Reev had thought gemstones should have been, in the pockets of the wall.

The tower was as bright as the outdoors in twilight, as through a dark passageway two men appeared.

Yet they were not men, but spirits, for their glowing forms were transparent. They looked like humans, but for their skin of greenish sallow hue, with flakes like scales. Their visages, surely hideous, were hidden by masks of baked clay, with holes for their yellowish eyes and their pale lips. From the sides of their masks, it was evident that their ears were pointed, and had the same greenish sallow hue as their skin.

One was holding a javelin, and was in the process of throwing it.

Farhad had been impaled, and was bleeding. The men in masks were transparent, but their weapons were not.

They raced for Fortunato and had drawn daggers. Reev screamed as Fortunato drew Danenhir, and parried once, and then again. Wrinn and Xan were fleeing. There was a way out, Reev saw, he hadn't noticed, a hollow in the tower bare to the outdoors. Fortunato struck and barreled past the ghostly figures and fled through the hollow, after Wrinn and Xan.

But Reev did not flee. He faced the ghostly figures, and he sensed they were afraid of him.

He strode toward them, bearing Doomblade, and their yellowish eyes were wide with fear. They licked their lips nervously, and Reev was surprised their tongues were not forked.

He realized why they were afraid of him — his kind had killed them before. They were the Sons of Nachash, and he was a Telantine.

"Are you afraid of me?" Reev said. "You should be!"

He raced at the ghostly figures and struck. One parried and his dagger shattered into pieces. He stabbed at one and his target dove away, but instead his sword pierced the other's chest.

The ghostly figure sank to the ground and his shimmering figure began to dim.

The other stood by in terror as Reev slashed his arm, then pierced his chest, then beheaded him. His ghostly form sank to the ground.

As the two figures evaporated into ghostly vapor, the red color of the flames of the tower turned to brilliant white.

A figure was approaching through the hollow in the tower, a woman in a dark leather vest, her black hair tied in a bun. She was gripping a dagger in her hand.

"Agent Secunda!" Reev shouted.

"The aegis shrine has been purified," she said. "Good work, son of Telantis."

~

Bran stood and stared at the six figures in black, as the howling winds and blowing sands of the sandstorm passed them by, and all was quiet amid the barrens.

"They escaped me," Bran said.

"And yet," whispered one of the six figures, one whom Bran guessed was their chief, whose iron mask he could barely make out, wrapped as it was in a black hood, "you have driven the party here, to their doom."

Bran looked at them, at their dark knives and swords of a blackish-gray color, and thought those weapons were not weapons of a normal kind, that they would cause a most deadly wound.

"Our plans have changed, Bran," said the chief of the men in black. "Events are conspiring in our favor in a way we have not seen in millennia. We have a new task for you, Bran, now that you have driven the boy and his party to doom. You must complete their doom, and the gold we promised will be delivered to you."

"What is that task?" Bran said.

"A shard of our master's sword has been unearthed not far from Qadirra, the largest shard ever uncovered," said the chief of the men in black. "A band of elves are transporting it through the wilds north of the Blue Khazan to ensure it does not fall into our hands. Even with the magic gloves they carry, they can only carry it an hour a day, for it burns their flesh. Nor do they dare share the burden, but have chosen a scapegoat. If we have possession of this shard, all the hopes of the boy and his party are over. And you will have your kingdom, Bran, under the suzerainty of our master."

"Who is your master?" Bran said.

Perhaps, Bran didn't want to know.

"And why don't you kill them yourselves, and take it?" Bran said.

If the chief of the men in black had a mouth, Bran guessed he was smiling beneath the folds of his cloak. "Doors and gates are open to you, Bran," he said. "But doors and gates are not open to us, and the elves know this."

He did not trust these men in black. No, Bran did not even like them. But for gold, and a kingdom, perhaps he'd do as they ask.

Chapter Eighteen: Hydropower

In the night, Ambrass had wept bitterly at the fate of her people. At the witching hour she had said a prayer. And now, as dawn broke, she had formed a plan.

She would use Artabanas's weaknesses against him. She had brushed her hair and braided it in plaits, as she had seen southron women wear. She had dabbed her face with red powder, and applied ochre to her lips. And she was dabbing Ink-of-Tyrrhenos on her eyes in the mirror, when a figure appeared through the door.

"You will dance for my husband," said Samira. "Let me offer you some advice. He does not like to be bored. Come with me."

~

Ambrass strode out into the King of Kings' throne without invitation, garbed in the flowered red robe of a Cathayan maiden. She had powdered her face with chalk, so white she looked like a pantomime. She did not wear a veil, but disguised her eyes with a hand fan as she sashayed before Artabanas and shouted to the lutist and the drummer, "Play *Kings of Wind and Water*!"

The lutist plucked his lute to a pentatonic tune. Flutes began to play, and when the drummer joined in, Ambrass let herself be carried away by the melody, prancing on her feet from one end of the room to the other before Artabanas's throne. As Ambrass danced, Artabanas's face changed from a look of fury to a look of interest.

The pentatonic tune built in on itself, cascading to new melodic heights, as Ambrass sashayed and then spun, waving her hand fan back and forth and trying to step gingerly and teasingly before the one who called himself the King of Kings.

The drum pounded and Ambrass struck her hairpiece. Her bundle of hair fell to her back.

A cymbal clanged and Ambrass struck the buttons of her robe, and it all unfurled, baring her smock.

The melody ended, and Ambrass removed her smock, casting the hand fan to the ground. She was in her loin-piece and brassiere. She slid to the floor.

At the sight of her, Artabanas seemed changed. He was looking at her in a new way, a way Ambrass hated, but what did she expect? All she could do for her people, she had done.

"You have pleased the king," said Artabanas. "What is your request?"

"Let my people pass through your kingdom," Ambrass said. "Let me accompany them."

Artabanas's mouth twisted to a sadistic grin. "Your people are gone, Ambrass. I have sold their wagons to the Imperial Bay Company. They are marching through the forests of Kash, now, and will be sold at high price to the slavers of Karthoon. And yet, for your dance, you shall be rewarded. My chief wife has displeased me, and so we will be wed, and you be made my chief wife."

It was the last thing Ambrass had wanted in the world.

~

As cataphracts pushed Julian and the other gypsies down a ridge through the thick growth of Kash, he said a prayer under his breath. Under his sleeve he still had his recurve dagger, and he intended not to give up hope, even as in the distance monkeys hooted and a rain began to pour, a sign of how far they had gone.

Amid the hot jungle, he looked about him. They were coming to the banks of a gushing river. As he walked, he eyed the river and its banks. He saw something gleaming — something metallic.

He turned to the cataphract beside him. "Sir! I must relieve myself!" he said.

Julian was not the best of liars, but the cataphract uttered some angry breath of assent, as Julian broached the undergrowth, pushing through tangled vines and thick bushes, amid the sweltering heat, to the gleam of something metallic in the water, and something, Julian sensed, magical.

He had seen such an eldritch gleam in the eyes of wizards back in Galiope, and in the eyes of magi in the Southern World. The gleam he saw in the water, he realized, was not just metal, but something more. As Julian pushed through the brush, he found himself by the crystal-clear water, and there amid a raging current, partially covered in mud, was a gold bracelet affixed with a shining blue gem.

The way it shone was so bright, it could not have been a reflection of the sun. It was brilliant, almost like fire. And Julian waited through the waters, and grasped ahold of it, but as he did the cataphract came storming through the brush on his horse.

"Stop this!" the cataphract hissed, and slashed with his scimitar.

But the cutting of his blade was met with Julian's recurve dagger. He slashed with his recurve dagger and the blade grazed the cataphract's chainmail. He struck him with the pommel and the cataphract gasped. He stabbed with the recurve dagger, and found a weakness in the chainmail, and the cataphract fell off his horse, bleeding to death.

Now an entire army of cataphracts was headed to Julian. As they pushed through the brush and were almost upon him, he dropped his recurve dagger and placed the blue-gemmed bracelet over his arm.

He felt something change. He felt something fill him.

The blue fire on the bracelet began to blaze. The cataphracts were now turning around, as a roar filed Julian's ears. He turned back, and saw trees crashing to the earth — beyond the river, a wall of water crushing all in its path, and amid that wall of water the shape of fangs and gaping teeth.

"Carnivorous waves!" Julian shouted, as the wall of water rushed over him and not on him, as it spewed through the jungle and decimated all in its path.

Julian walked beyond the flattened trees, to a landscape now flooded, and saw that the waters that the bracelet had summoned had bowled over and drowned the cataphracts, but not the gypsies they had captured and had intended to enslave.

The gypsies were standing in the jungle road, thousands of them in a line, and they had barely been sprayed with water. They were looking at Julian like he was a hero.

Chapter Nineteen: Her Hero

Past sandy earth and stands of dry grass, past ground that had not seen rain in months, perhaps years, Fortunato led Wrinn and Xan across the landscape, now beyond the tower in which they had taken shelter. Tyra Jade and Asté were following them.

"What about Reev?" Wrinn said.

"Reev has another task," said Fortunato. "A personal fight of his own."

How did Fortunato know that? He just knew.

But Wrinn and Xan listened to Fortunato, and believed him, as through the barren landscape appeared the shores of a great river.

It rushed across the dry dusty landscape, and though Farhad was dead and unable to tell, Fortunato guessed it was the Blue Khazan.

"The Blue Khazan," said Xan. "We cross it, and we will be in the land of Potam. The road to Bezakirah goes through the ruins of Qadirra. It will be easy to find that road…"

"Let's not worry about that road, Xan," Fortunato said, "until Reev finishes the fight ahead of him…"

"And what will we do in the meantime?" Xan said.

They forded the Blue Khazan in the afternoon, and found a settlement by its banks at dusk. There, they learned rumor — rumors of seven magic bracelets, of the Imperial Bay Company waging war, and of a gypsy queen who called herself Ambrass engaged to be married to the Fharese King of Kings.

It was that last rumor Fortunato set his heart against. Ambrass belonged to him, and to no one else.

~

Ambrass wept softly in her room, mourning her people, yes, but also mourning for herself. She had not wanted to be wed to Artabanas, and now she would be forced — at the end of a cataphract's scimitar. And so quietly she uttered prayers and asked what god could hear her, for her rescue. She prayed silently, and she was beginning to pray aloud, when the door to her room in the women's apartments opened, and standing there was a woman, an avatar of wrath.

Samira was glaring at Ambrass with boundless hate. "Chief wife," she said, and as she did her spittle crossed the room and struck Ambrass's face. "I help you, and you steal what I love best from me. Artabanas takes me from his highest place, and for a gypsy, not much better than a *lugal.* You will learn to rue the day you ever came to the land of Great Fharas, Ambrass. By the time I am done with you, you will learn to rue the day you were ever born."

That was a threat, Ambrass knew.

The boundless hate in Samira's eyes grew. "But before I do, Ambrass, my husband will learn to mourn what he lost, before I end you both.

"Do you know, Ambrass, that one of your people uncovered a magic bracelet that was thought lost? The magic bracelet called *Ab* is now in the possession of a gypsy. Most unfitting! The seven magic bracelets that the evil genie Arstibara forged are purposed for Qadirra's destruction. But instead, I will turn their power to destroy you."

It was a threat, indeed.

And Ambrass prayed she would be rescued. She prayed, and she thought, and she pondered. The figure in the back of her mind, the one who threatened to take control of her life and soul, was growing larger. What was his name? Who was he?

Was he her hero?

~

Samira had savored the look of terror on the gypsy queen's face. She knew that Artabanas had chosen Ambrass over her. She also knew that what Samira wanted was what Ambrass wanted least. So she would relish the fact that her enemy was in anguish as the wedding date approached, even as she tried to locate the bracelet called *Mainyu,* the bracelet that would allow her control over all of the genie Arstibara's powers.

Ab had been discovered by one of Ambrass's relatives. *Azar,* with powers over fire, was on Fenris's arm. One, *Satar,* with powers over star-fire and star-magic, was tucked away in a lockbox that Kavadh had hidden somewhere in the palace. Samira would not embark on her quest unarmed. So she supposed she would start with *Satar.*

She strode into her room. She opened her desk. She found the candelabra in which she had enslaved the genie who called himself Das. She beckoned with her mind, then shouted, "Das, come out."

He emerged, the hateful genie, a tendril of green smoke arising from the candelabra to his green body.

"Tell me where *Satar* is, and unlock the lockbox," said Samira.

Das's yellow eyes softened, as if to gain sympathy. It wouldn't work on Samira. No, it would not work at all. Samira glared at him with the fury that possessed anyone who worked with these creatures, who by wit and sharp ripostes of the tongue, and swift catchings of gold objects, forced genies into their service.

"If you free me," Das said. "I will do so."

Samira sighed. "Would you like a lash again, Das?"

"I will endure all your blows," Das said, "but I will not tell you where *Satar* is, nor unlock the lockbox, unless you promise to free me."

"I promise," said Samira.

Das gazed at her. "Promise, on the honor of your husband."

Samira smiled. Oh, the things that genies did not know, when they were trapped in a prison of gold. "I promise on the honor of my husband," she said.

The genie wafted away to his work.

Samira waited as her genie worked his magic on a lockbox that Kavadh had so desperately tried to hide away. When Das returned, and wafted again from the candelabra's fixture, his green body glowing, he eyed her. "It is hidden in the vault," said Das. "There is an entrance behind the throne. Now release me."

Samira smiled a sadistic smile. "I promised on the honor of my husband," she said, "but he has no honor, for he exchanged me for an outsider. Now go back into your prison, wicked genie."

Das's yellow eyes rolled up into the back of his head, and he vanished into the candelabra. Das had been thwarted again.

Samira donned her veil, and exited her room. Beyond the women's apartments, she moved quietly. The vault was not meant to be visited by anyone but the emperor and the marshal of the army, Kavadh.

But Artabanas, as was normal, was not on his throne, and the throne room was empty. Samira walked behind the throne, and saw the door she had seen a few times before, barely visible against a wall of white plaster. She opened it and descended down the stairs, down steps that were crafted of iron and had holes, to a room wherein was the scent of chemicals and moist air.

The stairs were taxing, and it beggared belief how deep they traveled, down a vault that was truly a chasm, like a bottomless pit. By the time she had reached the bottom of the vault, Samira was panting and sweating, completely exhausted. She could no longer bear to wear her veil, and removed it despite the law and the regulation.

How far had she traveled down the metal stairs? She had to be deep below Varda's surface.

In the vault, where she had never been before, there was not much, except a giant white tube that stretched up the entirety of the wall before vanishing into the darkness, with writing on it of inscrutable meaning — and on a metal desk, a lockbox, hanging open.

She walked up to the lockbox, and opened it. She saw within it something that was worth the cost of many kingdoms, a gold bracelet inset with a shining white gem. She knew what she did would displease Artabanas, for the seven bracelets of the genie Arstibara were pledged to destroy the city of Qadirra totally.

But Samira knew from experience, the designs of genies like Arstibara could be easily thwarted by anyone of a little cunning and wit. She could easily use the magical bracelet called *Satar* in a way opposite to what Arstibara had intended.

She eyed the bracelet greedily and took it in her hands. She marveled it as she slid it over her left arm. She felt power course through her.

The power of the stars was now at her fingertips.

Chapter Twenty: Hyperborean

Agent Secunda stood before Reev, a woman he had met once before.

He had been held captive in the Imperial Palace, and had discovered during his sojourn a brotherhood of spies that had operated since the Empire's founding and before, called the Oculus. The chief of the Oculus, Marius, had called Agent Secunda a woman of a silver tongue, and a master of disguises.

They stood amid the tower, what Agent Secunda had called an "aegis shrine."

"You followed me all this way?" Reev said. "All the way through the desert, through the Southern World?"

"On the contrary, Reev," said Agent Secunda, "as soon as you left our company, I was assigned here — to this part of the world. For the rebuilding of Qadirra, the city that once ruled the world, has attracted the interest of the Oculus. I was sent here to thwart its rebuilding, and I worried we were too late. But you did what none of us were capable of — you entered the aegis shrine, and you purified it."

"What do you mean?" Reev said.

"This tower is called the Aegis Shrine of Borean Hindrance," she said. "It is one of two poles that allow Qadirra's witchcraft to manifest, and for its ancient spells of protection and cursing to endure. Qadirrans built it to hinder the power of the gods and the power of the one coming — the hero pledged to destroy the city of Qadirra once and for all."

Reev guessed Agent Secunda was talking about him. But being called a hero or someone of importance would never be easy to Reev from Norwood.

"How did you enter it?" Agent Secunda said. "Its doors too are protected by an ancient Qadirran spell, that none may enter."

"You entered it yourself, without my help," Reev said.

"The hollow in the tower only manifested with the summoning of the tower's guardians," Agent Secunda said, "the guardians you were somehow able to slay and put to death."

Agent Secunda stirred and walked through the breadth of the tower. Reev saw a glass panel, and on it green writing aglow. The writing, though, was of a kind Reev could not understand. Yet Secunda was eyeing it, and it seemed legible to her.

"This is Telantine writing," Agent Secunda said. "Come, take a look. Try to perceive it."

Reev walked over to her, and fixed his eyes on the glass panel. He focused on the individual letters, and as he did, he felt something wash over him, understanding, insight — like he had known those letters, and writings, an age ago.

"It says," Reev said, " 'Sequence aborted. Hindrance two not lifted. Heaven's Spear — status, inert.' "

"Good work," said Agent Secunda. "The name Heaven's Spear seems promising. Tantalizing, even. Something called Heaven's Spear would work wonders against our enemy, Emperor Verrus…"

"My enemy is the Dark One," Reev said.

Agent Secunda said, "Will you not speak of Emperor Verrus and the Dark One in the same breath?" Reev supposed he would.

"The shrine is purified," said Agent Secunda, "and perhaps you will be able to grip Heaven's Spear in your hands if you purify the second shrine. This shrine, in the west, is called the Aegis Shrine of Borean Hindrance. But in the north is another tower, the Aegis Shrine of Hyperborean Hindrance."

"Where is this tower?" Reev said. "Do you know the way?"

~

Cobalt had wandered off, but the Blue Khazan and the rich grasslands that surrounded Qadirra were not far. They had left the desert and its dangers behind, and the dangers they faced would be new. But Cobalt would now have grass to eat, and water to drink, and Reev would not worry. Cobalt was one undulating song away.

They ventured, then, on foot, Reev in his loin cloth and coin amulet and Agent Secunda in her vest. Agent Secunda, Reev saw, was sporting a thick dagger at her side, and he wondered what other weapons the spies of the Oculus had in their arsenal. Back in the Imperial Palace, he had heard talk of "forgetfulness powder" and items that would allow a person to travel easily in jungle terrain. Yet their powers were not of magic or the arcane, but marvels of artisanship and engineering.

They were travelling the dry rocky ground north of Qadirra, days later, when Reev saw the ground begin to rise, and mountains veiled in hazy air. There, amid the rock of one low mountain, was the shape of a tower of a similar kind and style to the Aegis Shrine of Borean Hindrance.

On the ground surrounding the mountain, however, was an army. Agent Secunda handed Reev what appeared to be a tube of metal, and said, "Look into the glass."

He looked into the glass, and could see far away, as if he were standing just inches from his gathered foes.

"A spyglass," said Agent Secunda. "It's yours, if you want it."

"I want it," Reev said softly as he fixed the spyglass on the army.

He could see them, dressed varyingly of quilted cloth or of splint armor, arrayed with spears or with swords or axes, a motley assortment of weapons. But as he fixed his focus on their faces, bare to see in their light helmets, he noticed slight variations from the normal. Some had greenish, sallow skin, and others of more imperceptible greenish hue. Some had soupy eyes, or harsh features. When he spotted one with skin Reev would perhaps call clearly green, with yellow eyes and prominent canines, he knew what he was looking at.

"Anguipeds," Reev said.

During his captivity in the Imperial Palace, he had learned of a conspiracy against the Imperial people. A non-human species called anguipeds had been infiltrating the Empire's elite. Emperor Verrus was of anguiped blood, but the gathered soldiers arrayed before the army seemed of purer anguiped blood than he. Emperor Verrus's anguiped lineage was hardly to be seen.

"And where are they coming from?" said Agent Secunda. "Beyond here are wastes that none can travel, where no one lives. But the anguipeds must have a homeland. Their homeland has never been uncovered."

"Never uncovered," Reev said, "but they are massing at the aegis shrine. They are protecting it. They seem to know it is under threat."

"They have heard of your work," said Agent Secunda. "They know that Telantis's hero has arrived."

Chapter Twenty-One: Fire and Water

Julian led the gypsies through the rainforests of Kash after their triumph. The armies of the wicked king Artabanas had been utterly destroyed, and it was because of a magic bracelet Julian had retrieved from the river. They had been defending themselves; now, they would press the advantage and go to war.

The trees were vanishing behind them, replaced with grassland. Julian was at the head of them, leading them back to their wagons and then — he hoped — their victory. They would not stop now, armed with a magical weapon. They would rescue their queen, Julian's cousin, from the king Artabanas, and then they would be on their way. They would find Vharat. They would go home, where they belonged, to the ancient gypsy homeland, where Ambrass had insisted there was wine on the leaves of the trees like dew, and honey dripping down the trees' bark like sap.

Hours beyond the forest, through the scorching heat, and they were in grassland again as the sun was beginning its westward journey. They had come to the wagons, and the gypsies were not alone.

Soldiers were standing there, like Imperial soldiers, but their steel helmets and steel breastplates were contrasted by green rather than red, and the tops of their helmets were hooked. They were eyeing the wagons.

"What is this valued at?" said one of the soldiers before Julian and the gypsies made their presence known.

But Julian shouted and the soldiers looked up. Julian thought there were about three dozen. The soldiers drew their swords and rushed toward the gypsies, but Julian lifted his magic bracelet and cast his other hand forward.

A waterspout burst into existence underneath a soldier's leg, and he soared toward the heavens with the waterspout. Blasts of water burst the others, as there was a roaring sound, and a wall of water again appeared in the horizon, a wall of water with fangs and teeth, the carnivorous waves. In a fury of water and raging tempest, the soldiers were dead and scattered across the ground before the wagons. "To war! To war!" Julian shouted, as gypsies pilfered the soldiers' swords and shields, and then hopped into their own wagons, one by one.

~

Ambrass was eating silently. All life was gone from her, all life and all hope. She no longer wished to live another day, knowing she would be wed to Artabanas. She would be little better than his slave.

She could not bear to incline her head toward the gold-curtained dais, from whence Artabanas was surely staring at her. She could no longer bear much.

But as she ate her chicken stew, the doors to the dining chamber opened, and Kavadh came rushing out. "My king!" he cried. "The gypsies have uncovered the bracelet called *Ab*, and are using it against you... What's more, its power now works beyond the banks of the Black Khazan."

"Impossible," said Artabanas, now pushing through the gold curtain. "The ancient spell of Qadirra prevents it."

One rose from his table, one Samira had spoken of. He was covered head to toe in fur, Fenris, a former magus and now something else entirely, someone of a different, and Ambrass guessed, deadlier, power. Yet as he rose he took his magi's staff. As he spoke he gripped it in his furry hands. "Not impossible," said Fenris. "Two poles of power cause the spell of the Qadirrans to continue, two aegis shrines, one in the west and one in the north. If they are demolished, the spell will fail, and the Seven Bracelets of

Arstibara can do what they intended, bring about the final destruction of Qadirra."

Fenris's voice was deep and low, and Ambrass could almost imagine the man he would have been, were it not for the ray of moonlight that changed him.

Samira said he returned to his human form when he was "moonstruck." What was "moonstruck?"

"We must go to the aegis shrines," said Artabanas. "We must see to it that they are not demolished, that the spell endures."

"First things come first," said Fenris. "The gypsies are now armed with a powerful weapon, one that threatens to destroy us all. I must eliminate them…"

Ambrass wailed.

Fenris raised up the bracelet he carried on his arm, affixed with a glowing red gem. With a shake of his staff, he walked through the doors to work his magic on Ambrass's people.

~

Julian was riding in his wagon at the front of the caravan, toward Qadirra. He was speeding as fast as wagons could go toward the city where his cousin and the gypsies' queen, Ambrass, was being held captive. Beyond the tar-pocked landscape, there was nothing — nothing, except a figure riding toward them.

When Julian saw him, he was horrified.

The man riding toward Julian was covered in fur, and his mouth protruded so as to form a muzzle. In the man's hand was a staff shaped like a shepherd's crook, and over his body was a striped robe of many colors, red, green, yellow, blue and white. When Julian saw the bracelet on his right arm, he swallowed a scream, that there was another magic bracelet, and that his enemy possessed it.

Yet Julian wouldn't back down, nor would he give in to fear. He stood up in his wagon and shouted, "Carnivorous waves!" and as he heard a rush of water, the furry figure on the horse also raised up his magic bracelet. Fire swirled overhead — columns and jets — and the sky, it seemed was aflame.

And amid the battle, there was a struggle, fire against water, and the contest was not between the might of two men, but the might of two bracelets crafted by ancient power. The bracelets were battling against each other, and one would prevail — and it was not up to Julian or the furry creature to decide.

It was a contest — a bracelet of fire, against a bracelet of water.

And water was winning.

The fire was fading, clouds of water against clouds of fire, fire dissipating to smoke. Julian felt a buzzing about his hands, as the blue bracelet he wore on his arm prevailed over the red bracelet the furry creature wore on his.

When Julian looked down at the bracelet he wore, it was now silverish-gold, and the fiery gemstone was the color of a flaming emerald. Fire and water — what powers did Julian now possess?

The furry creature's arm was now bare, and he bore no bracelet.

Julian gave chase, and as he did, called down what his bracelet now allowed, not fire nor water but both — columns of steam and burning rain, as the furry creature fled on his horse, galloping at a breakneck pace.

The magic bracelet of steam was fading in power as they progressed, and as the wagons followed as fast as a wagon could, they had come in sight of the walls of Qadirra.

Julian could no longer summon columns of steam and boiling rain. The improved bracelet seemed to have no effect, so close to the city.

~

When Fenris had returned, most diners had returned to their rooms. But Ambrass had waited by the table with her empty bowl of stew, hoping Fenris would return with bad news. When she saw Fenris's grimace as he entered through the doors, she felt she would not be disappointed.

"Your Worship!" Fenris said. "Good news and bad. Which do you wish to hear first?"

"Out with it!" howled Artabanas behind the gold curtain.

"An aegis shrine holds. The city and its immediate outskirts are protected. The bracelets have power throughout much of our land, but you are safe here — we are safe. One of the aegis shrines must have been demolished. We must ensure the other one remains intact, or else we are done for," Fenris said.

"What was the good news?" Artabanas said.

"That was the good news," Fenris said nervously.

Artabanas hissed and uttered a string of curses behind the gold curtain.

"There was a battle of the bracelets, *Ab* the one they carry, and *Azar* the one I carried," Fenris said. "The one the gypsies carried prevailed."

Ambrass would try to hide her joy.

"Our bracelets were combined," said Fenris. "Fire and water makes steam. The gypsies have grown stronger. We must — "

"Silence!" howled Artabanas. "This is what we were afraid of. Of the Seven Bracelets being used, and inexplicably resulting in what is their goal, the destruction of our city. But you just *had* to bear *Azar*, didn't you?"

"I apologize, Your Worship," said Fenris.

"Kavadh has a bracelet in his lockbox," said Artabanas, "in the vault behind my throne. It has powers over stars. It is called *Satar*. Go get it. Perhaps, stars can prevail over steam."

"At once, Your Worship," said Fenris.

And Fenris rushed away, and Ambrass again waited, praying silently for disaster.

Again, she was not disappointed, when Fenris returned, and his face looked ashen — if a furry face could be ashen.

"Someone has taken it, Your Worship!" Fenris howled.

And the string of curses Artabanas let loose were fit for the history books.

Chapter Twenty-Two: Starfall

Samira was at the banks of the Blue Khazan. She did not know where *Mainyu* was. She had only an inkling.

Mainyu, the most powerful of the bracelets, would spell doom to the others, for in it Samira could gain control and forbid Qadirra's destruction forever. She could imagine it, as she dipped into the waters of the Black Khazan, how it all would go, and what she would say. She would rescue her husband's kingdom, but then she would have all powers of fire and water and earth, cloud and star and mind. Her husband would see what a cunning ally he had lost, and then she would destroy both her husband and the one with whom he had betrayed her.

What then? She would rule as an ancient Qadirran queen, unbridled and unmoored until the end of her days. As she climbed onto the opposite shore, she imagined what she would wear as queen regnant, a rich purple robe festooned with gemstones. She would have the richest stews, and she could eat all the stews she wanted. She would have it all — but first, she'd savor the look of terror on her husband's face.

Beyond her were scrub brush and bare rock. She was north of the land of Potam, what her husband called Great Fharas.

There was wilderness beyond it, stretches of wilderness, and here, Samira thought, the bracelets that were unaccounted for would be found. *Satar* had been discovered on the slopes of a high mountain. Fenris had discovered *Azar* in a ruin not far from the banks of the Black Khazan.

So where would she go? And how would she find it amid the wilderness?

Das, the wicked genie, knew — of that she was certain. But he was resistant to her inquests.

Another genie, weaker — someone of weaker will, would be able to tell her where to find *Mainyu.* Then, her fate would be sealed.

To trap a genie required two things. It required an object of gold that could fit them and seal them inside, and it required a sense beyond hearing or sight, one that few had, and one which almost exclusively was found in women. As Samira stood amid the air, she used that special sense, and as she tried to find feelings of anger or fear, she removed a golden tea kettle, and tried to follow it.

She felt fear coming from the north, great terrible fear. A fearful genie would be easy to bend to her will. Samira trekked on, at a rapid pace, following that feeling only she could sense.

~

Bran could see the elves below. From a cliff, he surveilled them, as they traversed three miles a day, carrying an object that would burn through common wood or metal, or anything that could contain it.

The elves were arrayed in silken robes of light colors. Their hair was long and varied from brown to blond. The scapegoat, as the six men in black had called him, was an elf with long blond hair, carrying a pair of magic gloves, with which he was carrying a large shard of green metal.

The six men in black wished Bran to waylay them, but Bran knew elves were possessed of magic, and among them there were great sorcerers that Bran — having no magical talent — would have to deal with.

And so he was merely waiting, merely watching, trying to understand all the factors they would face. When the elves stopped at twilight, they would set up a tent, a tent that prevented the six men in black from entering, but which would not hold against Bran.

There were about a hundred of them. At least one was a

sorcerer.

Bran would wait until the perfect moment, and no less.

~

Through the wilds, Samira followed the fear, the fear that caused in her no small amount of delight. She imagined battering and bruising the frightened genie with her words, until it did as she said, and told her where she could find what she wanted most of all, the magical bracelet called *Mainyu*. She followed the fear, and she sped along, as the day grew late, and the sun moved toward the west.

Hours later, and she was panting and sweating. Past a salt pan and a rocky ridge, she saw where the fear was emanating, and she found herself disappointed.

About a hundred *lugals* were moving through the wilds, dressed gaily in light silken robes. They bore swords and spears. But they did not have the power of *Satar*.

It had not been genies that were afraid. It had been *lugals*.

And yet — what were they carrying? A *lugal* was carrying an object in a pair of thick white gloves.

Samira knew that in history, the *lugals* and the Qadirrans had been polar opposites. Could they fear the power of *Mainyu*, too, falling into the wrong hands?

Samira had been taught from an early age, a *lugal* was worth one-eighth a Fharese woman. Their lives were not as valuable as hers, or even as her husband's, whom she now hated.

Could they be carrying *Mainyu*? Why risk giving it all away? Why, when *lugals* were worth so much less than she?

~

Bran crouched from his hiding place, as his eyes caught sight of a woman approaching in a yellow gown and a red veil. As he fixed his eyes on her, he saw that around her arm was a bracelet with a pulsing white gemstone. The hundred elves did not notice her, and Bran thought silently — *woe betide them* — as the pulsing white gemstone changed to a burning white fire.

The skies darkened. Bran looked up.

The skies, once covered in thin white clouds, had turned to dark gray, and were changing to black. Amid the blackness, stars burned into focus, until they were searing in their intensity.

The gathered elves looked up and a few began to scream.

When the first star fell, the wise elves went sprinting. Among them was the elf with the magic gloves, who was carrying the shard of *Serpentax*.

The star fell, and there was an explosion, and a crater in its wake. How many elves had died? Bran did not know. But the elf carrying the shard had escaped into the wilderness, and the woman in the veil was continuing to work her magic.

The magic, Bran realized, was coming from the bracelet.

Another star fell, fig-like, from the heavens, and this time every elf scrambled. They were running away in every direction, and before the second one hit, they had fled from the column of fire, the explosion of rocks and debris that followed. There were now two craters in the ground, and Bran — amid the panic of the moment — had lost track of his prey. The elf carrying the shard of *Serpentax* was nowhere to be seen, and the desert, and the newfound starry night hid him.

The woman in the veil was now facing Bran.

Another star began to fall, and Bran scrambled, before the sense of raging fire, before the explosion of rock and dirt, before the cave crumbled and fell in a rockslide to the wilderness below. He fled, and as he looked back, he locked eyes with an elf, and thought — in that brief moment, that they were of the same struggle.

He scrambled into the rocky hills. He was fleeing from the woman with the bracelet.

For an hour he ran, hoping to find somewhere to hide. At last, as darkness was setting in over the desert, he was in a cave. He thought the cave would shield him. He rested his massive hand against the stone. Something fell loose.

He looked down, and saw a bracelet on the ground.

Chapter Twenty-Three: The Three Thieves

Fortunato had ridden about the banks of the Black Khazan, trying to understand the battlefield he was swiftly moving into. The one he loved was in danger. The one he loved would not marry the Fharese King of Kings. She belonged to him, and he to her. And so he said a prayer as he reached the bounds of the land of Potam, which the wicked king Artabanas falsely called Great Fharas.

"What will we do?" Wrinn said.

Xan looked up. He was riding behind Wrinn, on Asté.

"What will we do?" Fortunato said. "We don't have an army. Advantage Artabanas. So we must get one, somehow."

"How do we get an army?" Wrinn said.

"If one is truly rich," Fortunato said, "an army can be bought in gold."

"How much gold?" Wrinn said.

"So much gold," Fortunato said, "and so we will have to take what this land gives us. We will have to don the mantle of the thief. The Three Thieves of Qadirra."

"The Three Thieves of Qadirra," Xan repeated.

"Good thieves," Fortunato said, "helping the ones Artabanas has under his sandal. The Imperial Bay Company is here, and they have a lot of ill-gotten wealth to share."

"The Three Thieves of Qadirra!" Wrinn said at a shout.

~

Along the river were small villages that grew up amid the fields of barley, amid the irrigation canals that were of necessity in the waterless hot plain of Potam. At a village called Shamshir,

Fortunato purchased the clothing he thought would be best for their new endeavor, black linens and black bandanas, to mask their faces and easily slip away. For a price much less than would be required in the Empire, they had the attire of thieves in their possession, and they donned them that night.

There was no tavern in Shamshir, no way to stir the senses or to forget life's troubles, but the three were invited by an elderly couple to a lamb roast on the village outskirts.

Between scattered bits of rumor, something about seven bracelets, about two bracelets being combined into one, Fortunato found an opportunity to ask the question he most desired.

"Where is the Imperial Bay Company encamped?" he said.

The woman's eyes looked away, peering into the darkness of the night, and seemed to have a revelation. As the fire burned in their yard, she said, "I saw them going westwards. I think our king has made a quiet agreement with them, and not for our good."

"Tell everyone you know," Fortunato said, "that Fortunato and his two thieves are here to bring justice where there is none, hope where no hope can be found."

"I will tell everyone I know," the woman answered, amid the fires of the night.

~

They rode, pressing westward, following the contours of the Black Khazan, the southern border of the land once called Potam but now called Great Fharas. Cobalt and Tyra Jade, having water available at every stop, were able to cross great distances without much trouble.

On the third day of their journey, they were coming to the westward terminus of the Black Khazan, to the meeting place of the Black Khazan and the Blue Khazan, where they joined and became the mighty Khazan River that everyone knew.

Amid the joining, there was an area of dense vegetation and —
Fortunato saw — camps and tents, and men walking about them in
the knockoff Imperial armor and the green horsehair crests of the
Imperial Bay Company. There, Fortunato on Tyra Jade made a
motion, and both she and Asté slowed to a stop.

"We are outnumbered," Wrinn said softly.

"Fortunato and his two thieves will find a way," Fortunato said.

Chapter Twenty-Four: Laying Siege

With his spyglass, Reev was able to observe the armies gathered before the aegis shrine from a distance, with no chance of them noticing him. Reev and Agent Secunda had erected a tent far from the armies under the shadow of a rock pinnacle, hidden from view.

As he surveilled the army, the masses of anguipeds guarding the shrine, he had come to realize two things: that as of now, he was incapable of storming past the defenses, and above all, that they were desperate to protect the shrine.

The glass panel with magic writing in the first aegis shrine, the Shrine of Borean Hindrance, had said that the impurity residing in these shrines was preventing the emergence of something called "Heaven's Spear." And such a spear, such a weapon, seemed perfect in Reev's hands, for he was fighting for Heaven, against the Dark One, whose destiny was Hell.

At least, that was how he had pieced together what he learned. The fact that anguipeds were so desperate to protect the shrine showed how terrified they were that Reev would breach the door, and remove the hindrance, and bear Heaven's Spear in his hand.

But now, his task was not understanding what Heaven's Spear was, or why the anguipeds were so desperate to guard it, but instead finding a way in, whether by force or by subterfuge. For days, they had been encamped, waiting for some sign that the anguipeds would depart from the shrine, or waiting for some idea to come to mind, some way to sneak past their defenses.

"What will we do, Agent Secunda?" Reev said.

"I'm trying to think," she replied. "In fact, I've been pondering it constantly. Perhaps, there is a way we could draw them away..."

But how could they draw the army? There were only two of

them, and thousands of anguipeds?

They seemed desperate to protect the aegis shrine, somehow knowing that its cleansing would lead them to grave danger.

"Stand here," said Agent Secunda. "Wait."

Reev stirred as Agent Secunda left, staring with his spyglass and looking closely at the anguipeds from so far a distance. He had tried to count them, to see how many protected the aegis shrine. So desperate were they to protect the shrine from Reev, they had amassed an army, an army that Reev could not penetrate. He had his sword and his Telantine amulet. He had Cobalt. He had Agent Secunda — and nothing else.

There was a flash of fire, a burning inferno, and Reev saw the anguipeds look up from their posts and give chase. Agent Secunda was now sprinting through the desert, and a handful of anguipeds were chasing her. As they chased her, Reev fixed his spyglass on them, and saw some had mounted horses.

But the horses they mounted were of a twisted kind — twisted like the anguipeds themselves. They were hairless and had no mane, and their tough hide was shades of white turning to green. On their heads were jagged sharp horns. They were like a perversion of Cobalt or Asté.

Reev's heart was beginning to race as he fixed his spyglass on Agent Secunda and the anguipeds approaching her.

The armies had shifted, but the bulk of them remained standing guard over the tower.

He watched as anguipeds on the anguiped horses drew back scimitars to strike, when Agent Secunda flicked white powder all over them. They looked about in confusion and Agent Secunda slipped off into the desert.

She returned an hour later. She was panting, clearly rattled. "I got so close," he said. "I thought fire would draw them out — allow you space to enter. I was wrong. But I learned something."

"What did you learn?" Reev said.

"The anguipeds are all gathered closely together," said Agent Secunda. "Something big, something forceful, could drive them all away."

But what force did they possess? Certainly nothing Reev had. All he had was his bravery, and his mettle, and the power that sometimes fell over him at unexpected moments.

That was the thing about those moments, they were unexpected. He had no control of them.

He uttered prayers that the power would come over him now, and he'd be able to dash the anguipeds to dust.

But instead, he heard a quiet voice, spoken it seemed at a whisper, audible only in his heart: *No, Reev, you must make a way. You must find a way to drive your enemies before you.*

And so, he would find that way, he vowed, somehow. But for now, he would wait underneath the desert sun.

Chapter Twenty-Five: Ob

When Bran emerged from the cave bearing his bracelet, it was dawn. He could see the gem fixed on the gold was a shining yellow.

He was amid caves and rocks, between cliffs, a barren wilderness where no one lived, north of the cursed land of Potam that was now called Great Fharas. The woman in the veil had tried to kill him, and it took all Bran's human blood to resist his rokahn urge to chase after her and deal vengeance. Instead, he remembered enough gold to buy a kingdom. *King Bran and his wife.*

If the woman with the bracelet tried anything, he could now answer it with powers of his own.

And what were those powers?

As he stood amid a scorching desert wind, he lifted the bracelet he held and allowed a power to swirl about him. An energy filled him, and the fingers of his now grazing the bracelet began to tingle. The blue skies vanished behind him, and clouds were moving in, clouds coming and clouds appearing out of nowhere. Soon the firmament overhead was gray, and the rain was beginning to pour.

As it rained, water began to collect on the dry ground and flow down in rivulets, giving life to the dry desert earth.

It wasn't much of a power, Bran thought, until lightning struck the ground. He inclined his mind to a tree standing alone, and pointed to it. Lightning struck it, and it bent and collapsed as it caught flame.

The power of clouds and storms was in this bracelet. He saw underneath the gem, writing in Fharese script. *Abrah*, it said.

And tomorrow, the desert would bloom.

~

Where had the elf with the magic gloves gone? Bran thought he hadn't gone far.

He could only carry the shard of *Serpentax* for an hour a day.

And so he returned, hiking through the wilderness for an hour, until he came to the wreckage that the woman with the bracelet had left, two craters in the sandy ground and a rocky ridge collapsed and pulverized to rubble.

He remembered — he recalled. The elf with the magic gloves had fled away from the group headed northeast. And so, gingerly making his way down the newfound crevasse, he hit the ground with his sandals, and stepped through the aftermath of the woman's magic.

In the dry dust, there were footprints leading every which way. Using his memory, he followed a set of footprints in the sand headed due northeast. Only able to carry the shard of *Serpentax* in his magic gloves for an hour per day before the pain became too great, the elf couldn't have gotten far.

Add to that the scorching desert sun, and the waterless places where he'd be traveling alone, and he had already been marching to his doom.

It was looking more and more likely that the elves had already failed.

He followed the footsteps through the desert sand, a bracelet on his right arm and a kukri-knife in his right hand.

~

In the dining chamber, Ambrass could hear Fenris and the man who wished to be her husband talking loudly.

Over a black blood stew, she eavesdropped.

"Your Worship," Fenris said before the curtained dais, "I must see which shrine has been demolished, and which remains, so that we ensure the protection of Qadirra holds."

"You are correct," boomed Artabanas behind the curtained dais.

"But I do not wish to venture to such dangerous territory unarmed," Fenris said. "Ever since I changed with that ray of moonlight, my powers as a magus have weakened. A bracelet has been lost — I must be armed with another. *Azar, Satar,* they are accounted for, or were. Now we know *Ab* is in existence, and has been found. Seven there are, and I will not venture unarmed to the Shrine of Borean or Hyperborean Hindrance."

"And where shall you search," said Artabanas, "in a kingdom of many hundreds of miles square, and a region far beyond where it could be lying under a tree, or buried under the sand."

"I will consult the astrologers," said Fenris. "They will surely heed my request."

"They are notoriously resistant to helping us," Artabanas said.

"But the kingdom is at risk," said Fenris. "If they do not help us, they do not love the king or the kingdom. They shall surely be put to death."

"I give you my consent, and my command," Artabanas said.

Ambrass watched as Fenris exited through the doors of the dining chamber, toward the city itself.

~

Fenris was glad his furry guise hid the expressions on his face. He was glad that King Artabanas and the others could not see his world-shattering fear.

For he knew what the demolishing of one of the aegis shrines meant. Or rather, he knew what an impossible task it was, to enter into the shrine and purify it. For in both the Borean and Hyperborean shrines were Qadirran spirits that none could kill, spirits who hindered Borea and Hyperborea. To enter in the door required something that none Fenris knew possessed, for the doors were sealed by Qadirran spells of sealing and forbidding. No siege weapon could burst through the metal doors, nor could all the fires in the world. None could enter.

But someone had entered through the door, and slain the Qadirran spirits, at one of the shrines. And so how could Fenris hope to stop him?

He would find a way.

Or at least, he hoped.

He gulped nervously, heading toward the astrologers' tower, hoping that the astrologers would help, and that also during the journey Fenris would not become moonstruck and vulnerable. The foe he faced had killed the ancient Qadirran spirits at one of the shrines, and how was that possible? Who was this person?

Religious texts claimed that Qadirra would be destroyed. But Fenris would ensure it never came to pass. For he could use the Seven Bracelets pledged against the city in the city's favor. Once they were all accounted for, Fenris would be in full control.

The rebuilt astrologers' tower was a work in progress. It had reached perhaps half its height when the city of Qadirra had been in existence in its ancient form.

Fenris was not a praying man. And so he crossed his furry fingers as he pressed through the doors, to rooms of gold and silver and diamond.

~

A man was there in a white robe and a blue turban. His black beard fell to the ground. In his hand was a crystal divining rod. He was frowning, apparently unhappy to see Fenris.

"Fenris," the chief astrologer Bahram said. "What brings you to the High House of the Stars?"

"A request," Fenris said. "And the penalty for refusal is death."

"Will you so break ancient Qadirran law and regulation? In Qadirra, astrologers were above the king," said Bahram.

"Nonetheless," said Fenris, "it is about the survival of the king and his kingdom. One of the aegis shrines has been purified — "

"Impossible!" cried Bahram.

"So, I thought," Fenris said, "but the powers of hindrance are weaker, and the bracelets now work throughout the land, up to the outskirts of the city. And yet, perhaps we are in a downward spiral, but we must use these bracelets in a manner opposite to their purpose. I must have the power to defeat this man, whoever he is, who purified one of the aegis shrines."

Bahram's face was downcast, and it seemed he would help even without the threat of death.

"Come with me, Fenris," said Bahram.

At the top of the tower, there were signs that construction was underway, piles of unlaid mudbrick and jars of dust that would be turned to mortar. But there was also the tools of astrology, glass walls to bear the starry expanse, and on a desk, and on shelves, leaves of parchment covered in charts.

"*Ab, Azar,* and *Satar* have been discovered," said Bahram as he took one of the charts in his hand. "Three walk about wielding the powers of water, fire and stars."

"Fire and water have been combined," said Fenris, "and in the hands of our enemy." Bahram's despairing look returned.

"There is one of great power I know, *Zam,* a bracelet unaccounted for, one which was in our possession as recently as last year, but which was lost.

"Let me see what the stars say. The constellation that the *lugals* call 'The Lovers' is now moving across the sky. It is not an earth sign, but a fire sign."

He was lost in the examination of charts, overwhelmed by what he was seeing.

"Its opposite," said Bahram. "I believe *Zam* is somewhere on the banks of the Blue Khazan. Yes, one mile and forty steps due east, along the shore, from the village of Arman."

"I thank you, astrologer," Fenris said.

"Chief Astrologer," Bahram said.

~

With the endorsement of the king, and all the earthly powers of the Fharese King of Kings behind him, Fenris rode on a warhorse due northeast of Qadira, along a winding road.

As the ancient Qadirrans, a layer of hardened black tar had been placed over the road and it glistened in the burning sun. A day into Fenris's journey, and the tar gave way to gravel and then to dirt. It would take a long time, and much effort, to restore the land of Potam, now Great Fharas, to its former glory.

At last the waters of the Blue Khazan appeared, irrigation canals dotted with date palms and covered in rows of barley — houses made of mudbrick with straw roofs. The village of Arman.

Due east along the shore, Fenris made a turn, and saw by the shores of the river, a mudbrick hut, beside it a boulder of black shiny rock, and at the edge of the black boulder, a woman with long gray hair dressed in black clothing.

As he approached, the woman looked to him.

"Why do you bother the Possessor of the Ob?" said the woman. "The woman who has all knowledge at her fingertips?" Her eyes seemed to have a wild magic.

Fenris, a former sorcerer himself, could not help but look away from those eyes.

"You possess more than a black stone," said Fenris. "You possess something that belongs to the King of Kings, Artabanas."

"Are you referring to this?" the woman said, and lifted up her left arm. On it was a gold bracelet, on it a gem that glowed brown.

The chief astrologer had led him here, to the correct path. There was something to their knowledge by starlight and constellation.

"The Ob told me where *Zam* was, and it told me when it would be unattended," said the woman. "Shall I ask the Ob where *Mainyu* is, so you can speed Qadirra's destruction?"

"Qadirra will never be destroyed," said Fenris.

"Ah, ah, it shall," the woman said, and she laughed. "It is so written."

"Give me *Zam*, woman, or I shall come back with an army, and cut you down, and break your Ob to pieces." Fenris shook his magus's staff menacingly.

"I shall give it to you, as you wish," said the woman, "and I will hasten Qadirra's destruction."

"Qadirra shall never be destroyed," said Fenris, as the woman walked over to him, removed *Zam* from her arm, and placed it about Fenris's left wrist.

The power of earth was now at Fenris's fingertips.

Chapter Twenty-Six: In the Garb of a Demon-Slayer

"What shall we do now, Fortunato?" Wrinn said.

Fortunato and his Two Thieves had been observing the motions of the Imperial Bay Company quietly for many days now, waiting for them to make a mistake, for a vulnerability that would allow an opening.

They were encamped, and Fortunato sensed they were profiting, that they had been pushed to the outer bounds of the region now called Great Fharas, but were adding to their shareholders' treasure. An agreement had been made with the one who called himself the Fharese King of Kings. It was the task of Fortunato and his Two Thieves to ensure their profit was small.

For the first time in days, as the morning light shone, there was motion from amid the greenery of the camp. A wagon was headed east down the road, rattling with its wheels as it crossed eastwards. Fortunato made a motion, and at a distance, he, Xan and Wrinn followed the cart.

It rattled on its wheels. It was being escorted by dozens of Imperial Bay Company soldiers, far more than Fortunato and his Two Thieves could take on by themselves. But they would follow, and hope they made a mistake. For as it rattled, Fortunato could make out the glimmer of gold, that it was transporting ill-gotten wealth pilfered from the rebuilt land of Potam, now called Great Fharas.

~

They followed the cart and its escort as it rattled east, then turned northward. It was broaching a village built near a bridge.

They watched the cart rattle over the bridge, and Fortunato resisted saying a curse. But he noticed something, then, that there was a commotion in the village square, and that the villagers had gathered.

They had lost the cart and its gold for now, but Fortunato wouldn't give up.

He wouldn't give up, and maybe the commotion would help him, somehow.

A stage had been set up in the midst of the village square. The Fharese peasants were looking at actors as they took positions on the stage.

There were two of them, in addition to stagehands nearby, all Imperials clearly, with short hair and clean-shaven faces. But they were garbed as the characters they intended to portray.

One wore the chiton of an Eloesian warrior. The other was painted with green paint, with horns plastered to his head. The actor playing the Eloesian warrior had a sword and shield in his hand, and the actor painted green was wielding a trident.

"The tale of Theron, Demon-Slayer!" shouted the actor playing the warrior, presumably Theron.

Theron then stood to the side as the green-painted actor strode up to the front of the stage. "For millennia I, Kronos, Prince of Chaos, have conspired against the people of Thénai, the inheritors of the glory of Stygidos. I have stood unopposed and my victory is at hand! Lo! Look! A warrior approaches."

Theron strode up to Kronos. "I, Theron, hero of the city of Thénai, fear none but the gods, least of all their enemy, Kronos. I bear in my hand the sword of the hero Phillipides, with which I will do battle, and slay you."

"You come not garbed in armor," said Kronos. "You cannot slay me."

"No armor shall I wear," said Theron. "Nay, I shall wear nothing at all, when I deal to the gods' enemies his defeat."

Theron pressed a button on his chiton, and he was bare — bare, save for a tight-fitting silken suit dyed to resemble human skin.

"Naked I shall fight you," said Theron. "In the garb of a demon-slayer…"

~

The actors were mixing with the crowds after their performance. As they did, Fortunato strode up to them.

"That skin-suit didn't look quite believable," Fortunato said to the actor playing Theron. "You aren't man enough to do the real thing?"

The actor smiled. "In Great Fharas," he said, "if a man so much as removes his shirt, he will be executed. It would break the law for me to perform as I do in Thénai. But if you ever come to our performances at the Queen Amara Theater in Thénai, you will know, I am man enough."

Fortunato didn't think he'd be taking up the actor on his offer.

Chapter Twenty-Seven: Cloudburst

Bran had scoured the desert for days under the blazing sun, and worried he was losing the elf's trail, the one the six men in black had called a scapegoat. Only able to travel three miles a day carrying the shard of *Serpentax*, Bran thought surely he would have found him by now.

He had passed beyond the ridges and entered a land abutting a river, what Bran thought was the northward branch of the Blue Khazan, the branch that took it beyond the cursed land of Potam, now called Great Fharas.

He would lose the trail for hours, and then see the mark of a sole amid the dry dust, but now it had been almost a day without any sign.

He thought it was possible that the elf had escaped him, and that Bran would never be King Bran, wealthy beyond measure.

No King Bran and his wife…

But as he stopped, exhausted, for a drink from the water, he saw figures approaching from the north.

Elves. He was on the right trail.

They were charging him, dressed in robes, and as they charged, the sunlight glittered on the breastplates beneath their wind-blown clothes. Some wielded swords, others curved knives. One, he saw, was dressed all in white, and bearing a staff in his hands. His eyes glowed with arcane power as he shot his hand, and a bolt of pure light zapped at Bran. Bran dodged, so narrowly he felt it singe the fur of his chest. At that point he called up the powers of his bracelet, and swiftly did it answer, the power of *Abrah*.

In moments the skies were dark and cloudy, and rain started, a drizzle and then suddenly a downpour. Before the magic weaver could strike again, Bran had summoned a lightning bolt that blackened and burned him, sending him dazed, then dead, to the ground.

The elves wailed, and one crossed the distance between them, striking with his sword — a blow Bran met with his kukri-knife. The blow was met, and Bran twisted, and the sword fell from the elf's grasp. Another spear of lightning, and the swordsman was dead.

More bolts of lightning struck, one after another, and the elves were no match for the powers of *Abrah,* the powers of cloud.

There was a flurry of flashes, and the elves that did not die were fleeing into the horizon.

The elf with the magic gloves, and the shard of *Serpentax,* had to be close.

~

Fenris traveled by horse from the village of Arman, following the course of the Blue Khazan. He knew that the weakest of the two shrines, the Aegis Shrine of Borean Hindrance, was not far from the banks of the Blue Khazan, north of it through the wilds. Amid rock and scrubland, it could be found, and though its defenses had held for the entirety of its existence, its spell had less strength than its sister. The shrine being purified was beyond the realm of what Fenris had thought possible, but the other shrine would beggar belief. And so he would start at the weakest, the one he thought was most likely to have fallen.

He passed over a bridge that had recently been rebuilt and entered the wilds, bearing *Zam* about his wrist. He could see the sun setting as he rode, galloping through dust-land in view of the burning sun and the bright blue sky. He could feel his nervousness growing, building toward fear, threatening toward panic he was trying mightily to control, for fear that the man who had purified the Shrine of Borean Hindrance was still nearby, and could undo him and the rebuilding of Qadirra that the King of Kings, Artabanas, had dedicated his life to.

But as the tower's form appeared in the horizon, he saw there was no one near it, only the remains of footsteps going in different directions, a portrait pressed into sand.

The footsteps were numerous. Three sets of prints went south toward the Blue Khazan and Great Fharas. Two sets of prints went north.

But Fenris sensed that whatever mighty man had purified the shrine was long gone. And so Fenris was safe, entering.

He passed through the doors, and shuddered at the thought that they were opened, that someone had opened them. The person who opened them had to have a power far beyond common magic.

When he passed under the doors, he saw that the tower was ransacked, and that on the flagstone floor were two masks — the masks, Fenris guessed, of the Qadirran guardians.

He saw that the sockets in the walls were aglow, confirming the shrine had been purified. He saw a glass panel with writing which Fenris couldn't read, magic letters glowing in green against the glass panel's darkness.

And at the thought, and at the sight, of the Aegis Shrine of Borean Hindrance being purified, Fenris allowed his welling panic to carry him away, out of the door.

Outside, Fenris wondered — was it possible somehow that he was wrong, that the hindrance had not been removed? There was only way to tell.

He raised up his newfound bracelet, *Zam,* and allowed the power to fill him. And as it filled him, and *Zam's* brown stone glowed like fire in the daylight, he thrust forth his right hand, and watched *Zam* at work.

The ground's shaking began as a slight quiver, a tenuous movement easy for the feet to navigate. It built to a shaking full and true, and then as an earthquake, cracks ripping through the earth, bits of the tower crumbing, all while Fenris's feet were sure.

At last, the tower, the Aegis Shrine of Borean Hindrance, collapsed in on itself, tumbling into an explosion of dirt and stone and dust. A cloud of dust rose, and then there was rubble. All sign of the Qadirrans' work, all sign of their witchcraft, was long gone.

The panic built to bursting.

Fenris could not contend with the man who purified this shrine with *Zam* alone, of that he was sure. He needed the greatest bracelet of all, *Mainyu,* to contend with such a threat. He shuddered in fear, in panic.

And then, hoping against hope he would not be moonstruck, he found his horse, quieted the powers of *Zam*, and rode eastward in the direction of the village of Arman.

The Possessor of the Ob said she could give Fenris the truth, and nothing she had done had proven otherwise.

Chapter Twenty-Eight: Paydirt

The gypsies were armed, but not all of them had swords and spears. Julian knew that had to change if they were to rescue their queen, his cousin, Ambrass.

He had heard, now possessing the powers of the combined bracelets of fire and water, now wielding a bracelet of steam, that the armies of the Imperial Bay Company were encamped where the waters of the Black Khazan and the Blue Khazan met.

And so they had ridden on their wagons at a swift but easy pace, from the outskirts of Qadirra to the horizon now appearing in view — green grassland where the rivers met, the western terminus of what was now called Great Fharas.

As the gypsies appeared, with Julian at the front, some Imperial Bay Company soldiers screamed orders and others began to flee, but not before Julian began to work his magic.

He lifted the bracelet, its gem now a bright green fire, its metal a whitish-gold hue, its powers containing the combined fury of *Azar* and *Ab*.

As a boiling rain fell, the air within the Imperial Bay Company camps turned sweltering, then scalding, then burning — like a tea kettle set to boil.

Some Imperial Bay Company soldiers shriveled within their armor, others fell to the ground to shield themselves. Others had fled in advance of the gypsies, taking with them bags of gold and gold objects, galloping away in every direction so as to avoid the threat posed by *Azar* and Ab.

At last, a wall of steam was pressing in from behind the gypsies. It would boil everything in its path, except the one the carrier of the bracelet wished to shield. And so it shielded Julian's brethren before passing through the Imperial Bay Company camps, everyone who had not fled in the wake of the gypsies' arrival.

They pilfered the camp, then, and realized the Imperial Bay Company had done a masterful job of sending away what they loved most, gold coin and treasure. But they had left behind their swords, their shields and their spears, and they had left behind their suits of armor and helmets. An army would now wander the land of Potam, an army of gypsies wielding swords and spears and shields, and wielding the deadliest power of all, *Ab* and *Azar*.

Yet the power of the bracelets did not work when they drew near the city of Qadirra. At least, it did not work for now.

~

Fortunato couldn't believe his luck.

Or rather — what had he been calling Xan and Wrinn? — Fortunato and his Two Thieves couldn't believe their luck, as the army of gypsies moved into the Imperial Bay Company camps, in the wake of men on horses who had fled with bags of gold.

Tyra Jade was much faster than a horse in short distances. And so Xan and Wrinn mounted Asté at Fortunato's signal, and Fortunato mounted Tyra Jade. They followed one of the fleeing horsemen as he galloped down along the shores of the Blue Khazan, going northward.

They followed a few paces at a distance, then raced forth at Asté's gallop and Tyra Jade's sprint.

They were gaining on the soldier with the bag of gold, and then they were upon him.

Tyra Jade ripped open the horse's throat and the soldier crashed with the horse to the ground. Xan leapt from Asté and drew his butterfly blade in one motion, struck with one end and severed the soldier's right arm, struck with the other and severed the soldier's head.

A bag of gold, not a bad payday for Fortunato and his Two Thieves. He dismounted and checked through the bag, seeing countless gold coins worth a fortune, and amid the gold coins a gold ring.

He pocketed the gold ring. He thought he would need it.

Chapter Twenty-Nine: Sky Battle

Samira wandered the desert alone, bearing the bracelet called *Satar*. She had devastated the *lugals* and scattered them when she had seen something she had not thought possible, one who was half a *lugal*, and half a rokahn. Now she looked for him, to quench a threat to her future queendom, armed with a bracelet that could destroy him.

Satar had powers of stars, and she had witnessed its effects. But she knew that the further she traveled from Qadirra, the weaker the powers would grow. At the hundred-mile mark, they would cease their power entirely, for the evil genie Arstibara had purposed them for the destruction of her future queendom. What use were they, in the evil genie Arstibara's mind, so far away from the city he had hoped to destroy forever?

She had seen the monster escape her. She knew the monster yet lived. And as long as half-rokahn, half-*lugal* lived, Samira was not safe. Of that, she was sure.

She followed a sense, not fear nor anger, but dissonance — the sense of two desires battling and attempting to take control. That was the feeling she followed, the feeling the monster experienced as he traversed the barren landscape.

As she strode, faster and faster, she worried she wouldn't be able to catch up with his long legs. But the monster was stopping frequently, searching for something. Was he searching for *Mainyu?*

Was he searching for what belonged to Samira? Such behavior she would expect from a troublesome genie, not a half-lugal, half-rokahn.

A lump of fear grew in Samira's throat as the fearful sense grew stronger, as she realized she was at the doorstep of the feeling of dissonance.

She caught sight of him, bending over a set of footprints in the desert sand. And before she could react, he had turned, and met her gaze head on.

How could a half-rokahn have such lovely eyes?

He was wearing a bracelet.

Samira fought mad terror. She watched as he raised his bracelet, and in a frenzy she lifted her own. *Satar*, the bracelet she was wearing, glowed with a white fire gemstone.

The one he was wielding glowed yellow. She recalled — the bracelet named *Abrah*, with power over clouds, and winds, and rain.

She raised *Satar* and as the skies darkened with clouds, the forms of stars burned through the clouds' veil. The powers of stars and clouds were now battling, and Samira did not know which would win, which order of bracelet was higher.

Yet *Satar* was not *Abrah's* opposite. They could not and would not combine.

A star fell and exploded in the distance, leaving a crater in the desert earth. Another fell, and she called it down toward the half-rokahn, half-*lugal* with a trembling hand.

But there was a gust of wind, and the flaming sphere seemed to catch a fire of its own. It was dust before it hit the ground.

A spear of lightning struck inches from Samira's feet, and she screamed and fled. She fled clouds and rain. She fled thunder and storm. She had sprinted a mile, perhaps, and looked back, and saw the storm continuing, but the half-rokahn, half-*lugal*, was gone.

~

Fenris galloped with all due speed through Arman, to the hut where the Possessor of the Ob lived. The woman, he saw, was still sitting before the shiny black boulder, amid the scorching sun, not bothering to shield herself from the sun's rays.

"My lady!" Fenris said. "I come for truth."

"The signs of earth and cloud are ahead," said the Possessor of the Ob, "and the constellation called 'The Lovers' is in apogee. What does this mean? The Ob shall not tell me."

"It will not tell you," Fenris said, "but it will tell me where *Mainyu* is. You said so yourself."

The woman arose from her seat. "You seek the chief bracelet, so as to forestall Qadirra's doom. But Qadirra's destruction is coming. That is what writings say."

"Forget the writings," said Fenris. "Where is *Mainyu?* Tell me!"

The woman arose, and stared at the black boulder. "*Mainyu* is in the desert. I shall write your destiny on your heart. It shall take you to *Mainyu's* gate. Then, can you enter?"

It was madness, but Fenris felt something fill him, an inkling of one way or another. His destiny, he sensed, was beyond the Blue Khazan. His destiny was in the midst of the desert sands.

~

After the woman with the bracelet had tried to slay Bran, and Bran's bracelet, *Abrah*, prevailed over hers, he had an inkling he had scared her off, that she knew now she could not contend with him. Now the path was clear, to locate the elf carrying the shard of *Serpentax*.

King Bran and his wife — it was almost a certainty, now.

Chapter Thirty: His Name

The gold Fortunato had pilfered from the Imperial Bay Company soldier was more money than he had earned in his entire life.

He counted within it three-hundred and eighty-seven gold libra, and that wasn't counting the diamond necklaces and the emerald brooches, the assorted jewel-studded rings and objects of pearl and lapis lazuli he had found in the bag.

But he didn't just want to take money from the ill-gotten coffers of the Imperial Bay Company. He wanted to send a message to the so-called King of Kings, Artabanas, who had dared to try to steal his beloved from him.

The Imperial Bay Company, who had fled in the wake of the army of gypsies, was now scattered in every direction throughout Potam, now Greater Fharas, and the wildernesses beyond. So how would he frighten Artabanas, and tell him that Fortunato was coming.

Perhaps, his two thieves could help.

For Fortunato had discovered amid the gold a bracelet with an especially shiny diamond. When he had placed it over his arm, it granted him now power, but he didn't think that Artabanas would know any better.

~

They purchased firewood and oil at a village called Arman, in addition to wooden planks. They rode with haste toward the city of Qadirra, as afternoon turned to dusk, and dusk turned to night. In the dark, Fortunato and his Two Thieves set to work, building pyres in a circle, one by one, around Qadirra's hateful rebuilt walls.

Fortunato knew Ambrass was behind those walls. He could sense her. And he could sense her anguish.

He took a torch when the pyres had been assembled and took the oil dispenser and handed it to Wrinn. With a flint and tinder he lit the torch and set to work, and mounted on Tyra Jade he began to light them, one after another, turning them to blazing beacons, surrounding the city one fire at a time. And as they burned in the night, the moon arose, and the stars. The moon was a crescent.

The fires burned, and Fortunato, Wrinn and Xan were mounted at their steeds, in view of Qadirra's gate.

~

"My king!" Kavadh came sprinting into the dining chamber, in view of Ambrass and of Artabanas behind his curtained dais. "The enemies of Qadirra have at last arrived, the ones promised to destroy it… Their leader bears a bracelet in his hand."

"And will you not fight, Kavadh? Will you not be a man?" Artabanas said. "Will you not take all our soldiers, and ensure Qadirra never falls?"

"Of course, my king!" Kavadh sprinted through the doors of the chamber, into the distance.

~

The gates opened, and an army was leaving. Thousands of cataphracts were pouring out of the gate to face Fortunato, and behind him, Xan and Wrinn.

Fortunato faced them with no fear. He could see the terror on the face of their captain.

He flexed his bracelet, and the captain shuddered further. "Tell Artabanas that the doom of Qadirra is almost here," Fortunato said.

"And tell the one he has taken captive, her beloved is coming, and none shall stop him."

The cataphracts' faces had melted in terror. The captain managed to speak. "I shall tell him," said the captain. "I shall tell him, *lugal.*"

And he howled at the sight of the burning fires, surrounding Qadirra. He eyed Tyra Jade. He looked into Fortunato's eyes and wheeled his horse around in a panic.

"Retreat!" cried the captain. "Retreat…"

~

Kavadh had returned to the dining chamber. He was doing his best to hide his wild terror, but his face was ashen and pale. "Your Worship, we drove them off, and they fled, but their fires still burn…"

Ambrass relished his terror.

"Their leader rides mounted on a black wolf," Kavadh said.

Ambrass fainted.

When she came to, she was in her room in the women's apartments. The eunuch had taken her there.

But she remembered what Kavadh had said.

The towering being in the back of her mind, the one who threatened to take control of her life and soul, the one she feared to love, was at the gates.

What was his name?

She remembered — Fortunato.

"Fortunato," she said, and she fainted again, now on her bed.

Chapter Thirty-One: Natural Allies

Reev stirred before the aegis shrine, the anguipeds gathered that had not noticed him but threatened to notice him every day. Far away, with his spyglass, he was unseen by his foes, but the anguipeds were crafty, and the fact that they were massing at the aegis shrine showed they knew they were under threat.

They were afraid, of him, of Fortunato, of Agent Secunda. And Agent Secunda had departed days ago, promising him she would be back with assistance. They would try to dislodge the army protecting the shrine, the army attempting to stop its purification.

Why? Reev only had glimpses. He had seen the words "Heaven's Spear" in a language he but not Agent Secunda could read, a language he could read intuitively, which he didn't remember Gastreel teaching him back in Norwood.

In his loin cloth, with Doomblade at his side, his neck tattooed with Telantine lightning marks, his appearance would cause the anguipeds to flee. But some of them would stay and fight. Enough of them to prevent him from broaching the shrine's doors and purifying the shrine.

For now, Reev was unable to do what he wished, to purify the Aegis Shrine of Hyperborean Hindrance, and loose Heaven's Spear — whatever that was.

He could tell Heaven's Spear would harm the anguipeds' cause because of the way they massed around the shrine.

He heard a noise, and looked back, and saw through the desert sands forms appearing, forms cloaked in white. It was a southron army, and Agent Secunda was leading the charge.

She, with the Oculus's funds, had hired mercenaries to displace these anguipeds. It was anyone's guess if the gambit would work.

Reev steeled himself, and drew a breath, and said a prayer. He drew Doomblade as the mercenaries walked through the desert sands, bearing scimitars and wicker shields, an army in size — Reev noted — was double the force of anguipeds.

The anguipeds noticed, and drew their swords and shields. The splint armor of their warriors glistened in the sun, as they brandished their weapons. Trumpets blew, sounds of alarm, as Reev had a feeling — a voice, a quiet voice, telling himself that now was not the right time to charge forth and bear his sword, that now was not the time to do battle against the anguipeds.

Despite his coin amulet, despite his *estirion* sword Doomblade worth the cost of many kingdoms, he had a feeling the mercenaries Agent Secunda had hired were no match for the anguipeds. And as they charged, and the anguipeds charged in turn, he saw evidence he was right.

The anguipeds struck with their swords with serpentine grace, stabbing and beheading the lightly armored southron mercenaries. The southron's scimitars bounced off their shining splint armor, and though the southrons outnumbered the anguipeds two to one, the anguipeds had met them face to face, and at first did battle, and then started cutting through them.

The southrons were being slaughtered, and being hired mercenaries, not invested in the fight, there was little incentive not to escape with their lives. Scimitars flashed and swords struck, and blood was spilled in the desert sand.

It had quickly turned to a rout, the southrons against the anguipeds, and within an hour of battle, countless southrons lay dead and bleeding, and the rest were fleeing. Where was Agent Secunda?

Reev, now feeling a bit of raw nerves, fixed his spyglass on the scene of battle. He scanned the bodies, anguiped and southron both, and could see no sign of the agent of the Oculus who had taken him under her wing.

He supposed not seeing her was what he wanted. He felt a tap on his shoulder.

He looked back and saw her, her black hair ruffled, her face speckled with blood. "The mercs failed," she said. "They cost the Oculus a fortune."

"How did you escape?" Reev said.

"Forgetfulness powder works in a pinch," Agent Secunda said. "Let us mourn their lives. Their hearts were not in the fight, but they did battle with the anguipeds."

How many had died and how many had scattered? Reev guessed, a countless number.

The hired mercenaries had barely made a dent in the anguiped lines.

~

In the dark, in the cool of the desert night, Agent Secunda was shaken. "I'm out of ideas," she said. "Perhaps, Spymaster Marius will come up with something."

There was no fire, nor had there been, since they arrived at this lonely desert shrine. In the dark, concealed by the night, they ate their road-bread and jerky, enough food to last them through a day of surveillance and waiting.

"And what now?" Agent Secunda said.

"We wait for them to make a mistake," Reev said. "They're anguipeds. They'll make one."

"They are clearly skilled at war," Agent Secunda said. "Far more skilled than the hired swords we paid for. But I think Imperial soldiers would make quick work of them."

"The Imperials won't help us," Reev said. "They care about peace and the maintenance of order. And now, the emperor himself is an anguiped. He will not send his troops against his own kind."

"No," Agent Secunda said softly. "No, he won't. It's him we

fight against."

"The Dark One," Reev corrected.

"Again, the same breath," Agent Secunda said.

Reev took a bite of his jerky. He had tired of the same fare every night, the same fare that filled his stomach but did little to tantalize the appetite.

"The Empire," Reev said, "allows the city of Qadirra to be rebuilt."

"Fharas tries to rebuild itself, and Qadirra," Agent Secunda said. "By human effort, they try to recapture what the gods have taken from them. But they are doomed to fail, for they both are condemned. Fharas can never recover its strength, nor will Qadirra ever be reborn."

Agent Secunda spoke grandly. But Emperor Verrus was enabling Qadirra's reconstruction. Emperor Verrus was looking the other way as Fharas, the Empire's old enemy, staked out a new life for itself amid haunted earth.

"And what now?" Reev said. "We fight — Emperor Verrus and the Dark One. How will we ever breach the gates of the shrine and and purify it?"

"Perhaps, we should abandon this quest and look elsewhere," Agent Secunda said. "There are other ways to bring about Qadirra's ruin. There are seven magic bracelets, recently uncovered, pledged for the city's destruction. Perhaps, we could uncover one of them and use it against the city."

"No," Reev said. He was resolved. "We will enter in the shrine somehow. We will purify it. But first, I must drive the anguipeds before me."

"Then we will try to find a way," said Agent Secunda. "But it doesn't seem that there is any way."

"We must make a way," Reev said.

~

In the morning, it was evident even without his spyglass — the anguipeds had reinforcement. Bands of anguipeds were entering from the north, and interspersed among them were rokahn. With shouts and the cracks of whips, the anguipeds dealt with the rokahns harshly. But it seemed that anguipeds and rokahn were natural allies.

Chapter Thirty-Two: Only Him

Garbed in a veil, now in the courtyard of the palace, Ambrass watched as the actors exited the stage. She was seated next to Artabanas and she had hated every moment of the play because she was so near to him.

The actors, one dressed as Theron and the other as a demon, had made the gathered court ooh and ah, laugh and weep, but all Ambrass could remember, enveloped in disgust for the one seated next to her, was high dudgeon and language that was too flowery, and an ill-fitting skin suit that made a mockery of the artistic restrictions of Great Fharas.

Artabanas laid out his hand before hers as the actors departed, inviting her to grip it. When she refused, he gripped her hand tight, aggressively, so hard his bony fingers pierced the soft flesh of her wrist.

She despised Artabanas, and in that moment she vowed she would die before she ever married him.

After all, the one she loved was in the cursed land of Potam, the land that Ambrass also vowed to never call Great Fharas. The one she loved — Fortunato. At the very sound of his name in her mind, her heart sang, and her heart ventured to lofty places.

A kiss on the battlements of Galiope. A promise of love, one she hoped with all of her heart would come true.

Fortunato had strode on his black wolf up to Qadirra's gate. He had made a show, so as to know Ambrass knew.

Her beloved was here. Her beloved would not rest until they were together. And Ambrass would gladly receive him.

She tried to worm her way out of Artabanas's bony grip, but the more she pulled, the more forcefully he gripped her.

"How did you like the play?" Artabanas said.

"I hated it," Ambrass said, and when she said it, she tried to imply, *because I'm sitting next to you.*

"You will learn to be obedient, Ambrass," Artabanas said. "You will learn, like others before you. You will learn to be appreciative you are the wife of the King of Kings."

Fortunato was coming for her. She knew this. She had heard word already. And when she had pulled with all her might, to the point of tears, Artabanas finally relinquished his grip, and her hand was free.

What would she do, and how would she find him? She could not easily escape the palace or the city gates. Artabanas knew how she felt about him and would prevent easy escape. But her beloved would find a way. Somehow, some way, Ambrass and Fortunato would find each other.

She knew it. She knew it in her heart.

Artabanas was glaring at her with a fiery glare.

"You will learn," Artabanas said at a hiss, and the glare in his eyes was like a burning fire.

It took all of Ambrass's strength not to stick his tongue out at him and spit in his face.

"A wedding, we shall have," said Artabanas. "We shall have it soon. This long period of betrothal is clearly not good for you."

Ambrass despaired at the thought. She needed to flee. She needed to flee now, into Fortunato's arms.

~

In her room at the women's apartments, Ambrass packed what she needed, a desert shawl, a waterskin. Perhaps, she should bring a fire signal to alert Fortunato. He could not have gotten far, for the Land of Potam was not vast, and he would surely be easy to find.

Into a sack she threw her sparse belongings. She would wait until night.

~

In the night they ate a stew richer than before, one with boiled capon and simmered onions, leeks and bits of beef stomach. So rich was it, so hearty, that Ambrass almost forgot the plan of action she had developed, the moment she'd flee into Fortunato's arms.

So rich was indeed, so thick with fat and meat, that a horrible feeling settled within her that it was a special occasion.

Kavadh rose up amid the diners. "Distinguished guests of His Worship, the King of Kings," said Kavadh, "the King of Kings has good news, an announcement only he could make himself."

Hands Ambrass hated opened the curtain, and a man she despised now stepped out, in two-piece linen clothing that bared a sickly stomach. Artabanas was wearing his golden circlet.

"We have moved up the wedding date of Ambrass and I," said Artabanas. "She shall become my chief wife no later than the thirteenth day of the month of Arah."

That was two weeks from now. Ambrass went pale.

"Coincidentally," said Artabanas, "the day of Qadirra's ancient founding."

Ambrass's stomach turned, and she fled from the room, unable to withhold a wail. She could sense the eyes of the diners upon her she rushed through the doors, toward her room in the women's apartments — her prison.

Not long after, despite all rule and regulation, Artabanas stormed through the women's apartments into her room. His eyes glared with a fiery wrath. "You embarrassed me," she said, "in front of the Governor of Great Fharas."

"Potam," Ambrass said. "A cursed land is all it will ever be."

She realized Artabanas was holding a birch rod.

And when he struck her, Ambrass feared it would be the first of many times. That night, a guard was placed at her door. She was now a prisoner in every sense of the word.

Only Fortunato could save her now.

Chapter Thirty-Three: Orders

In a village called Cyra, a herald was shouting and speaking in a bold   voice. Fortunato and his Two Thieves watched as he delivered a message from the one who called himself the King of Kings.

"His Worship, King of Kings, His Majesty, the Padisha of Fharas and the Great King of Qadirra, Artabanas, announces a wedding on the thirteenth day of the month of Arah, to his beloved, Ambrass, Queen of the Gypsies," the herald said. "On the day, all the king's subjects are invited to make a sacrificial offering for the king and queen's beneficence."

Fortunato had less than two weeks to make things right. How would he rescue his love?

~

The gypsies were armed, and now, even without the combined powers of *Ab* and *Azar*, the King of Kings of Great Fharas feared them. They dared not send troops after them as they made their way across the land of Great Fharas, pillaging and besieging towns, gaining wealth and also weapons.

The gypsies, led by Julian, were now armed to the teeth

But Qadirra was still protected by the ancient Qadirrans' witchcraft, and the powers of *Ab* and *Azar* would not work on the city itself. The King of Kings of Great Fharas seemed to know this, and he knew the gypsies' limitations. All along the hateful walls of Qadirra were soldiers in armor, with scimitars at wicker shields at the ready, prepared at any moment to defend against siege.

The gypsies had little experience in besieging towns. Indeed, the enemies they faced during their journeys tended to be bandits and robbers, highwaymen who could easily be dispatched by force of numbers.

So how would they overcome the defenses, Julian wondered as he led the wagon train around Qadirra's walls?

He could see the burnt remains of beacons surrounding the city, firewood that had blackened and turned to ash.

So how would he breach the gate without the power of *Ab* and *Azar*?

The gypsies had managed to pillage some ten talents worth of gold and silver from the Imperial Bay Company camps. Perhaps, they could pay for what they did not know how to do.

On the shores of the Black Khazan, far from Qadirra, Julian announced his plan to his brother Anton.

Anton, wearing a bandana and now armed with an Imperial Bay Company short-sword, nodded his head in approval.

"Beyond Kash," said Anton, "south of it, is Udara. Their towns are experienced with siege. I'll take a few of us, and some money, and hire a few people who know — there are forests to build towers in the east."

"You go with my blessing," Julian said, "and the blessing of our god Kama."

That night, Julian departed for the cities of Udara, a region well versed in war. But Julian knew Anton went into danger, without the aid of the power of *Ab* and *Azar*. The power of *Ab* and *Azar* were the only reason the armies of Great Fharas did not attack the gypsies. The power of *Ab* and *Azar* would not avail Anton in the land of Udara, and only his own wit, and the blessing of the gods, would keep him from danger.

Julian announced that all gypsies should pray, pray for Anton's success, and for the rescue of their cousin, the gypsies' queen

Ambrass.

~

How could Fortunato storm the gates of Qadirra? He thought it would take evasion, quick wit, to rescue his beloved from her captor's hands.

He would cause chaos and hope the chaos would provide an opportunity for victory.

He had built beacons to intimidate the King of Kings of Great Fharas, but since then they had remained behind the city gates, the city with its spell of protection and with its army that could not be defeated handily without a much larger army of their own.

Fortunato, now rich by his standards, had enough to purchase a few mercenaries, but mercenaries in the Southern World were notoriously untrustworthy? And so what would he do?

On Tyra Jade, he and Xan and Wrinn, whom they called their Two Thieves, found themselves again where the rivers met, amid greenery and grass and date palms, and tents and the remains of camps that had been thoroughly pilfered. Little remained, now, of the Imperial Bay Company encampment that had been in the process of robbing Great Fharas.

But as they broached the bridge, amid the tall grass so tall as to hide them, they saw they were not alone. Imperial soldiers full and true were in the process of crossing, a line two by two, thousands perhaps in number — streaming into Great Fharas, a land now at war.

The troubles that Fortunato and the gypsies had created had drawn the eye of the unworthy anguiped emperor, Verrus.

Fortunato made a signal, and those whom he called his two thieves dismounted and hid in the grass.

~

An Imperial soldier had stridden through the doors of the dining chamber.

Ambrass had hoped it was Fortunato entering through the door, as she always hoped when the doors opened.

She was dreading each day that passed, for fear of the wedding date she abhorred.

But no, it was not Fortunato, but an Imperial soldier in a breastplate and a red half-cape, his brown hair and green eyes bare. He wore no helmet.

"From the proconsul of Shakrath, *namsita*," the soldier said. "I am Legate Paulus."

He stared a while, and Ambrass was sure that Artabanas was fuming behind the gold curtain.

"Pardon," said Legate Paulus, "open the curtain. I will not speak to a length of cloth."

"It is against our law," said Kavadh from a corner table, "for the King of Kings to be seen whilst he eats."

"Open it," Legate Paulus said, and after a moment of hesitation, Ambrass watched two wiry hands tear open the gold curtains, baring Artabanas's visage.

She savored his embarrassment.

"The consulary legate of the Imperial Bay Company has brought a massive theft to our attention," said Legate Paulus. "A theft, and damages, of some two-hundred and eighty talents, from its operations in the land of Potam."

"Great Fharas," Artabanas said at a hiss.

"They are entitled to damages," said Legate Paulus, "and I am trying to determine the offending party."

Artabanas wailed his disapproval. "We are a sovereign land," said Artabanas. "A sovereign kingdom."

"You cast your crown before the emperor's image," Legate Paulus said, "and so you are a tributary kingdom with rights of self-government. Those rights are not unlimited, however."

Artabanas's face had twisted into a grimace. Ambrass appreciated his embarrassment, but what she wanted was Fortunato to rescue her.

Would he rescue her?

"The gypsies were the ones who destroyed the Imperial Bay Company camps and pilfered their belongings," said Artabanas. "It was not our fault. They are in the possession of a magic bracelet that can wield powers of water, fire and steam. They are the ones who robbed the Imperial Bay Company and none other."

"That is not what our reports have indicated," Legate Paulus said. "We have eyewitness reports of three thieves, acting alone, who have personally taken a treasure hoard of the Imperial Bay Company's wealth. Men dressed darkly, with black bandanas."

"Then we shall seize these three thieves," Artabanas said, "and put them to death."

"Until the investigation is completed by the Imperial Council," the Legate Paulus said, "you should prepare to pay an indemnity. For you are charged with the Imperial Bay Company's defense, and the fault — it seems — is at least partially your own."

A string of curses escaped Artabanas's lips.

"But until then, send all your forces to capture these three thieves," the Legate Paulus said. "You have His Excellency Emperor Verrus's demand to capture them and to put them to death."

Artabanas watched the Legate Paulus exit through the doors.

As soon as the doors had shut, Artabanas shouted, "As soon as Qadirra is rebuilt, we shall restore our people's fortunes. The *lugal* empire will fall."

"But we should capture those three thieves," Kavadh said.

"Yes," Artabanas said, "we will capture them and surely put them to death. For they steal from the Imperial Bay Company now, but they will rob the King of Kings of Great Fharas, the Great King of Qadirra, later."

~

In the grass, Fortunato made a signal. As the Imperial soldiers departed, they moved south through grassland.

How to cause chaos, and find an opening? Fortunato would find a way.

He would not allow Ambrass to fall to her captors. He would take Ambrass from Artabanas, and their love would be complete.

Chapter Thirty-Four: What Was Promised

The elf with the shard could not have gone far. At three miles a day, he was barely moving across the desert landscape. Unless he had some burst of strength, some newfound power to grasp the shard, he was somewhere amid this landscape of dry dust and sand, these mountains stretching all about. Beside Bran was the river, one he guessed was the northward branch of the Blue Khazan. The elf, now separated from his brethren, had surely run out of water many times now, and would not stray from a water source.

Bran's prey could not have gotten far. Raw logic proved that to be true.

Yet as he wandered, he had not seen footsteps in more than a day, and he was beginning to wonder if he had taken a wrong turn, or if he was looking in the wrong place entirely. The elf with the shard, and the magic gloves, could have fled in the opposite direction.

But in the opposite direction was Qadirra.

Bran was a warrior, and his skills at tracking were secondary to his kukri-knife. With his fingers, he touched the cold waters of the Blue Khazan. He sensed the river flowed down from the Sky Moutains far north of here.

The power of his bracelet was waning as he approached a land where no one lived. He realized, he was not far from the Pashupat Plateau, where he had killed a man and taken his kukri-knife, the kukri-knife that was his most prized possession.

The footsteps were gone. The trail had been lost.

And as Bran stirred in the wind, he had a sense he didn't understand, one that beckoned southwards, toward the city of Qadirra.

He sensed he was going in the wrong direction. For all he knew, he could be mistaken.

But he turned at that moment and headed south, toward Qadirra and the cursed land of Potam.

~

The fight with the half-rokahn, half-*lugal* had sent Samira into a tailspin.

She feared her bracelet, *Satar*, was of the lesser orders of bracelet. How could the powers of wind and cloud overcome the powers of the stars, the stars that the Qadirrans worshiped as gods?

Yet the bracelet *Abrah*, with powers over cloud, had indeed overcome *Satar*.

What then could she do? She worried someone else had found *Mainyu* and gained the powers of Arstibara. If someone else found *Mainyu*, it was they and not her who would reign over rebuilt Qadirra.

For now, though, she was fleeing south, fleeing the half-rokahn, half-lugal, who had defeated her.

~

Anton was passing through the greenness of Kash. Amid the brilliant verdancy, he saw the bewitching eyes of a snake peering directly at him from a tree branch.

Then, the bewitching eyes were gone, and there was the sound of a bone crunching.

Anton made a signal. The twenty gypsy warriors behind him also stopped.

And he saw amid the greenery, humans cutting a path with machetes through the dense undergrowth. The chief of them was holding a snake with a snapped neck in his hands.

He saw they were what southrons would call *lugals*. Some wore trousers and some wore loin cloths, but all of them had chests bare to the jungle heat. And on their necks were tattoos of black lightning marks. Their hair ranged from brown to blond, and in their hands were swords.

The chief of them met Anton's gaze with his eyes of blue.

Anton feared they would rob him, and the gypsies were carrying almost all the wealth they had taken from the Imperial Bay Company.

"Gypsy," said the chief of the men, "where are you going?"

Anton didn't want to answer. He wanted to be on his way. But the man's overpowering gaze broke past Anton's defenses.

"To find an engineer to besiege Qadirra," Anton said.

"Come with us, gypsy," said the man, "for the destruction of Qadirra was promised to our people and to our people alone. Come, witness it with us, what was promised. Among us are those who know how to build engines of siege."

And Anton trusted these people somehow, for power of their gaze, for confidence of their speech. Perhaps, instead of venturing so far to Udara, they would spend their gold in other ways.

And as the men further cut their way through the jungle, Anton followed them. He would follow them, he hoped, to the destruction of Qadirra, but not before they rescued their queen.

Their queen, Anton knew, was in great danger.

Chapter Thirty-Five: Heart-Path

The Possessor of the Ob had done something to Fenris, something inexplicable. He walked a path through the dry dust-land, and when he strayed, he found an overpowering sense he was going the wrong way. Yet it was leading him through waterless places, and the waterskin he had brought was running low. But it would lead him to *Mainyu*, to the most powerful bracelet of the Seven Bracelets of Arstibara. It would lead him to what he most desired, a way to forestall the destruction of Qadirra forever. The Possessor of the Ob had already proven her worth.

Yet as his heart led him amid the barren lands, he began to question and to wonder, if the destiny she had placed on him would end in a way he feared would come to pass.

A battle was coming — it was already here. Forces conspired to destroy Qadirra, the great city, and the Great King who now ruled it. But Qadirra would not fall; it was beloved above all.

He had at last come to the waters of the Blue Khazan as it trickled south from the Sky Mountains. He could see the crystal blue waters and the reeds growing alongside it. And he could see something else — a *lugal* In a robe colored rose, his long blond hair flowing down his back. His hands were covered in white gloves and in his left hand he was carrying something, a shard of blackish-green metal. On his right arm was a bracelet, its gold studded with a gem that was a flaming black.

He bore *Mah*, a bracelet unaccounted for. He must have found it in the desert, or his kindred.

But *Mah* was not opposed to *Zam*, which Fenris wore, nor were the powers of the moon in his estimation mightier than the powers of earth. Even with *Mah* and *Zam* on his arms, he would not be able to contend with a man mighty enough to enter the Aegis Shrine of Borean Hindrance, a man mighty enough to slay its two guardian spirits.

And though Fenris's liege would not look well on a *lugal* headed southwards toward Qadirra, least of all one wearing a bracelet, Fenris allowed him to pass him by.

He needed *Mainyu.*

Only *Mainyu* was mighty enough to confront such a man, who had purified the aegis shrine.

Besides, his heart inclined not to the *lugal,* but beyond.

~

The tall grass cloaked Fortunato and his Two Thieves. As the days progressed, he saw signs that the Imperial Bay Company was returning to its old haunt. They dared not return with a full army, nor take their precious wealth, for fear of the gypsies returning, but there were a few wandering the tall grasses, fortifying areas and building walls, scattered and few — perfect for three skilled warriors to waylay.

Amid the sound of insects buzzing, amid the stinging heat and midges swirling about Fortunato's eyes, he saw there was a pair of five Imperial Bay Company soldiers gathered just yards away.

He was getting ready to make a signal to attack when amid the thick heat, there was motion — the glittering of chainmail, a man in thick armor, the one who had confronted Fortunato at Qadirra's gate.

Hidden in the grass, he watched as the cataphract captain rode up to the Imperial Bay Company soldiers, then reared up on his warhorse.

"Any sign of them?" he said.

"No, Kavadh," said a consulary soldier. "They have escaped our notice. But we will lay a trap… they stole a bag of gold, and we will try to draw them out of their hiding places with wealth."

Were they speaking of the gypsies? No, Fortunato thought they were talking about Fortunato and his Two Thieves.

"And what of our plans," said the consulary soldier, "the eighth of Arah?"

"The eighth of Arah," said Kavadh, "shall be an infamous day."

"Are you ready to be King Kavadh?" said the consulary soldier.

"Better regicide, and a fifty percent tax on tar," said Kavadh, "than a Great King of Qadirra who casts his crown before a *lugal*."

"You sound so royal, Kavadh," the consulary soldier said. "I can picture you with a gold circlet now."

~

Fenris had followed his heart to his destiny a few paces.

And then he thought, the *lugal* would bring harm to the rebuilt Qadirra. For *lugals* had no love for Qadirra, and the *lugal*'s heart would be set against Artabanas, the Great King.

He turned, seeing the *lugal* venturing southward along the river, and realized he could not allow him to escape. It would be irresponsible. Were the powers of earth not greater than the powers of moon?

Fenris would dispatch him quickly, and then he would have the powers of *Zam* and *Mah,* in addition to *Mainyu.* Three bracelets could fit on his arm, with a little legerdemain.

And so he turned, and as the *lugal* walked — not having noticed him — Fenris raised up his bracelet, and its glowing brown gem turned to fire.

The earth began to shake, and the *lugal* looked about in a panic, then turned, and locked eyes with Fenris.

The black-gemmed bracelet the *lugal* wore was now liquid with black flames.

There was a crack in the earth, then, as the earth shook and rifts began to open up in the soil.

But above head, the white-blue sky darkened to purple, and then to black.

The moon appeared, and it was an angry moon, glowing some shade between white and orange, powerful in its majesty — the whole of the moon, a wrathful circle.

Fenris despaired at the sight of the moon, even as the ground grew unstable, and the *lugal* stumbled, then fell.

But the moon was aglow, and the waters of the Blue Khazan were kicking up froth. Waves were appearing in the Blue Khazan, massive waves, and as they waxed with the size of the moon, there was a roaring sound as the moon grew closer and closer, larger than any moon Fenris had ever seen, larger than any moon Fenris thought there had ever been.

A wall of water passed over the *lugal's* head and knocked Fenris to the ground. His bracelet loosened and almost slipped from his arm. The waters turned the cracks in the earth to mud, and as Fenris turned, he slipped and fell.

Mah was stronger than *Zam*. A stronger bracelet than *Zam* was in the hands of a *lugal*.

And Fenris fled into the desert. He would follow his heart. He would find *Mainyu* and he would kill the man who had purified the aegis shrine.

~

The bodies of the Imperial Bay Company soldiers lay about Fortunato, but he had left one alive. He was kneeling on the consulary soldier's chest, the last to survive. The consulary soldier was bleeding from his shoulders, from incisions that Fortunato had made with Danenhir.

"You were saying," Fortunato snapped, "a conspiracy to install Kavadh as king…"

"Please! Let me live!" the consulary soldier wailed.

So close to him, Fortunato detected a slight greenish hue to his skin. He had to be an anguiped.

"And how will this conspiracy unravel?" Fortunato said. "Tell me…"

"The actors are performing a play," the consulary soldier wheezed, "the king will be led to his private box. There, the conspirators in the Royal Guard will kill him, take his crown, and place it on Kavadh's head. Kavadh already has the support of his soldiers…"

"I thank you, soldier," Fortunato said. He sliced one of the consulary's cheeks, then the other. "When you go about bearing these wounds, tell them that Fortunato and his Two Thieves dealt them to you, and that Fortunato is coming for his beloved."

Fortunato stood up and kicked dirt at the consulary soldier as he stumbled to the ground and then staggered off, into the horizon.

Fortunato did not have an army behind him, but he could create chaos. And in chaos, he thought, there would be a chance for him to thrive.

The consulary soldier fled into the grassland, and at last disappeared into the distance.

Chapter Thirty-Six: As Before

As Reev stared at the walls of the aegis shrine, he continued to wait, and hope, and pray.

At some time, he thought, an opportunity would arise, but opportunities were few amid the desert wastes.

A mercenary army twice the size of the anguipeds' host had been dashed like water against rocks, and now, as they redoubled, growing in size by the day to protect the shrine, Reev could see the armies massing.

With his spyglass fixed on massing host, he saw one morning, for the first time, the bluish-green face of a kobold among the anguipeds.

Kobolds were abominations of the Dark One, crafted in his servant Lothan's forge, beings half-elf and half-rokahn, their bodies fused in unholy synergy. They were possessed of magic, and greater skill with the sword than common rokahn. As Reev watched their falchions gleam, as more kobolds were to be seen, Reev fought a sense of hopelessness that they'd never penetrate the doors of the aegis shrine.

Now, the army knew he was here, that Reev was not far.

Behind Reev, Agent Secunda stirred.

"We could try subterfuge," Agent Secunda said. "A pinch of forgetfulness powder, a dash through the dark."

"Rokahn will smell you," Reev said. "They can pick up your scent. Kobolds, I suppose, even more so."

So what could Reev do, then, and hope to accomplish? How could he possibly hope to scatter such an impregnable foe? The army, aware of the threat, was strengthening its defenses, and as Reev fixed the spyglass from one horizon to another, he saw some kobolds were engaged in construction, that they were building the beginnings of walls.

When the wall was built, how would Reev be able to penetrate the gate?

They knew Reev was here, they knew what he intended to do — to purify the shrine.

His kind struck terror in the hearts of anguipeds long ago. He would do his best to strike terror in them now.

He saw the anguipeds had anguiped horses, hairless with tough hides of whitish green. He would ride forth as a Son of Telantis.

"I'm going to rattle them," Reev said.

He put a finger to his lips, and let out an undulating song.

Amid the vast expanse, Cobalt came galloping, his hooves pounding against the sand and kicking up a cloud of dust.

"Let them fear the Sons of Telantis, like they did long ago," Reev said.

As Cobalt drew near, Reev swept himself onto his saddle, and then Cobalt galloped away, leaving behind Agent Secunda's cries of protest.

~

Reev stopped before the gathered anguipeds and brandished Doomblade.

Anguipeds cried and some fled.

The kobolds looked up with their glistening eyes, and ceased their construction of the wall.

Reev sat astride Cobalt before them, his amulet glistening in the sun, his Telantine lightning marks bare to see. And as some anguipeds steeled themselves, and brandished their swords, managing to withhold panic, others mounted anguiped horses and drew scimitars.

Anguiped against Telantine, and Reev would see who had the

better steed.

He galloped forth through the sand, and Cobalt kicked up a cloud of dust. He galloped through the desert, horse and rider as one unit, and Reev knew the anguipeds were right behind him.

They galloped through the desert, Reev and the ones pursuing him. Reev did not look back, but he heard their furious shouts. Through sand and dust Reev and Cobalt galloped, underneath a burning sun, as the ground began to rise, slowly at first then sharply. Reev was traversing, then, up rocks, and then a rocky hill. He had come to a rocky ridge, and when he did he turned around to face them.

He was high above the anguipeds, and the sun was shining on him. His coin amulet was flashing in the bright light of day.

There were hundreds of anguipeds mounted on horses, but when Reev turned to face them, and brandished Doomblade, they cried out in fear at the sight of him, wreathed in sunlight.

They turned, then, the hundreds of anguipeds, and fled on anguiped horses back in the direction of the tower.

"Tell your master that Qadirra's doom is sure!" Reev shouted. And the anguipeds, fleeing from Reev's sight, kicked up clouds of dust as they galled at a manic pace back toward where they had come.

Who would they send after Reev now? Who would face him, now that, one against a hundred, they had fled from the sight of him in mad terror?

~

When he returned to Agent Secunda, he returned to grumbling. Agent Secunda was beside herself at the display.

"You could have gotten yourself killed," Agent Secunda said.

"That was an undue risk. Spymaster Marius would be so displeased…"

"But I'm alive," Reev said, "and they fled from me. They really are scared of the sight of me."

But through the sunlight, the masses of anguipeds and rokahn were growing by the day, and though the anguipeds had fled from them in isolation, Reev was certain that they would not flee from him if he charged, alone, to the gate.

He was certain… almost certain, anyway.

Out in the open, beyond the hiding place, bare to see, he rode out. He fixed his spyglass on the anguipeds in full view of them. He saw the kobolds had ceased their work on the wall.

Perhaps, they now thought the wall would not hold against him.

Would he put their fears to the test?

Chapter Thirty-Seven: Message Sent

Fortunato had spent the day hunting down the scattered remnants of the Imperial Bay Company, the ones who had dared to continue to operate in the territory staked out by him and his Two Thieves — the grassland in the west of Potam, where the Blue Khazan and Black Khazan joined as one.

On Tyra Jade, he made a survey, riding amid abandoned tents and pilfered crates, the remains of the Imperial Bay Company's ill-gotten wealth that had either been secreted away, or taken by the gypsies or by Fortunato and his Two Thieves.

He had made an accounting of the area, and he thought there were no consulary soldiers who dared to remain.

And so Fortunato looked to Wrinn and then to Xan, the ones he called his Two Thieves, and wheeled about on Tyra Jade. Our base of operations is secured. "We must take territory, now," Fortunato said.

And leading Wrinn and Xan, who were riding two-a-saddle on Asté, Fortunato rode on Tyra Jade as she sprinted, until the grassland had become dry dust.

And there was someone on the road, someone going east in the direction of Qadirra. It was a cart and not a gypsy cart, a slight sleek cart made for speedy travel and not for living. A team of five horses were pulling the cart as it sped across the road, so fast the wheels seemed to just barely graze the ground. Painted on the wagon, Fortunato saw, was a four-pointed star, the symbol of the Kingdom of Great Fharas. This wagon belonged to the one who had taken captive his beloved.

He sprinted on Tyra Jade, and the team of horses was no match for Tyra at short distances. He raced in front of them, and then sat astride Tyra in the midst of the road. The horses neighed in fear at the sight of Tyra and then ground to a stop.

"I have heard of you!" said the man sitting at the front of the wagon with his whip, a southron in a white turban. "You are Fortunato."

Wrinn galloped ahead, in view. He shouted, "And we are his Two Thieves."

"I am a postman and nothing more," said the man. "I have no gold for you to pilfer."

"But perhaps, you can deliver a message to the king," Fortunato said.

~

With paper and a quill the postman had provided, Fortunato wrote down what he thought would initially help, and then doom Artabanas.

From Fortunato and his Two Thieves:

Kavadh intends to betray you on the eighth of Arah. He and traitors in the Royal Guard will kill you while you watch a play.
Be warned.
Also, Qadirra's doom is sure.

"Have this read to him in public," Fortunato said, "or else I and my two Thieves will hunt you down and put an end to you.

The postman took the paper and nodded frantically his assent. Fortunato thought he really believed it was true, that Fortunato and his Two Thieves were powerful enough to hunt him down.

His quick wit, his laying of ambushes, was paying dividends.

And the name of Fortunato and his Two Thieves were feared across the cursed land of Potam.

~

Samira had been defeated by the half-rokahn, half-*lugal*. She still had not recovered from that smarting wound… indeed, when she was not taken with fear at the thought, she was aggrieved.

She was nursing that bitterness as she stood on a desert hill overlooking the waters of the Blue Khazan.

She feared her opportunity to be Queen of Qadirra was slipping from her.

And then she saw she was not alone.

When she saw motion, a lump of panic moved from her heart to her throat, for fear it was the half-rokahn, half-*lugal*.

Instead it was a *lugal*, one of the varieties with pointed ears, garbed in a robe the color of roses. His hair was the color of gold.

He was wearing white gloves, and carrying something that was hurting him, a shard of metal. And then Samira saw it, first in fear — but when she saw the black color if its gem, delight.

The *lugal* bore the bracelet called *Mah* in his hands. The powers of the moon were at the *lugal*'s fingertips. And then Samira realized, the bracelet she wore and the bracelet the *lugal* bore were opposites.

The battle began, between two bracelets and not two wielders, before the *lugal* locked eyes with her, and panic consumed them both.

As the bracelets did battle, the blue skies turned to inky black, and stars appeared even in daylight, and turned to brilliant white, and then contorted to ochre, tilting toward red.

For then the moon appeared, and it was almost full, white at first, then orange.

The moon was blood red as the two bracelets battled against each other.

The powers of the moon had to be more powerful than the powers of the stars. The stars were to Qadirrans' eyes gods to be worshiped.

But when Samira looked at her hand, her bracelet was gone, and on the *lugal*'s arm, his bracelet had changed to glittering white, and the combined gems was a glowing gray.

A darkness like a cloud appeared, threatening to suck Samira into its vacuum, as powers of stars and moon were combined into powers of void — of the space between the heavenly bodies.

Samira sprinted into the desert, looking back constantly, fearing the void would claim her.

She could feel the vacuum pulling at her as she ran away.

~

On Tyra Jade Fortunato rode, and his Two Thieves rode behind. As the dusk settled on the eighth of Arah, he could see the postman's cart rattling through the gates of Qadirra.

Fortunato said a prayer that his warning would hurt, not help, Artabanas.

He said a prayer that it would provide an opening for him to rescue his beloved.

The death of Artabanas belonged to him, not Kavadh, and it was he who would rescue his love. The night was coming, and he did not know when the play would be.

But he sensed Ambrass's anguish from afar.

He sensed her longing for him, and he knew that she knew he was here.

He was at the gates.

Chapter Thirty-Eight: The Gods Of Qadirra

When the postman read the letter, and panic filled the dining chamber, all Ambrass thought about, all Ambrass cared about, was its sender. "Fortunato and his Two Thieves."

She knew Fortunato had a sense of humor, and he wondered who his two thieves were. Was it Reev? Was it Bala?

Bala, Ambrass knew, had taken a liking to Fortunato. The vampire child had to be ten years old by now. He had shown the beginnings of latching on to Fortunato before Ambrass had departed from Galiope.

She imagined Bala, his little body dressed up in a black suit and bandana, and smiled, as Artabanas tore open the curtain, having turned pale, and looked near to faint.

And she laid bare her smile, her joy, for all to see, as Artabanas fixed his impotent fury on Kavadh.

Kavadh's eyes were so wide, he looked like a deer before an oncoming cart.

"Is this true?" Artabanas said. "Is this true, Kavadh?"

The Eloesian actors were supposed to be performing a play this night, *Fhareedi's Quest*. Ambrass recalled Kavadh intimately involved in the details of where Artabanas would be sitting, and who would be sitting with him.

She savored the terror and the pandemonium. But she wondered why Fortunato had intervened. Didn't he love her?

Ambrass wondered if he wanted to take on Artabanas, personally, himself.

She did not mask her joy, as members of the Royal Guard seized Kavadh.

"It's true," Artabanas said. "And we shall uncover every last traitor in this palace. I shall be Great King of Qadirra! I will rule over rebuilt Qadirra, and no other!"

But in Fortunato's letter, he had declared, Qadirra's doom was sure. That was more trustworthy than Artabanas's petty cries.

"Kill the actors, too," Artabanas said. "Anyone suspect, any possible conspirators must be killed. But Kavadh will receive the worst. The court shall see what happens to one who tries to kill the Great King. And the gods of Qadirra will be honored in the manner of his death."

~

Outside, in the brisk night air, there was an altar that had been unearthed from the Qadirran ruins. The slabs were carved with reliefs of horned gods with tongues flaring, of gods with the heads of humans and the bodies of lions, or gods with serpents for legs.

There, Artabanas had brought a bound and weeping Kavadh, as the gathered members of the court watched, and the members of the Royal Guard who had not been executed wielded torches.

In the torchlight, in the light of the moon, which was a waning gibbous, Ambrass stood by with a cold gasp as Kavadh was slammed face up on the altar, and then his hands and feet bound to the stone. "We have one with us who is a master of the ancient rites of Qadirra," said Artabanas, "who will sacrifice him according to all ritual and all proper method. We honor the gods of Qadirra tonight."

A man was before the altar, then, a man in a scintillating gold robe and a horned headdress. His eyes were wild, and his eyes seemed filled with a dark madness. He carried in his hand a stone knife.

"To Tamtum Lady of Chaos we dedicate this offering," the priest said. "Let the blood of Kavadh please her, and usher her back into the world of mortals. Let her black scales glisten, the fire of her breath make Qadirra new."

And Ambrass looked away before the blow landed. Kavadh's blood sprayed everywhere.

What a wicked city, and what a wicked company, Ambrass had found herself in.

She prayed to the gods for rescue. She said softly under her breath, "Quicker, Fortunato, quicker… there is no time."

The wedding date was approaching, the wedding when her life could end, and all hope. She despised Artabanas with all she had in her.

What would she do if he had his way?

She could not bear to think of it. She could not bear to go to that dark place.

~

Fortunato could see the air of Qadirra change, a sense of terror building in the air. He knew now that Artabanas would be paranoid, looking through every dark place, every closet door. In every room he'd fear an assassin. And he knew his rule was tenuous, and his kingship would be brief.

Fortunato, astride Tyra Jade, took stock of the city's walls, so proud, so insolent. He believed in his heart they would fall.

Ambrass lay out of his grip. He had no army. Could he find one?

No… he could not.

And the dire day approached, the day when all would be threatened, when all hope for he and Ambrass would be lost.

They would ride together to the Dark Land, or their love would never be complete.

At least, that was what Fortunato thought.

Chapter Thirty-Nine: The Bracelets' Purpose

Samira had been afraid, and now she was terrified. In the cold of the desert night, under the light of the moon which she looked upon now with terror, she could see her hands trembling.

So much had been taken from her. Now, all had been taken from her. She was no longer the King of Kings' chief wife, and now, she no longer had the powers of the bracelet called *Satar* in her hands.

She thought her foes, the half-*lugal* and the *lugal*, were far enough away for her to catch her breath. And though she felt hunted, she thought she would stop and pause, to recalibrate and think anew on all that had transpired, and form a new plan.

A mighty bracelet was now in the hands of the *lugal*. Were the combined powers of *Ab* and *Azar* the mightiest, or were the combined might of *Mah* and *Abrah* stronger whose power now was void?

All Samira knew was that she had come close to death, and that moreover, she had been thwarted. She had almost died, and now she had nothing, nothing at all.

But in the cold air of the desert night, the raw momentum of the panic was fading, the hard edges that prevented thought and purpose. The wild panic was fading to horrible fear, and in horrible fear, she could think, and dream up a new plan?

Whether *Mah, Abra, Azar or Ab* were strongest was unknown even to the wise. They had not been tested. But what was beyond dispute, something in common knowledge, was that the greatest of the Seven Bracelets of Arstibara was *Mainyu,* and in it was a power far stronger than all the others.

The wicked genie Arstibara had fashioned them all for

Qadirra's destruction, but Qadirra's walls had been rebuilt, and other buildings were being constructed every day. The city was rising from the ashes, and wherever Arstibara was, Samira was sure he was filled with wrath, that his plans were faltering.

When Qadirra was rebuilt, Qadirra would rule the world. The *lugal* empire would vanish and would be no more, when the gods of Qadirra reemerged in the world of mortals, when their temples were unearthed, and the magic of Qadirra spread throughout the whole of the world.

Arstibara, a crafter of wonders, a masterful metallurge, was not the only genie in the world, however. One lived in the candelabra Samira had brought with her, one she corralled at the edge of her sharp tongue, who shuddered at the sight of her face.

She was in no mood to be beguiled or defied. She was angry, and she would not allow her captured genie to deceive her.

As the panic began to fade to a fear she could control, and seeing no sign of *lugals* or half-*lugals* in the desert night, she took her candelabra out and clapped her hands and said, "Come out, Das!"

There was the telltale billow of green smoke as the genie emerged from his prison.

When Das had emerged fully, and his green body glowed in the desert night, Samira worried he could sense her fear, that he knew she was just recovering from a severe defeat.

She tried to put on the taunting face from before, but her fear and defeat was spilling through.

"What's wrong?" Das said.

"Nothing," Samira said, and spittle hit the desert sand. "Quiet, you."

Das's massive green body seemed to shrink, and inch toward the fixture of the candelabra he was emerging from.

"I can tell you are afraid, Samira," Das said.

"Where is *Mainyu*?" Samira said. "Tell me, and I will free you."

"You must swear an oath," Das said.

And Samira thought perhaps she had to be truthful now, that perhaps the recovery of *Mainyu* was worth losing her genie servant.

And yet, she couldn't help herself. She loved the look on Das's face when he was thwarted.

"I swear an oath," said Samira, "by the bracelet *Satar* and its power, if you tell me where *Mainyu* is, I will free you."

Das's yellow eyes examined her, but he was just a troublesome genie and nothing more.

"Go to the village of Arman. Walk one mile and forty steps due east. There, you shall find *Mainyu*."

Das looked at her. "Now free me," said Das.

Samira smiled a sadistic smile. "I shall not, Das, for *Satar* is gone. The powers of stars and moon have combined unto void."

"Woe betide Qadirra, then," Das dared to say, as his yellow eyes rolled into the back of his head, and he turned to billows of green smoke that vanished into the candelabra's fixture.

~

Bran had only become more convinced he was on the right track the closer he got to Potam. He was treading near footsteps that were fresh, footsteps formed from the leather soles of elven shoes. And so he had quickened his pace, and was half-running, half-walking, down the shore, when he at last spotted his prey.

The elf had been moving quicker than he had thought. And when he saw the elf, he realized he was no longer wearing the magic white gloves.

The shard of *Serpentax* was no longer in the elf's possession. Something else was.

And long before Bran spied the silverish-white bracelet and the shining gray gem, the stars had burned through the clouds, and the form of an orange moon had appeared overhead. As a black cloud descended toward the heavens, and Bran felt himself pulled toward it, he eyed the elf one more time, thoroughly.

The magic gloves were discarded. The shard of *Serpentax* was gone.

Had he tossed it in the river? Had the elf disposed of it somehow?

No, that was not possible.

Bran called up his bracelet, but though the sky shimmered, the clouds failed to cover the bracelet of a higher order. He rushed, despite the descending black void, and drew his kukri-knife. As the black void covered him, he slashed with its edge and struck a dolorous blow.

The elf fell limp to the ground, and the powers of the bracelet without a wearer vanished. Clouds again covered the night sky, as the stars were veiled again with an astral thunder.

By quickness and a deft blow, he had slain the elf. His blood was pooling on the dirt, but as Bran looked about, he saw he was not alone.

Despite the darkness he could see six figures approaching from the desert sands, for the cloaks they wore were darker than the night, blacker than any pitch or tar, seeming to suck in all light. Bran shuddered at the sight of them, and then he looked to the bracelet with its gray star aglow.

"You have dealt the Telantines a severe blow, Bran," said the chief of the six men, whose grayish-black blade was a sword. "The rokahn in you has proved strong. Our master is proud."

Who was their master? They still had not told.

"And yet, a rokahn would not charge at a moment of deepest peril, when void was sinking from the night sky, and the combined powers of star and moon descended. It was your bravery, perhaps recklessness, that saved your life."

Bran eyed the white bracelet, whose power was far greater than the one he wielded.

"Leave the bracelet of star and moon behind," said the chief of the six men. "Its power can be wielded, but its end will make its way to the destruction of our cause.

"Therefore, also, cast the bracelet you wear, *Zam,* to the ground, and think of it no more."

Bran was not one to obey orders from anyone, but he eyed the blackish-gray blades the six men bore and feared what they could do. He removed *Zam* and cast it into the waters of the river.

"Our enemies have now removed *Serpentax* from our sight," the man in black continued. "An elven magic is now over it, preventing us from finding it. But if you find it, Bran, you will have gold enough for a kingdom. Our master promises it."

Who was their master?

For now, it didn't matter. He had to find the shard.

King Bran, and his wife.

Chapter Forty: Stronger

Through the desert, Fenris followed the inkling the Possessor of the Ob had instilled in him, and one burning afternoon, the inkling reversed, and he found himself facing the opposite direction. Had the Possessor of the Ob done this to torment him, to humiliate the King of Kings' chief advisor? Was she playing with him like a puppet on her string, trying to delay the rebuilding of Qadirra?

Qadirra was beloved above all; it would be rebuilt. Its gods would reign again in Varda, and the *lugal* empire would be decimated.

But despite what could have been a crafty woman's dark trick, Fenris did turn around and follow the same inkling that had been guiding him in the opposite direction before.

It would take him to *Mainyu,* she had said.

He followed the inkling, first walking through the desert soil, then running, then sprinting, for the inkling was stronger than it had ever been. As he reached the top of a high ridge, he saw crystal clear waters down below, the gushing of the Blue Khazan as it pierced the desert, flowing north to south.

Something was glittering in the water.

Its gleam was not mere metal, but eldritch. A bracelet was in the water.

It was surely *Mainyu.*

But when Fenris waded in, he saw the gleam was not purple as *Mainyu* was said to be, but brown. When he removed the bracelet from the water, he saw it was *Zam*, the bracelet of earth, and when he saw it was *Zam — Abrah's* opposite — he fixed it to his right wrist, and commanded them to do battle.

The earth beneath Fenris shook. The clouds above him turned

dark and stormy. Lightning flashed, and rain poured. Rivulets ran through the dirt, giving moisture to the sandy soil that had not been seen in surely ages. The earth quaked, but the sky was fixed above, and lightning pierced the dirt, and the earth was flooded.

The bracelet on Fenris's left wrist was now white, and fixed with an orange gem. The powers of earth and cloud were at his fingertips — but what power would such a combination produce?

The inkling in Fenris's heart was gone.

The Possessor of the Ob had not led him to *Mainyu*.

Or had she?

~

In the days since the attempted assassination, Artabanas seemed to be consumed in paranoia. The Royal Guard had been halved, but even the survivors he did not seem to trust. He did not trust Ambrass, surely, but she knew that assassinations were not her method, but sharp words and cutting remarks, and the truth that was made obvious when he asked questions about the wedding.

Ambrass knew she couldn't escape, that every door was watched, and so she sat in the women's apartments quietly, praying prayers and making requests, that Fortunato her love would rescue her.

But all was stillness — all silence. All, save a sense of hate that lingered. Her eyes inclined to the door.

~

Samira had traveled with haste to the village of Arman. Its peasants were at work in the barley fields.

Das said *Mainyu* could be found one mile and forty steps east from this village, this collection of huts and mudbrick houses.

Samira did not disguise her disgust at the sight of the peasants, so beneath her, but she was wearing a veil.

So she removed her veil, against all law and regulation, and let the peasants see her scornful grimace.

The peasants had barely noticed her.

She crossed east, walking a mile, and then she counted the forty steps. She had come to a house that had been burned to the ground. Near the house was a large black stone, one that Samira had a sense was no ordinary stone.

Not a stone it was, but a boulder. She could see the reflection of her unveiled face within it.

She stared at the glistening rock, at her face.

She stared at the black shiny surface. She stared, and felt she was entering a trance, like the black boulder was staring into her.

She saw, then, her husband in an intimate embrace with the queen of the gypsies. Her despair won out over her desire for *Mainyu*.

She fell back and struggled not to weep.

She had to win him back. She had to abandon this quest. She wanted Artabanas's love. She would be Queen of Qadirra through him, not without him.

She turned and saw *lugals* in breastplates, with green crests on their helmets. There were about a dozen of them, and they were looking at her angrily.

Samira, though, was beside herself at the vision, at the thought of losing Artabanas forever.

"Signora," said one of the *lugal* soldiers — she recalled, a member of the Imperial Bay Company. "This rock is being transported to our quarry for processing. Please step aside."

Behind the *lugals* she saw carts and a wooden crane.

She looked into the shiny rock again.

What truth would it lay bare, what reality would it show, to shatter her heart?

Her heart was already in pieces.

In the rock she saw the reflection of a bracelet on a gray arm, its gem shining purple.

Mainyu.

The consulary soldiers seized her by the arm and heaved her aside.

~

Ambrass had a terrible feeling as she sat in her room, like a phantom threatening her, a dark hand arising from the grave. Fortunato, it seemed, had never been so far away, the hopes of their love so far gone. For she felt a wrath fixed on her, a wrath that would not cease until she was dead, or worse. What was worse than death?

She prayed. "Fortunato, rescue me," she said, in the privacy of her room.

What was worse than death? Being separated from Fortunato, forever.

~

Fortunato stared at the hateful walls of Qadirra, not knowing what to do. The gate was sealed, and he had his Two Thieves.

He wondered if he was too bold, to save Artabanas's death for Danenhir. But he wished it to be his blade that was plunged through Artabanas's heart, and not Kavadh's. He didn't want an unworthy king to replace an unworthy king. He wanted to be the avenger, the gods' avenger. He wanted to be the one to engineer Artabanas's fall.

He knew time was running out. He knew Ambrass was about to be wed, at the end of a sword.

She was Artabanas's captive, and Fortunato, sitting astride Tyra Jade with Xan and Wrinn behind him, was at a loss for what to do, at how to bring about the outcome he desired.

As the sun set, he fought despair at the helpless feeling. He did not know what to do. The days he could act were numbered, to rescue his beloved. Xan was skilled with the butterfly blade, and Wrinn was skilled with his quarterstaff, but the walls of Qadirra were tall, and they were defended.

Even now, amid the growing dark, Fortunato could see countless men in chainmail along the walls' battlements. Artabanas knew that his was a city under siege, that though the world they knew loved Qadirra, there were some that hated it. Artabanas knew there were enemies, waiting to lay his city waste.

And so what would happen? Could Fortunato find a way? He always had before. But now he was fighting fear, fear he wouldn't be able to achieve the outcome he desired, fear that Ambrass would be married to Artabanas at the end of a sword.

The folk of Great Fharas called men like Fortunato and Xan *lugals*, and treated them with contempt. They knew, *lugals* were Qadirra's enemy, opposed by their very natures.

The city that had once ruled the world, in the time before the Empire was even a thought in its founders' minds, was being rebuilt. And Fortunato, from where he sat astride Tyra Jade, could see each day new towers rising, and new buildings built upon what just years ago were ruins.

Could he rescue Ambrass? He drew his sword, and uttered a vow, that he would.

"Qadirra, Qadirra! You shall fall, and my beloved will fall into my hands!" Fortunato shouted to the city, the city that rose above the desert plain.

The moon above-head, as darkness fell deep and true, was partially obscured in shadow. The moon too, it seemed, was filled with loathing for Qadirra. It just had that look.

"Qadirra, Qadirra! You shall fall!" Wrinn shouted after him.

"It shall!" said Xan.

"And Ambrass will fall into Fortunato's hands," Wrinn said.

They were alone amid the desert night. At least, it seemed that way.

The wedding of Artabanas and Ambrass was at the door. If Fortunato did not find a way in, it all would be over for him.

"Qadirra, Qadirra, you shall fall," Fortunato said one last time, "and my beloved will fall into my hands…"

~

When Anton arrived, on foot, where the gypsy wagons had gathered, he was not alone.

Julian, having expected his brother, walked out beyond the caravan, amid the moonlit desert night.

The forms behind Julian were taller than most gypsies. There were about a hundred of them, by Julian's count.

"Who are these folk?" Julian said.

It was not possible for Anton to have traveled to Udara and back in all this time.

"Telantines," Anton explained.

They were tall, and some wore trousers, and others wore loin cloths. None wore a shirt or a tunic.

Some bore swords at their belts. But others were carrying other objects, objects of wood — it seemed.

"Are they siege engineers?" Julian said.

"No," Anton said.

Julian would try not to utter curses at his brother. They had precious little time, for the wedding of Ambrass and Artabanas was at the door.

As the men that Anton called Telantines drew near, Julian saw the wooden objects they were carrying were chairs. Chairs could not breach the gates of Qadirra. What could chairs do? "What is this?" Julian said, and he did not disguise his confusion.

"We've brought chairs," one of the Telantines said, "to witness the destruction of Qadirra that was promised to us."

Julian marveled at the men. He saw their necks were tattooed with lightning marks.

As they set their chairs into the sand and sat down before a view of Qadirra, Julian wondered if they were too bold.

But they were so confident, he wouldn't question them.

Chapter Forty-One: Moonstruck

Fenris had tried to activate the bracelet's powers, but the combined strength of earth and cloud seemed to be something that would not manifest in his environment. Its magic was present, and its powers were in Fenris, and he knew that there was power because of the magic glow of its orange gem — but Fenris could not seem to activate it.

The Possessor of the Ob had said it was *Mainyu*. But Fenris was a student of the Seven Bracelets of Arstibara, and he knew the gem of *Mainyu's* bracelet was purple.

The bracelet Fenris wore was not *Mainyu*.

But as he trekked through the desert, he still felt he did not have enough to confront a man so mighty as to enter into the borean shrine and slay its two guardian spirits, especially not knowing what powers the bracelet possessed.

Some would call Fenris a coward, but he was only crafty and wise. He wouldn't rush in like a fool and risk failure. No, he would enter into battle with the mighty man with all knowledge and all the might available to him.

Where could he start? He supposed he could start with the one who wrote the inkling on his heart. Surely she could be able to tell him what powers the bracelet of cloud and earth contained, what hidden power it had, so that Fenris would enter into battle boldly.

A mile and forty steps, east along the Blue Khazan from the village of Arman, and he would have his answer.

~

When he had gone a mile, and was counting his ginger steps,

his breath was a cold gasp in his lungs, and he was trembling. His magi's staff, which he hadn't made much use of since his transformation in the temple of the moon, shook along with his sweaty grip.

And when he saw the woman's house burnt to the ground, and the Ob the woman possessed standing by the waters, and consulary soldiers beside it, he felt himself shudder.

There was a crane beside the ob, and the consulary soldiers were looking at Fenris with contemptuous faces.

He saw marks in the dirt all about the ob, the grass pulverized to bare the dirt.

"What is this?" Fenris said.

"The boulder has been sold by your liege to the Imperial Bay Company," said a consulary soldier. "But it is so large, our crane cannot dislodge it.

It didn't look that large to Fenris.

"And what of the woman?" Fenris said.

"Any who resists the king is put to death," the consulary soldier said, "according to the laws of Great Fharas. The consulary army is permitted to carry out executions, as per Imperial Council Resolution, 'Granting Acts,' Section 5."

It was a pity. The woman would have helped him.

But he strode up to the black stone and eyed its shining dark facets, facets in which he could see clear reflections of whatever was behind him.

He could see the furry face he had been stricken with since he entered the temple of the moon god. He could see the striped robe that was a mimicry of what the god had worn in the same temple. He could see his shepherd's crook staff. He asked the black stone to tell him the truth, silently.

And the image of himself changed to that of a mighty man, his biceps struggling to fit into the striped robe he wore, so muscular was he.

He strode up to the giant black stone, what the woman had called an Ob, and laid a hold of it.

He pulled, and when he did, the orange gemstone turned to a bright orange flame.

He could feel great resistance, but the strength that the bracelet had given him was stronger, He could feel the dirt crumbling as the Ob was pulled through its earth tomb, up around Fenris's head, bearing a flat-shaped bottom that would have made it impossible for a crane to dislodge.

A hole was now in the ground, and the boulder, which the woman had called an Ob, was being held aloft over Fenris's head.

The Imperial Bay Company soldiers, did not have looks of appreciation or marvel, but instead a cool businesslike demanding gaze.

"Please set it in the cart, Fenris," said a consulary soldier, "or else you will be in violation of Imperial Council resolution 'Caro's Day Addendum,' Section 9."

Fenris was now a mighty man. But he did not think he was mighty enough to contend with the one who purified the shrine.

As he took the boulder and set it in a cart the consulary soldiers were motioning to, like it was the weight of a pebble, he vowed — he would not confront the purifier of the shrine with the powers of a lesser bracelet.

As the cart strained under the weight, he caught sight of another image in the Ob's facets, the form of a gray arm, a bracelet about it with a purple gleam.

Mainyu.

~

In the dining chamber, sick of stews, Ambrass was barely eating. The lutists and drummers were playing a tune they had played before.

Ambrass knew the days were growing later, that their wedding was almost set to begin. At the thought, she felt her eyes begin to water, when the worst happened, the gold curtain of Artabanas's dais opened, and Artabanas stepped out.

He was dressed in that two-piece suit that Ambrass hated.

"I shall dine with my bride," said Artabanas, carrying his bowl of stew. His silver spoon glittered in the light of the lamps and the candles.

The construction of the dining room had about finished, and the walls were sealed with plaster. Paintings of symmetrical shapes had been lined on the wall, but no forms of men or beasts, no brilliant color or signs of life.

Ambrass tried not to weep.

When Artabanas sat next to her, she fought against her tears all the more, for fear he'd sense weakness. He set his bowl on the ground.

"Our wedding is in three days," said Artabanas. "Are you excited?"

"My beloved will come for me," said Ambrass. "And you cannot stop him. Not with an army, not with all the power of Qadirra's gods. Our love is destined; it is written. You will not stop my beloved's arrival."

"And who is your beloved?" Artabanas said.

He placed a wiry hand on hers and she shuddered at the touch.

"I am your beloved," Artabanas said.

"No," Ambrass said, "my beloved is strong, and he is good. His hair is dark and his eyes are bright. He is kind, and he is a hero. He is your opposite."

Artabanas struck her across the cheek and tears fell unbidden from Ambrass's eyes.

The door had opened.

Standing there was someone Ambrass had not seen in days, Fenris with his striped robe and his magus's staff. He was carrying a bracelet, and at the sight of the magic bracelet she shuddered, but then she remembered it had no power within Qadirra's walls.

"Your Worship," said Fenris, "I would like to make a request."

The gemstone of Fenris's bracelet was orange.

"What is your request, Fenris?" Artabanas said. At Fenris's appearance, he was distracted, so Ambrass removed her hands from the table entirely, to avoid his touch.

"The magic of Qadirra holds," said Fenris. "The ancient witchcraft they uttered over the Land of Potam, however, has dissipated, as you know, by the purification of the Aegis Shrine of Borean Hindrance. I do not know where the purifier is, but I know what his goal is set on, the purification of the Aegis Shrine of Hyperborean Hindrance. I believe he is there."

"Thousands of *huls* guard it," said Artabanas, "with our consent."

"But as long as the purifier lives, we in Qadirra should quake in fear," Fenris said. "We must kill him before he purifies the last shrine, and all the defenses of Qadirra are gone. For then, the writings would be true, and the city, the beloved most of all, will fall."

"Go kill him," said Artabanas. "You have my command."

"I require more to kill someone strong enough to purify an aegis shrine, and slay its two guardians," said Fenris.

"You have a bracelet," Artabanas said. "And the army of *huls* are strong. *Huls*, after all, are descended from ancient Qadirrans."

"*Huls* are strong," said Fenris, "but if I am to kill the purifier, who slew two Qadirran guardian spirits, I will need even more… an army. A thousand cataphracts, at a minimum."

"Quiet, fool," Artabanas said. "An army of gypsies roams freely through the land of Great Fharas, threatening to besiege the city at any moment. The city's defenses hold not just because of Qadirran magic and the remaining aegis shrine, but also because of force of arms.

"Be a man, Fenris. I know you are something else, now, in the temple of the moon. But don all your courage."

"Something else, now," Fenris said. "That reminds me of something…"

~

Fenris exited the palace, disappointed. The bracelet with the orange gemstone glistened in the hot desert sun. The Bracelet of Might would avail him, and Artabanas had been correct that thousands of *huls* would be an asset, but Fenris had a weakness, one he hoped to assuage.

When he approached the rebuilt temple of Utuk and its mounting levels, Fenris hoped the ancient magic of the Qadirran gods would avail him.

"What do you want?" said the priest in his billowing headdress. The rebuilt altar he stood before was wet with sacrificial blood.

"What is your request of Great Utuk?" said the priest.

"That I not be moonstruck, as I go forth to slay the Telantines' hero," Fenris said.

"A gift of blood," the priest growled.

"Whose blood?" Fenris said.

The priest beckoned. An attendant appeared with a stone knife.

Fenris winced as he extended his hand over the altar. He shut his eyes as he felt a slashing sharp pain.

And when it happened, he felt his hands tremble, the sign of an episode threatening to overtake him.

But when he shut his eyes his hands were not trembling. He could focus, just barely.

He felt weakened, somehow, as he exited the rebuilt temple of

Utuk, now dripping blood from his right hand.

Chapter Forty-Two: Hul Ally

As Reev stood before the Aegis Shrine of Hyperborean Hindrance, he had an inexplicable sense that time was running out.

The doors were sealed, and the armies of anguipeds, rokahn and kobolds were growing by the day. The armies were growing, as if they too knew that time was running out for Reev, that if they held on a little longer, it would be over for him, and for the cause of light.

That was the inexplicable sense Reev got as he stared into the massing army from his hiding place, with Agent Secunda behind him.

As he watched and waited, hand gripping Doomblade's hilt in its sheath, there was a storm of dust, and noise.

As he sat, crouching, in the waning light of day, a warhorse passed by, just inches from his hiding place.

~

The King of Kings, Artabanas, had not provided Fenris with an army, but he had provided him with a fresh horse. And so he had ridden with all due speed from Qadirra to the Aegis Shrine of Hyperborean Hindrance.

Here, as he said, thousands of *huls* were gathered. Amid them were rokahn of various kinds, and strange beings Fenris had not seen before, beings of green or blue complexion, with serpentine yellow eyes that threatened to steal one's life when one's gazes met.

Yet *huls* and the warriors of Great Fharas were allies, for they both wished for Qadirra's rebuilding, and Qadirra's rule. The *huls* knew Fenris was an ally, and did not draw their swords or axcs as

Fenris galloped through the beginnings of wooden fortifications and kicked up a cloud of dust.

Amid the massing army, he thought it impossible that even a man who purified the Aegis Shrine of Borean Hindrance could dash to pieces this gathered force.

Yet on the gathered *huls'* faces there seemed to be looks of disquiet and worry, a tenseness and an unbidden fear.

Their leader approached, one of purer lineage, whose skin had a green hue without looking at it closely, whose facial features were sharp, whose eyes were yellow. He had a sword, and the crossbar was forged in the form of a serpent's head. His sword was in its sheath.

"The Receiver of the Blessing of Enzu approaches," said the *hul* captain.

He was referring to the incident at the temple of the moon, the one which changed him and gave him his furry guise.

"And you are?" Fenris said. He felt uncharacteristically rattled.

The blood had ceased dripping in great volume, but he felt disturbed, worried even more than the moon would strike him.

"Mawt," said the captain of the *huls*. "Why have you come, Fenris?"

Fenris raised up the bracelet with the orange gemstone. "I bear the combined powers of earth and cloud," Fenris said, "making a Bracelet of Might. I come to deal death to the one who purified the Aegis Shrine of Borean Hindrance, so that he may not destroy the aegis shrine you now guard."

"The power of Hyperborea is hindered," said Mawt. "Heaven's Spear, wherever it is, is almost eliminated. And the Telantine will not bear it against us. Only a little while longer."

A Telantine… Fenris had only a little recollection of what that word meant. He knew that the Telantines were like *lugals*, but like hyper-*lugals*, the spirit and flesh of the *lugals* embodied.

And one was here. One had been mighty enough to purify the

shrine.

"We must act," said Fenris. "We must kill him. It is the King of Kings' command."

"When Heaven's Spear is no more," said Mawt. "There will be no hope for Telantis to be reborn."

But Fenris wished to attack. He wished to find the Telantine and kill him, as the King of Kings demanded.

~

The inexplicable sense that time was running out was only growing stronger in Reev Nax.

Agent Secunda wished to depart and seek another way to bring about Qadirra's destruction.

But Reev's eyes were fixed on the shrine. He felt compelled to act, a stirring in his heart that would not go away.

He eyed the army, and the shrine that hindered Hyperborea, and set his heart against them.

Chapter Forty-Three:
Astral Language

In the night, in her room, Ambrass stirred, fearful of what was to come, dreading the dread day.

Did Fortunato still love her?

Why, then, had he not arrived? Why then, had he not stormed the gates? For surely, since their love was written, the gates will not hold against him.

She eyed the night sky, and saw a starry band.

"Come to me, love," Ambrass said.

~

A band of stars were moving across the night sky, prominently.

Fortunato felt that they were speaking to him an astral language as they twinkled. "I will come to you," Fortunato said to them. "A little while longer, my beloved…"

But the walls of Qadirra were tall, and the gate was strong. To the walls, turrets were being added every day, and fortifications strengthened, as the phantom city arose from its ruins.

Would the city be rebuilt? Would its gods return?

Fortunato knew, the wedding was tomorrow. But the gate was strong.

So how would he get past it? How could he rescue his love from her fate?

He pondered. He would pray, perchance to dream. But how could he rescue her? How could he avoid this fate?

~

"I will see you soon," Ambrass said to the stary band. "I know I will."

~

"You know," Fortunato breathed. "You know, and that is enough for me."

~

Amid the starry expanse, the gypsies were gathered in their wagons.

Julian knew that time was running out, that the wedding of Artabanas and Ambrass was at the door. Yet they had swords and swords only, and they had no way to besiege the city, nor force of numbers to surround it.

Julian had only the inexplicable hope that the Telantine warriors had brought, as they sat encamped with the gypsies, the confidence that Qadirra would fall. So confident were they, they had come as spectators and not warriors of a literal sense. They were with the gypsies, but in the night, one of them was stirring.

The Telantine man, his blond hair a silverish-gold under the light of the waning crescent moon, had a sword in his hand. "Gypsy," he said, and his lightning mark tattoos stood out in the silver light on his neck, "I have a sense — a stirring in my heart. I must depart, for I sense a hindrance."

"You go with the blessing of the gypsies," said Julian.

And it was true. Anton would not disagree.

As the Telantine man, the leader of the Telantines' party, whose name Julian did not know, departed, Julian uttered a prayer that he would be guided to success, that the gods would grant speed and certainty to his feet.

But what hope was there, now? The wedding was almost here.

~

It was the twelfth of Arah, Fortunato knew. Behind him were his two thieves.

His eyes fixed to the starry band.

"I will see you soon," he said, "but how? The gates are strong."

~

Ambrass knew her wedding was two days away. She had little time. They had to be bold, she knew. She said to the starry band, "The gates cannot hold against you, my beloved. You know this. As our love is written, so too it is written on your heart, that the gates cannot hold against you."

~

"The gates cannot hold against me," Fortunato said, and Wrinn and Xan heard.

It was madness, to storm the gates of the rising phantom city.

It was utter madness, but the desert landscape was cast in moonlight.

He was astride Tyra Jade, and Xan and Wrinn were mounted on Asté behind.

The gates would not hold against him. The stars had told them in their astral language that it was written upon his heart.

Fortunato fixed his eyes on the hateful gates of the phantom city, which Artabanas was trying to rise anew.

The gates would not hold against him — it was written on his heart, it was true.

He rode forth on Tyra Jade to Wrinn and Xan's protests, as she walked and then she sprinted, and then she pranced before

Qadirra's massive gate.

Fortunato could sense Wrinn and Xan behind him, amid the waxing crescent moon.

He stood, and the soldiers on the battlements of the wall looked down upon him. To Fortunato's eyes, they were dark shapes and not much more.

The gate did not burst before him, nor did it disintegrate before his gaze, as he had half expected. But there were shouts among the soldiers, the dark shapes on the battlements of the wall, and movement in the light of the desert moon.

Fortunato had stridden forth boldly. But perhaps it had not been written on his heart after all.

"Who are you?" he heard a soldier shout on the battlements.

"Fortunato," he shouted in turn.

"And his Two Thieves!" shouted Xan a moment later.

And the shapes began to stir, a blur of motion in the desert moonlight. A guard departed from his post.

Fortunato waited, and hoped, and prayed.

~

She could sense him, she could sense him not far. She knew, he was at the gates.

She prayed. She looked again to the stars. "Will I see you soon?" she said.

~

"You will," Fortunato said.

And as he sat astride Tyra Jade, for what seemed like an hour, he waited patiently.

The guard on the post reappeared as a chill night wind blew.

The gates began to grind open, and at first Fortunato couldn't believe his luck, until he saw a storm of soldiers, cataphracts mounted on horses.

"Fortunato and the two thieves," said one of the cataphracts, "you are wanted for robbery. The sentence is death."

Fortunato could flee, and maybe outrun them. But he had a destiny beyond Qadirra's gates.

He dismounted from Tyra, and clucked, and Tyra Jade fled away, into the desert night.

As Fortunato eyed the storm of cataphracts, he touched his pocket to make sure the ring he had brought was where he had buried it. He could feel it, deep in his trouser pocket.

Wrinn, then Xan, dismounted.

"Fortunato of Ríva enters the gates of Qadirra," Fortunato narrated, "on the twelfth of Arah."

"It is the eleventh of Arah," the cataphract said.

The calendar of Qadirra was foreign to Fortunato. The date he had appended, these days of Albos, must have been off by one. There was another day, and another night, before all hope would be lost.

What did that mean for him?

"You come and present yourself for justice," said the cataphract. "You have brought yourself no benefit. You will be executed at sundown tomorrow, as all the laws of Great Fharas and beloved Qadirra demand."

Fortunato's gut clenched. And then he vowed — he would survive.

He eyed the starry band, and as the guards cinched his hands behind his back in rope, he said, "I am here."

~

He was here, beyond the gate, and Ambrass knew it. She would find him. She would find her love.

~

The cataphracts had beaten Fortunato with a birch rod and thrown him into a cell.

The mudbrick walls of his cell were layered in plaster, and as Fortunato looked about, from the mudbrick walls to the iron bar separating him from freedom, and from his love, he could see no way to escape, no way to get out. He laid hold of the the iron bars and pulled, and they were masterfully built, with no sign of crumbling.

So where, then, did hope lay, and how could he hope to escape?

Escape, it seemed, was beyond them.

He had hoped to interrupt the wedding, but he had been a day late. Would Fortunato receive a blow from the executioner, and be gone from Varda, knowing that Ambrass was about to wed Artabanas?

Fortunato could not abide the thought.

He sat upon his hard cot, which had been placed on an alcove, and prayed quietly. He sensed something as he stood, amid lamplight, a presence growing, one he knew.

~

Ambrass had taken an oil lamp and passed by the sleeping eunuch. In her veil she had exited the women's apartments, and ventured down the corridors. It was late and the night was lit by moonlight outside, and Artabanas was fast asleep. He always retired early.

But Ambraass was awake, and she could not sleep, for she knew her love was here.

She had seen the mail of cataphracts glittering in the palace yard. That was where her love had to be, Fortunato her beloved.

By lamplight she traversed the palace yard in the cool desert night air, as she saw the door to the palace prison shutting, and a cataphract on foot exiting.

In the prison — he had been taken here for execution.

Her love could not die. Could he?

She passed through, to the prison, and there was a guard standing there.

"My lady," he said.

Ambrass removed her veil. She lied, "It is I, soon to be your queen."

The guard stood by as she passed through the door, to a hall of cells with iron bars, and on tables, many lamps burning.

She passed through the cells, and when she turned to her right, she saw the one who possessed her heart.

Fair, handsome was he, in the flower of his youth, virile and full of male vigor. Her heart dropped at the sight of him, as she laid hold of the bars, and wanted to enter in to the cell where Fortunato was being held.

Her heart sang; her soul protested that iron bars separated her from her love.

"Fortunato," she said.

~

His love was beautiful. His love was kind.

Though she had discarded her veil, she was garbed in a light southron raiment, colored like a desert rose. At the sight of her, his heart sang, and his soul protested that they could not be close.

But there was space between the bars, and he reached out his hand. Their fingers touched, and his desire grew stronger.

He pulled at the bars, but he could not break free of this prison wall.

"Ambrass," Fortunato said. "I love you."

Ambrass, transfixed, was motionless and silent, caught up in her gaze, overcome with passion, and emotion, and love.

"Fortunato," she said, "you are all I have ever wanted. I realize that, now."

"And Gaius?" Fortunato said.

"Gaius is dead," Ambrass replied.

"And Nocturne?" Fortunato said.

"Nocturne is nothing," Ambrass said.

"Artabanas," Fortunato said.

Disgust was written on Ambrass's face.

"I must kill him," Fortunato said.

"I would hand you the sword," Ambrass said, "but I have no sword."

Fortunato paused. "I will be executed tomorrow."

"I know the one who dares wish to be my husband all too well," Ambrass said. "I know his weaknesses. I know how to get him to delay."

But delay, without a plan, didn't seem profitable.

~

She told him what to do. She exited the doors of the prison. She prayed that they would be together, in love. And as she strode out into the cold desert night, under the waxing crescent moon, she saw the doors of the palace yard open, and a figure Ambrass knew walking hurriedly between the mirrored pools.

It was Samira, whom Artabanas had scorned, whom Ambrass had not seen in weeks. She was hurrying in view of the moonlit water.

Ambrass could see the candelabra peeking out of her pocket.

She could also see that about her neck was a necklace with a fiery red gemstone.

~

As Samira entered, she pledged to the gods of Qadirra she would win her husband back. She would return into his graces and his love.

She would be his chief wife again, no matter what she had to do.

She would stop at nothing. She would pour her very life, her very soul, into this effort.

Chapter Forty-Four: A Needle in a Haystack

Bran was awake as light began to appear in the desert, as dawn began to make itself known. He had fallen asleep in the shade of a tamarisk tree.

He was now searching for something beyond his ken, a more impossible task than finding a needle in a haystack — as the folk of Redman Territory would call it. He was trying to find a metal shard in the midst of a vast desert expanse, a windblown landscape where nothing could be found.

He had tried to retrace the steps of the elf whom he had killed, the one who had been carrying the metal shard of *Serpentax* and then abandoned it somewhere. Had he buried it? Was a layer of sand now covering the metal shard, making it all the more impossible to find?

Under the rising sun, as the chill air began to dissipate, beyond the shade of the tamarisk tree, he began his arduous search.

His eyes scanned the horizon, the barren landscape that stretched for countless miles before terminating in the Sky Mountains.

The task quite literally seemed impossible.

But as he traversed, following the footsteps, he thought he might spy out of the corner of his eye a bit of displaced dust, footsteps that had not been hidden, footsteps that would lead him to the elves' hiding place, and the metal shard, and gold enough for a kingdom, and King Bran's wife.

But as he traversed the desert, he was having a hopeless sense, following the waters of the Blue Khazan.

And something else troubled him, the nature of the six men in black which he had not discerned, the "master" they were working for and spoke of, whom they would not identify.

What would the six men in black do with the shard of *Serpentax* once they got it? Bran had a sense that whatever they intended to do with it, it wasn't good.

The waters were near him, available for a drink whenever Bran wanted it. The crystal clear waters, gushing down from their lofty source in the Sky Mountains, would be available all along this quest.

But perhaps that was the problem.

The elves would have hidden the shard of *Serpentax* far away. And Bran, though possessed of a sense of heightened smell from his rokahn blood, could only see as well as the average human. Metal shards didn't possess a smell he would be able to detect, not even metal shards of a twisted, abominable origin.

And so he trod through the desert sand, as the sun rose truly over the western horizon, and amid the barren desert there were signs of life, the chirping of a distant bird.

Bran wondered if it was even possible to locate the shard amid a landscape so vast and so barren. The places the elves could hide the shard were without count, amid a desert so large, and so difficult to navigate there was no place, really, to begin.

His mother back in Redman Territory had encouraged him to seek after things that had seemed impossible, to run for mayor despite his rokahn blood, to start a business and become a tycoon. But his mother, he thought, would not want him to do the bidding of the six men in black, with the iron masks.

The Redman Territory folk had not treated him ill. But he had seen himself in a mirror, and thought there was no way that they could possibly love him. He thought there was no way their kind faces told the truth. Bran knew he was a monster.

He was a monster, and he knew it, so at age sixteen he had run away from home and joined a band of rokahn. He had spent much of his youth pillaging and living among them, building dark-holds and storing away loot.

Yet there, too, he had not felt accepted. The rokahn did not hide their distrust of him, their belief that he was not of them. He had departed from the rokahn, and ventured here, amid desert landscapes and tyrant kings, and tried to seek his fortune.

He had profited greatly, but he spent every denara or libra or Fharese mina he made. But he thought perhaps, gold enough for a kingdom, would be such a great amount as to make it impossible to throw away.

Up above him, he could see a rocky ridge rising above the landscape, a small cliff with a view. At a higher point, perhaps, he could see a larger breadth of the desert, and perhaps find that needle in a haystack, as his mother would call it, amid such vast extent.

He trudged through the sand and the dust, over rocks, and the Blue Khazan was behind him.

What would his mother think, this trail he had found himself on?

He could see her now, in her house in Redman Territory, telling her, "Bran, I got a feeling those six men are up to no good."

But gold enough for a kingdom, King Bran and his wife, was too good a prospect for him to pass up. In Redman Territory, Bran had never dared approach girls, knowing he was a monster, but perhaps a monster such as Bran, if named king, would be wealthy enough to find a wife.

"King Bran and his wife," he said, and eyed the rocky ridge, further than it had seemed. A tract of desert separated it from the crystal clear waters of the Blue Khazan behind.

~

Bran had made it up to the bottom of the cliffs when he tripped.

A cloud of dust wafted up into the air. Tripping was unlike him. He had navigated rocky and sandy terrain for years now.

He turned about as he hastened to his feet. He could see, in the sand and the dust, something sticking out of the redness.

There was something brighter than the red sand, something sticking out, just barely to be seen.

He pushed apart the layer of dust, and unearthed it. He could see white gloves sticking out of the sand.

Chapter Forty-Five: The Builder

In the cool morning air, Reev's inexplicable sense that time was running out was building to urgency, to something he could no longer control. He could see the anguipeds, the rokahn and the kobolds, massing, and he felt, despite Agent Secunda's disagreement, that such a force would not stay there guarding the shrine indefinitely, that they were waiting for something, and that their victory was about at hand.

As the heat built, and the sun began its daily journey, Reev turned and saw a figure striding boldly toward them. He carried himself confidently. His shoulders were broad and large. The sun cast his blond hair so as to make it shining gold. He was wearing a loin cloth and nothing more, and there were tattoos of lighting marks on his neck. At his side was a sword.

Was this a Telantine, living and breathing?

Reev knew it was.

And Reev strode forth, and felt almost unworthy to be in his presence. Was he truly descended from such blood?

Reev was. And as the man strode out confidently, Reev strode out confidently to meet him, or at least tried to don the same confidence that the man exhibited.

"Reev Nax," said the man. "We have an obstruction, here. I'm here to help. But we'll have to wait until night. In the meantime, we can prepare."

In addition to a sword at the man's side, Reev could see that strapped to his back was a hatchet for chopping wood.

"I know how to do this," said the man. "I have experience."

~

Fenris had argued with the captain of the *huls*, Mawt, about whether they should pursue and kill the Telantine now, or whether to wait. He had argued, and, it seemed, Mawt wouldn't listen.

But the more Mawt had talked, the more Fenris had been disabused of his notions, and thought craftiness and cunning was not driving his emotions, but fear.

Fear, mad fear… that was what drove Mawt. He was terrified of the man who had purified the aegis shrine, and Mawt's terror made Fenris's fear seem well-founded.

The fear was beginning to take control of him, but Mawt had insisted — they wait a little while longer, and the victory of the *huls*, and the Qadirrans, and the Fharese, was assured.

"For all time," Mawt had said, in the fires of the camps.

Fenris would trust that fear did not drive those words too.

The Telantine, standing far off, seemed to know where the armies had been massing. When scouts rode to secure the perimeter, he had been unseen in all this time.

And so, Fenris stood as guardian and nothing more, joining to the strength of the gathered *huls* and their rokahn thralls the powers of earth and cloud, the Bracelet of Might.

He was a guardian, but he was a troubled guardian, fearing at every moment that disaster would fall upon him.

Disaster — a sense of impending doom. It was everywhere, and it was all about him.

~

Reev had followed the Telantine through the dry dust-land, and Agent Secunda was following a step behind.

Agent Secunda grumbled about walking so boldly, in view of anguipeds and their rokahn minions.

But the Telantine's confidence had washed over Reev like light in a dark place, and wherever he went, Reev felt safe and secure.

"There is a cedar forest," said the Telantine, "not far from the shrine…"

And when the green boughs and the dense forest appeared, surrounding the waters of a spring, the Telantine turned and smiled a bright smile.

"Reev Nax," he said, "do you have experience chopping wood?"

Reev didn't, but he was eager to learn.

Chapter Forty-Six: By the Gods of Qadirra

Each hour Fortunato and Ambrass were apart was torture. Each moment they were separated was agony. They faced a dreadful enemy, she knew, one backed by the swords and shields of thousands of cataphracts.

But swords could not sever their love.

No, nothing could. The night on the battlements, when she had sent him away, was her life's greatest mistake. But the gods had given her a chance to correct it.

She would take that chance. Else, she'd be dead.

In her room in the women's apartments, the door opened, and the eunuch appeared. "Your soon-to-be husband wishes to see you," the eunuch said.

"He will never be," Ambrass said.

And yet, the eunuch's arm was stronger than hers, and he had a dagger at his side. She had to be practical.

She stood up from her bed and followed the eunuch out of her room, past the women's apartments, to winding corridors and hallways, the maze that was the palace of the one who aspired to be Great King of Qadirra.

~

In a room of mudbrick walls was a sight that filled Ambrass with disgust.

A woman in a veil was holding up a white gown to the lamplight.

Artabanas dared to smile. "Your wedding gown," he said.

Ambrass grimaced and stuck out her tongue. "I will not wear

it," she said. "I would rather die."

"At the end of a scimitar," Artabanas said, and his smile turned to a sadistic smile, "whatever needs to be done, you shall be the King of Kings' wife. By the gods of Qadirra, I swear it."

"My beloved is coming," Ambrass said. "He is beyond the gate. He is in the city itself."

"Who is your beloved?" Artabanas said. "Tell me, so I may kill him."

"Fortunato," she said, but when she spoke Artabanas didn't seem to be listening. He had looked away.

Artabanas turned, and his eyes were avatars of wrath.

"You will be the chief wife," said Artabanas. "Dutiful…. Obedient. An example to others in the kingdom."

"My beloved is coming," said Ambrass, "and you will not stop him. He is already here!"

As Artabanas exited the doors and the woman carrying the dress followed him, she shouted as the door closed, "Fortunato! Fortunato is his name!"

But Artabanas hadn't heard.

~

Fortunato stirred within his prison of mudbrick and iron, desperate to escape and find his love.

But his love was beyond these iron bars, beyond these mudbrick walls, and he knew time was running out. Time was running out for their love to be complete.

Fortunato knew in his heart, if Artabanas and Ambrass were wed, than he and Ambrass would never be together.

Wrinn and Xan, down another hall, had their minds on other things, the execution that Artabanas intended but which Ambrass had formed a plan to thwart. Whether the plan would work was impossible to know, but what he did know that he and Ambrass were meant to be together, that they were meant to be as one.

There were no stars to talk to. There was no way for her to hear. So Fortunato uttered a vow to the gods that it would be his sword that plunged through Artabanas's chest, that it would be him who slew the one who claimed to be Great King of Qadirra. It would be Fortunato and none other, not his Two Thieves, but Fortunato and no other.

"I am coming, Ambrass!" Fortunato shouted, but the prison guard seemed to be looking the other way.

He hadn't heard.

~

Samira had lost her status as chief wife. The wedding was any day now. And though it was a risk to approach the King of Kings without invitation, and she felt her husband would not take it well, she endeavored to give it her all.

She had seen, after all, what she feared most in the reflection of the shining black boulder. She had seen what she feared most of all, Artabanas and the gypsy queen in a loving embrace. She had seen the sum of all her fears, or so she realized when she saw it, a bottomless pit she could not escape from, at the sight of Artabanas in another's embrace.

She had pushed through the corridors beyond the women's apartments. She had donned her veil. She had reached the doors of the throne room, and wondered if she should have asked Das for his help.

But what help was there to give her? What could a genie's hand truly do?

An inexplicable sense, a horrible feeling… but she pushed through the doors, and saw her husband seated on the throne.

She slid before him, kneeling. She tore her veil aside. "My beloved Artabanas," she said to him. "Do not make a mistake. The queen of the gypsies entices you, but it is me you love, not her."

Artabanas's fury was sudden and the fire of the fury in his eyes was complete. He reached for his scepter and Samira knew what that meant. She eyed the soldiers standing by with scimitars at either side of the throne.

But Artabanas stayed his hand, and on the seat looked up, looking upon Samira with a fury had not lessened, but which had reached a plateau beneath murder.

"Samira," said Artabanas. "You were a dutiful chief wife. But you I did not love like Ambrass. For I know the secret you hide, that you are a sorceress…"

"I am not a sorceress," Samira wailed. "I trapped genies in gold, and have them do my bidding. I have no power over earth or fire or water on my own."

"But you had power over stars," said Artabanas. "You disappeared, and you returned. I know it was you, who took the bracelet called *Satar* from its place."

"I am sorry!" Samira wailed. "I beg your forgiveness, my husband. I wished to impress you, that I might find *Mainyu* and forestall Qadirra's doom."

"Qadirra is not doomed," Artabanas said. "And you said you wished to find *Mainyu*. So where is it?"

"It cannot be found," Samira said. "No one knows where it is. But I saw an image of it, a bracelet with a purple gemstone upon a gray arm."

"You see visions," said Artabanas. "Another lie. You are a sorceress, after all, and not a magus. You should be put to death…"

"I looked into a black stone," Samira said. "'I did not see the vision by my own eye."

"The Ob," Artabanas said. "The possessor of whom I put to death, for sorcery. You shall join her in death…"

He reached for the scepter, and this time she sensed he would hold it up, and there would be no hope for Samira anymore.

Artabanas gripped the scepter as Samira wailed, "Think of Darian and Syrus. What will they do if they know you killed their mother?"

And Artabanas did not raise his scepter. "I will think of Darian and Syrus," he said. "You will not be killed." The scepter fell from his grip. "According to the Qadirran formula, 'I divorce you. I divorce you. I divorce you.'"

Samira let out a wail that came from the bottom of her belly, all the pain, of the ages, of her heart.

But Artabanas's fury had hardened to hate.

Who was this man, now seated at the throne of Great Fharas? Who was this man? Samira did not recognize him.

"A few days I will give you to prepare to depart," Artabanas said. "The story of our love is over…"

Samira would not give up. She would win back her husband's love. Else, she was sure, she would dissipate into thin air, and there would be nothing left.

Chapter Forty-Seven: Hungry for Gold

As the gentle warmth of the morning built to scorching new heat, Bran saw his work, and wiped the sweat from his brow.

With his bare hands he had dug through the sand, an unbelievable distance around where he had found the discarded magic gloves. He took a step back, panting and sweating, and saw it looked like a crater, not something possible with human or rokahn hands.

But Bran, he supposed, just had a way about him.

He stepped amid his work, and realized he hadn't got very far. Though the magic gloves had been discarded, they could have been discarded far from where the shard of *Serpentax* was deposited. For all Bran knew, the shard of *Serpentax*, was thirty miles west through the barren sands.

The thought troubled him. He scanned the dirt again, the crater his hands had made, and amid the vastness, he wondered if there was a better way.

In the schoolhouse in Redman Territory, he had struggled to keep up with the other children, and he'd had help from his friend Jasmine, but he thought — surely — there was something he was missing, some easy way to locate the shard of *Serpentax*.

He wiped some more sweat off his brow, sweat that was quickly collecting. It was running down his skin in rivulets and rivers.

He needed a drink.

He could hear the river babbling over rocks. Its crystal clear waters would provide refreshment.

But as he stepped, he tripped again, and something burned his hand.

As it did, he thought he saw a bottomless black void, and then the flash of an image of a throne crafted out of skulls.

Through a thin veil of dust he dared not uncover, a little ways beyond the crater he had made, was a shard of dark green metal, peeking out of the desert sands.

Bran had found the shard — a shard that looked, by his estimation, more like glass than metal. But Bran supposed the shard of a sword called *Serpentax* would be made of strange stuff.

He eyed the shard amid the windblown sand. He knew he couldn't transport the shard. He also knew his giant half-rokahn fists wouldn't fit within those dainty white gloves.

He would never touch that thing again.

But as he stood in view of the shard, he could feel a wind blowing, a wind he didn't like, one that reminded him of trouble and portent. He turned around, and when he had turned, he wasn't alone.

The six men in black had arrived. The blades they had in their possession, whether dagger or sword, did not glisten in the sunlight. They were colored blackish-gray, and Bran feared those blades, almost as much as the shard directly behind him.

"You have done well, Bran," said the chief of the six men. "How did you do it?"

Despite the burning desert heat, the man's voice was like an icy wind in the middle of winter.

In winter, though, all the folks in Redman Territory had to suffer through was a little rain, and sleet if they were unlucky.

So what could he point to, to relate to this icy feeling, this frost-rimed hand gripping his heart?

"I don't know how I did it," Bran answered the man.

In Redman Territory, he was to say, "Yes, sir" and "No, sir." But Bran couldn't bring to give these men any respect.

He had no respect for them, but he was afraid of those blades they carried.

"You don't know how you did it," the chief of the six men

continued. "Dumb luck is not a trait of rokahn. It must have come from your other lineage.

"*Starla…*"

"Don't say my mother's name," Bran insisted.

But he watched as the six men walked around him, seeming to glide rather than to step, as the chief of them laid two iron-gauntleted hands around the shard of the sword called *Serpentax*, and picked it up as is if it were mere metal.

It didn't hurt them.

These weren't men, and now Bran was sure.

"Come with us, Bran," said the chief of the six men. "You will get your gold. But first, you must witness our smith beating the metal into our swords. You have ensured that there is no hope for the Telantines."

The Telantines…. What was that? Bran had a terrible sinking feeling.

Chapter Forty-Eight: A Dance of the Streets

The afternoon was growing late. Fortunato knew that Ambrass was struggling. He could sense her fear, her worries that their love would not come to fruition.

But Fortunato was thinking of something else, now, as through the halls of the prison came walking in a man in glittering chainmail. Fortunato knew, he and two others had a date with twisted justice.

~

The court had gathered to witness the execution.

In their black clothing, Fortunato and the two men he had called his thieves were walking before the faces of men in rich red and purple robes, of women in veils, and in the highest seat Artabanas.

Before them was a stone block, and at the stone block was a man in a black hood. In the executioner's hand was a bulky scimitar designed for clean cuts.

Fortunato, tied in binds, was kicked before the executioner. "Artabanas," he said, "before you put I and my Two Thieves to death, recall that we saved your life. Also, I would like to make a last request, if it were possible. For I and my Two Thieves are professional dancers, and we would like to perform one last dance, if it would please the king… a show that you will not forget, that will set your heart to racing, and your feet to tapping.

"We have entertained countless *lugals* on *lugal* stages. But we have never performed for an audience so high as you…"

Fortunato eyed Artabanas, and saw his lips purse.

"You are in our custody," said Artabanas. "What is another day, when you cannot escape?

"A dance would please me…"

~

Samira had curled into a ball on her bed. She had thought she had nothing, but now — she realized she really did. The sorrow and bottomless despair was consuming her, a void that had already undone her, and ended her.

What was left for her, now?

She could scarcely think, or catch a moment to breathe. She wasn't sure the shallow breaths she was taking, curled on her bed, were breaths at all, but only light intakes of air that were not providing her sustenance.

But amid the void, there was something else, something else besides loss, something she tried to stop her panicked breathing to discern. Amid void, with her eyes shut, she searched. She thought she knew what it was. It was beginning to come to her.

It was hate.

Hate, yes, that was what else she felt. But it was not hate for Artabanas. It was hate for someone else.

She thought of a red shirt and a brown skirt, of long flowing hair and a beautiful face.

Samira hated the queen of the gypsies, and she would get her revenge.

If she could not have Artabanas, she would have that.

~

It was the eve of the wedding, and Ambrass was fighting off fear. She knew she would be wed to Artabanas, but for the feeling in her heart, words written upon it, that she and Fortunato would know love.

It was written on her heart, despite her knowledge of what a terrible situation they had found themselves in, for fear — yes, for fear — that all was lost.

As she took her seat in the dining chamber, and kitchen servants strode out with bowls of stew, Ambrass realized she had developed a taste for the stews of Qadirra, their liquid thick with globules of hot fat, the meat and the salt and the taste of long peppers and curry. She felt her stomach growl, despite her fear that she and Fortunato and their love would be no more. She felt somehow she should eat — eat richly even… even celebrate.

But a look at the curtained dais behind her, and she knew that such thoughts were madness. The one who dared try to become her husband was behind that curtained dais, the one who had her under his iron thumb. That man was watching her, and he would never allow her to escape the grip of his wiry hands.

Despair returned anew, fighting against the knowledge of her heart. She prayed silently. She could think of her plight and nothing else.

But she imagined Fortunato's face, and she gained her bearings enough to grip her silver spoon, and eat the stew hungrily.

The despair threatened to return at the sound of spoons clinking against bowls, and idle chatter surrounding her. For then what she knew in her heart seemed impossible, that she and Fortunato would be together in love.

She ate, and the stew seemed fattier than any stew before it. Beef with glistening fat was floating amid the red broth. The spices had been especially thick, and each spoonful of broth was a delectable complexity of flavors, gained from the cooking of meats and vegetables of various kinds.

But Fortunato… where was he? Ambrass wondered if Fortunato would like this stew. Ambrass thought that he would love it. Perhaps, she should save some for him.

Oh, what idle fancies she had, at the thought of what was

written upon her heart.

She had met Fortunato five years ago, taking care of him like he was a baby as he recovered from a dark iron wound. Like his recovery had been impossible, so, it seemed had been their love — Imperial and gypsy. But Fortunato had recovered from a wound that none had before, and on the battlements of the city wall in Galiope, Ambrass — a gypsy — and Fortunato — an Imperial — had kissed.

That kiss had been all she thought about for long periods. During her marriage to Gaius, which had been brief, so often she had thought about him.

And now, the thought of Fortunato's face consumed her, and the thought of him, she believed, would control her until the end of her days. She and Fortunato would be together, or she would be dead. She and Fortunato would be together, or else the world of Varda would end, and the Dark One reign on his throne of skulls.

Ambrass and Fortunato not together was impossible.

But where was he?

The doors to the dining chamber opened.

And he was there.

The men he called his two thieves were Wrinn and Ivan Xandrast, both dressed like him in black clothing and black bandanas.

As Xan and Wrinn entered, then Fortunato, a guitar began to play from the dining chamber's hidden corners, and on drums, a tantalizing rhythm that tempted everyone — Ambrass most of all — to leap to their feet and dance.

"To Artabanas, the one who calls himself the King of Kings," Fortunato said, "Fortunato and his Two Thieves dedicate this dance… a dance of the streets. If you took a turn down Imperial Square, you might see three men doing a dance just like this."

Fortunato dropped to the ground as Wrinn and Xan spun and began to sing.

Wherever, you go,
Namsita… Namsita…

Fortunato danced on the ground athletically, pulling his body and contorting it, sticking out his legs perfectly to each blast of the guitar, each pulse of the drum.

Whatever you do,
Namsita… Namsita…
My king!

Fortunato was dancing like a wild animal, seeming to hover about the ground as he pulled and twisted his legs and arms. Ambrass had never seen this from Fortunato, and she wondered why he had hid it from the world.

Namsita, yes, Namsita…
In the Northern World that's hello…
Wherever you go, namsita, namsita,
My king

Fortunato was carried away, dancing on the ground, twisting his limbs, contorting and then jerking his body up, but never getting far off the floor. The diners had been transfixed, and were shouting, as Artabanas pulled the gold curtains back, so as to get the perfect view.

Wherever you go,
Namsita… Namsita…
My king

Fortunato's limbs were a storm as the melody built to its peak, and others were chanting and cheering him on, as limbs shot out and then twisted back, and the melody at last began to ease.

How was what Fortunato was doing possible?

Wherever you go,
Namsita… Namsita…
My king

When the Fortunato yanked himself back to his feet, the dining chamber was consumed with applause, and as he stood up, Artabanas was looking at him with a respect that verged on reverence.

"Fortunato and his Two Thieves," Artabanas said, "have greatly pleased the king. And he may have any request, but for his life. The law is the law…"

"I will stay here, and feast with you, this night," Fortunato said, "and tonight — a room of my own, a bed to lay my head."

"It shall be granted to you, Fortunato," Artabanas said.

And Ambrass was consumed with wonder in addition to love, as Fortunato and his Two Thieves, Xan and Wrinn, took a seat at a table across the room.

Her love was just yards away. And what was written in her heart now seemed possible. She fought elation, that by pride it might not come true.

But her love was just yards away. She could see him. She could see his face.

Chapter Forty-Nine: Ancestral Memory

Night had set in, and Reev, following the Telantine's lead, had nailed together wooden beacons, and they were fixing them to the sand in view of the Aegis Shrine of Hyperborean Hindrance.

As the Telantine set them in the sand, Agent Secunda would douse them with oil until they dripped in the night. Between the beacons, as they surrounded the gathered anguipeds, the rokahn and the kobolds, Reev laid a length of rope that Agent Secunda also covered it in oil.

Reev wasn't sure how this would work, but the Telantine said it would, and Reev trusted him.

The crescent moon was beginning to arise over the desert night, and the stars were brilliant, unspoiled by city lights. Reev had a feeling in his heart, a feeling of purpose, a feeling that what he was doing in this night was of immeasurable purpose, as he followed the Telantine's lead every step of the way.

When the Telantine planted the last of their beacons in the sand, he looked with his eyes to Reev and said, "It's time. I won't go where you go. But trust me. When they're lit, wait until you can see the fires reflecting in their eyes. And then charge."

Reev would trust him. He knew the Telantine was trustworthy. He would trust him with his life and more.

"They know what it means," said the Telantine. "They have a memory, by their blood."

Reev stepped back and nodded, then walked toward the middle of the where the beacons had set up. He was facing the gate of the Shrine of Hyperborean Hindrance.

He drew Doomblade and took a breath, as the light of a fire burned — a torch in the Telantine's hand. No sooner had the torch been lit, than the beacon blazed into fire, and in the span of moments, all beacons surrounding the aegis shrine were towering and flaming.

Reev saw in the anguipeds' eyes the reflection of the burning beacons, and having drawn Doomblade, he charged.

Before he had reached their front lines, they were scattering and fleeing in terror, shrieking at the top of their lungs.

And when he had pushed past the remnants of their camp, now alone, he saw a man covered in fur, wearing a striped robe, with a bracelet fixed with an orange gem.

The fire of the beacons was in his eyes. He was frozen in terror.

Then his body began to quiver and shake, and dribble escape his mouth.

He fell to the floor, gyrating and twisting, and as he did, he was changed in the moonlight. As he bit with his jaws, and wriggled uncontrolledly with his limbs, his fur was gone, and he was a man with a black plaited beard, a man consumed by this frenzy.

Reev would show no mercy. The Telantine would be disappointed if he did.

He took Doomblade and stabbed the man in the heart, and when he did, as he died, the bracelet with the fiery orange gemstone slipped from his grip.

He turned and saw the vanishing anguipeds, fleeing into the distance. He could see the Telantine standing far-off in the light of the burning beacons, nodding his approval.

Agent Secunda was running up to Reev, amid the blazing fires, her face pallid, breathing raggedly as she sprinted. "It worked," she at last howled, now steps from him. "It worked, somehow."

"An ancestral memory," Reev said in the light of the burning beacons.

"Now we enter," Agent Secunda said. "Now, we purify the shrine."

Reev strode up to the great metal doors and laid his hands in the handholds. He pulled, and it was like trying to pull a mountain up by its roots. Not only did it not open, it showed no sign of budging. It was perfectly still, perfectly resistant.

"How did you enter the other shrine, Reev?" Agent Secunda said.

"I had help… My friend, Ivan Xandrast, has the Skeleton Key."

"Where is he?" Agent Secunda was peering into the darkness beyond the beacons, as if she were worried the anguipeds would return.

But Reev wasn't worried. The fear he had seen in the anguipeds' eyes had been bottomless.

"I don't know," Reev said. "I don't know where he is. He must be far, and I don't know where to find him."

"Curses," Agent Secunda grumbled.

But Reev looked about, to the door, to the beacons and the disappearing form of the Telantine as he walked south toward Qadirra, then to the body of the once-furry man who in death had returned to human form.

Then, he looked to the orange-gemmed bracelet he was wearing.

The bracelet clearly had magical properties.

Reev stooped down and took it in his hands. He placed it about his right wrist. He felt a power swirl about and then settle within him.

"One of the Seven Bracelets of Arstibara," said Agent Secunda. "Now, the power of cloud and earth combined. Yellow and brown, and now it is orange. What power does it contain?"

Reev did not know. But armed with the bracelet, he laid his hands again in the handhold.

He pulled, and then he yanked, and then he pulled with all his might.

Filled with a supernal strength, he felt the metal doors give way again.

He pulled with all he had in him, until sweat was dripping from his brow and his biceps were flexing to their maximum size. He shouted "Forth Telantis!" as he pulled even harder, as the doors cracked, and hinges whined, and the metal doors fell with a deafening clatter onto the rocky ground.

"A Bracelet of Might," Agent Secunda said. "We shall not go into the Aegis Shrine of Hyperborean Hindrance unarmed."

Reev strode in through the doors and Agent Secunda followed a step behind. There was a torch in the dark, just barely visible from the moonlight wafting in. Agent Secunda reached for her tinderbox.

And as they strode in, Reev uttered a prayer for success, that their mission would not fail.

"Heaven's Spear," Reev said, "I give you my blessing."

Chapter Fifty: Commitment

The gypsies were gathered on the twelfth day of Arah, by *lugal* reckoning the seventh day of Albos. The desert night was cool, and all seemed at peace, the gypsies gathered in their wagons and surveying Qadirra's mighty walls under starlight and moonlight. The Telantines, in their wooden seats they had brought, had insisted they would not lay siege, but wait, and watch, for what was promised.

As for Julian, he had to think more practically than promises written in texts, for his cousin Ambrass was behind those walls – Ambrass, their queen. And if the texts were true, then Ambrass too was in danger, being as she was behind Qadirra's mighty walls.

In the dark, a man was striding through the sand, the man who had departed to deal with a "hindrance." His body was speckled with ash and dust. "Gypsy," he said, "I was coming from the west. There is an army on its way... an army with green crests on their helmets, and green capes."

"The Imperial Bay Company," Julian said. "Haven't they learned their lesson?"

Julian whipped at his horses and raised his recurve dagger, a sign for his fellow gypsies to draw swords, that they were about to go to war.

His bracelet with its green gem, the combined powers of *Ab* and *Azar*, with powers over fire, water, and steam, was gleaming — indicating that magic was nearby.

But Julian couldn't afford to worry. He wouldn't allow the Imperial Bay Company to get anywhere near Qadirra.

~

As the feasting died down, the air in the palace was peaceful and quiet, though dark. Ambrass could see Artabanas chatting with members of the court, distracted about some palatial or national problem. She rose and dared to take off her veil, and looked to Fortunato's seat.

But Fortunato wasn't there.

She searched for him in the dining chamber, but saw no sign of him. She feared — had her love slipped away from her, or had Artabanas's reassurances been false?

It was anyone's guess. But Ambrass was full of a quiet confidence now, the confidence that the words written on her heart were true, that she and Fortunato were destined to be together.

And so she exited the dining chamber's doors with the same quiet confidence, passing down a corridor in the light of oil lamps and candles on sconces.

She thought — she should follow her heart.

And so tossing aside all common sense, all wit and wisdom, she passed down corridors she did not know, darkened halls she had never dared to venture through.

She saw at last a room, and beyond a door, a window with a view of the plain of Potam and the crescent moon.

Fortunato was sitting on his bed. "Ambrass," he said, and his smile was bright. His smile took her breath away. His smile was everything.

"Wrinn claims he has happened upon a keg of wine in this joyless land," Fortunato said. "He's in the process of hauling it to his room down the hall."

"Wine would be nice," Ambrass said. "It's been a while since I've had a drink."

Fortunato's gazed out the window to the desert landscape, to the crescent moon.

"Xan managed to take his Skeleton Key from the prison

guard," Fortunato said. "He's in the process of getting our weapons. Then, a trip to the stable to fetch Asté, and we'll find the perfect moment to run out of here.

"I'd like you to come with us, Ambrass."

"I won't run off with someone who hasn't made a commitment," Ambrass said.

"A commitment," Fortunato said, and he reached into his pocket. When his hand emerged again, he was holding a gold ring. "Like this?"

Ambrass gasped, and felt her eyes water.

"Will you marry me, Ambrass?" Fortunato said.

"I will," Ambrass said. "Nothing would make me happier in the world."

And Ambrass allowed him to slide the gold ring over her finger.

And her heart soared, and she felt complete. Almost. "Kiss me, Fortunato."

And he rose, and took her by the shoulders, and met her in a passionate embrace. He kissed her, and fires coursed through her veins, fires like she felt on the battlements of the City of Galiope, where this had happened before.

It had happened before, but for her ring.

And she saw Wrinn was peeking his head through the door, hauling a keg of wine in his hands.

"How will we leave?" Ambrass said. "And where are we going?"

"To the Dark Land," Fortunato said.

Ambrass shuddered. So close to the Desert of Hamma, she had heard tell of the Dark Land, a region beyond sand and an impassible sea, one where evil reigned and good was not allowed to prosper, one where the minions of the Dark One ruled as kings.

"I will follow you to the Dark Land," Ambrass said, "yes, to the ends of Varda…"

"But we must wait for the perfect moment," Fortunato said.

"The perfect moment, and no later…"

~

Wearing her engagement ring, she walked, and Fortunato followed, down the hall to where Wrinn had hauled the wine keg. She told him of their engagement, and he congratulated them both.

And they poured themselves tall glasses of wine, filled to the brim, overflowing. They drank deeply, and Ambrass's joy was complete.

~

The gypsies had ridden out on their wagons to face the Imperial Bay Company. Miles from the city, the two armies were in sight.

The consulary soldiers in their green-crested helmets and their green capes, in every way an inferior mimicry of the Imperial Army, were marching on foot or riding on horses. They greatly outnumbered the gypsies, but that hadn't stopped the gypsies before.

They stretched from one horizon to the other, and Julian couldn't believe that the Empire allowed a separate army to operate alongside it. But he knew that Emperor Verrus was unworthy of the throne.

A man strode forth on a speckled horse, his horsehair crest sideways so as to mark his rank as legate. There was a hungry, sadistic look in his eyes as he raised his left hand. About his arm was a bracelet colored silverish-white, inset with a glowing gray gem.

"Gypsies!" he shouted. "Vengeance has arrived!"

Chapter Fifty-One: Bran Breaks Free

Bran stood amid a landscape that had changed rapidly, from sand and dust in a flat plain to high ridges and rocky cliffs, in view of mountains so high they seemed impossible.

He was on the Pashupat Plateau, having ridden on the back of one of the six phantoms' hell-beasts, and there was snow on the ground.

They were not far from a lamasery. Mountain guides in thick woolens walked about amid the silent scene, the snow drifting from the sky, as a smith fed a blazing fire, and the six phantoms in black looked upon the flame with a hungry gaze.

Bran had so many questions, questions that had not been answered. Who did these six phantoms serve? And what were they?

He had seen the hellish gleam in the eyes of the beasts they rode, like the spawn of a wolf and some monstrous jackal. He knew, whatever the six phantoms intended, it was not for good.

As the fire raged, the chief of the six phantoms, whom the smith had called "Gogg!" took the shard of *Serpentax*, and tossed it amid the flames. There, the green shard began to emit smoke, and then glow with a yellow glow.

As Bran stared, he wondered, and as he wondered, he imagined. He saw brown hair and brown brows, bright loving eyes.

Mother…

Gogg had said this shard of *Serpentax* would put an end to the hope of all Telantines forever. But who, and what, was a Telantine?

The six phantoms' blades were also being heated in the flames, and the blackish-gray blades were turning to red hot.

Then, as the six phantoms looked on, the Pashupat smith began to beat the molten shard of Serpentax into the other six blades, starting with the knives and the daggers.

"Gogg!" Bran shouted. "What is a Telantine?"

An image flashed in his mind, brown hair, brown eyes.

Mother!

"What is a Telantine?" Bran screamed, but as the blades now imbued with the poison shard of *Serpentax* began to settle to a greenish-black color, he thought he had already received the answer in his mind.

And as the Pashupat smith reached for Gogg's sword, to beat the remains of *Serpentax* into it, Bran knew that the gods could not love him because of his rokahn blood, that he could never enter Heaven.

But he could do good in the here and now.

He drew his kukri-knife from his side, and as Gogg looked on, he struck at Gogg.

But Gogg pulled his molten sword out of the fire and parried. With a perfect strike, he pierced Bran in the shoulder, and the wound seemed more than he could bear, the pain more than he could fathom.

He turned and ran, fearing what he had done, grieving for what he had caused to happen.

~

The wound was weakening him as he staggered from the heights of the Pashupat Plateau down toward the desert. He touched his mouth and realized it was foaming.

He was occasionally grazing his ground with his knees, striking the sand. But where would he go? Who would take him in?

He ran into the desert night with the plateau and its snows far behind.

~

He had gone a mile, or had he gone two? Where was he going? He realized he was going northeast, away from Qadirra.

The pain in his shoulder threatened to end him if he thought about it. But he braced himself, and kept running.

Where was he going?

~

He would stagger a few steps, and then run a few steps, but he was making progress, running by desert ways. He didn't know what he was running to, but he knew he was not running away from something. He had a destination in mind.

The desert night was cool and the crescent moon was bare to see. The moon and the stars seemed to be looking down on Bran favorably, yes, on Bran. And he looked up at them and watched them twinkle.

He clutched his wound. He touched his mouth and saw he was still dribbling. He kept running.

He would run all night if he had to. He had to leave the six phantoms behind.

Would they come calling?

If they did, he'd strike with his kukri-knife again, and this time, he'd hit them.

~

Had he run ten miles?

He would endure the wound's pain, the terrible wound such as he had never endured.

Treading through sand and dust and dry dirt, under the starry sky, he felt possessed of a second wind, that he could run all night, and perhaps he would.

Every step took him further away from the phantoms and their evil.

He was thinking as he ran, mile ten or eleven, or was it twenty? Their master was the Dark One. Bran really couldn't get to Heaven, now.

He would endure the wound.

He would run… to where?

~

He had collapsed by the shores of the Blue Khazan. He sank into sleep.

As he slept, there was a vision of bright white light, and beyond the white light, a young man in a loin cloth, with a coin necklace about his neck, his neck tattooed with lightning marks.

"Bran," said the young man, "the gods can love you — in fact, they do. And Heaven is waiting for you.

"Do not worry about the wound you received. It cannot kill you, of such blood. For you are not just the offspring of Urok War-Caller, but also Starla. And of human lineages, there are none so good as yours.

"Sleep well. Rest. Rise in the morning and go home. For your mother has left a candle burning in her back porch all this time, to let you know you are welcome. All these days, she has hoped for your return."

Chapter Fifty-Two:
A Gray Arm

On a battlefield outside of Qadirra, two peoples and two bracelets did battle. As gypsies charged forth on their wagons bearing swords and shields, consulary soldiers met them, racing with swords, axes and polearms, gleaming in the crescent moon.

But Julian and the consulary legate stood back, standing far apart, now facing each other.

The gray gem of the consulary legate's bracelet turned to liquid fire, and the darkness of the sky turned into inestimable blackness. The stars now were white beacons, as the crescent moon darkened to orange, and then to a fiery blood red. As meteors fell toward the gypsies, exploding and leaving craters of dust and billows of sand, Julian activated his green bracelet and heard the rush of water.

Walls of water began to cross a plain so vast, and then columns of fire burning down upon the consulary armies. Fireballs lit up the night, setting fire to the consulary army's ballistae and scorpions, as under the blazing beacons of the astral bodies, gypsy warrior fought against consulary soldier to a man.

The air seemed changed, and the moon was growing larger. The dark spaces of the moon, which made it a crescent, were being revealed by pulsing light.

"Carnivorous waves!" Julian shouted, as walls of many-fanged and many-mouthed water rushed over the consulary soldiers, and as he realized the tide of battle was slowly driving them backward, in view of Qadirra.

Arstibara, the genie who crafted the bracelets, wished for Qadirra's destruction. Julian and the legate were wielding his creations against each other, but Julian knew that in the end they were pawns.

To the falling meteors, now swallowed up in wind and water, were added bursts of moonlight that seemed to stir madness in consulary soldier and gypsy warrior alike, to send them one by one, racing backwards toward Qadirra's walls and the fate that the gypsy Arstibara had designed.

Under red moonlight and burning starlight, Julian looked back, and could see the walls that the genie Arstibara wished to lay low.

But still, the witchcraft of the Qadirrans held firm, the spell that prevented the bracelets from leveling it to the ground.

"Woe betide Qadirra," Julian said.

~

With cups of wine, Fortunato, Ambrass and Wrinn had found themselves in the throne room, now tipsy, verging on inebriated.

Whether they broke the law Ambrass was uncertain, but it was difficult to worry about anything when you'd had your third glass of wine.

Laughing at something Fortunato had said, Ambrass fell back before the throne, as her gown caught on something — a knob.

"A door," Fortunato said.

There was a white door painted to blend into the plaster.

"What is Artabanas hiding?" Ambrass said.

"Something we don't want to find," Wrinn insisted. "Something that would help us."

She opened the door and walked in. She could see metal stairs descending down a vault. She wondered where it would lead them.

At the bottom of a taxing climb, one that had taken all her energy, she saw a lockbox that had been opened and pilfered, and dominating much of the room, a massive white tube that stretched upwards into the inestimable distance, before vanishing into the darkness.

There was writing on the edge of the tube in black letters.

"What does it say?" Ambrass asked.

"It says, 'Heaven's Spear,' " Fortunato answered.

~

"There is a way to summon the guardian spirits," said Reev.

His eyes scanned the Aegis Shrine of Hyperborean Hindrance, now illuminated by Agent Secunda's torch.

It seemed larger than the other aegis shrine, with more pockets of darkness, and more places for things to hide. But he turned and saw in the far corner, near a hollow that had opened up in the shrine, baring the outdoors, writing of a strange kind, which Reev couldn't read.

Reev pointed to it. "It's anguiped writing," said Agent Secunda.

"*Ka a na ga wasa nachshli*," Agent Secunda read.

"I summon the daughters of Nachash," Reev said, guessing at the translation, from what Farhad had read before.

And Agent Secunda and Reev were not alone.

Beings blinked into existence, beings that glowed amid the darkness of the room. Two translucent women approached Reev, women of buxom form, their skin green, their ears pointed. And yet, looking at them, Reev was fighting off an overpowering passion, at their symmetrical faces, the way they stepped toward him teasingly, eyeing him with lust.

He resisted with all he had in them as the women approached him and laid hold of his shoulders. When they tried to kiss him, he looked away, and pushed them off of him.

The translucent women looked at him in disbelief, and in shock, and then, their forms began to vanish away in flame.

The air in the shrine had changed. It felt empty, pure, clean.

Light was now spreading from small sockets in a circle around the roof of the shrine, blue lights glowing with a quiet fire.

"The aegis shrine is purified," Agent Secunda said.

Like in the other shrine, there was a glass with magic green writing glowing amid the black color.

Agent Secunda rushed to it, and took Reev by the arm.

"You can read it," she said.

Reev fixed his eyes on the writing, and the letters made sense to him, though Gastreel had never taught him.

"Sequence engaged. Hindrances eliminated," he read the writing. "Awaiting engagement at Argent Point."

And below the magic glowing green text, Reev saw a map of the walls of a city, below it a blinking green dot.

"South of Qadirra," Agent Secunda. "South of Qadirra, your destiny lies."

But Reev turned, and saw the aegis shrine was now lit brightly. The guardian spirits had been defeated, but Reev and Agent Secunda were still not alone.

There was a statue of an anguiped woman with pointed ears. On the granite arm of the statue was a bracelet with a purple gem.

Agent Secunda noticed, and began walking toward it.

~

The party's weapons were stowed away in Asté's saddlebags. Asté herself was waiting between the mirrored pools in the palace yard. The gates to the palace were unguarded. It was the perfect moment, Xan thought, but as he passed through to the dining chamber, he saw it might not have been.

There were panicked looks amid the members of the court. "The city is undefended," said Artabanas. "I can feel it in the air — the witchcraft gone. The bracelets will lay us all waste!"

"The gypsies and the consulary armies are not far away," said one of the Royal Guard. "Their bracelets are doing battle."

~

Outside, under apocalyptic scenes, as meteors fell and waters crashed overhead, under stars that burned like beacons against a canvas of inestimable darkness, and wonders to amaze mortal men, Julian saw that his bracelet was being pulled in a direction by a force unseen. He was facing the walls of Qadirra, and the walls of Qadirra were unprotected.

Fire, water, steam, sun and moon and void, would all be wielded against her. But Ambrass was inside.

He tried to remove his bracelet, but the bracelet, it seemed had melded to Julian's skin. He was fixed, then, on Qadirra, and Qadirra's doom.

Poor Ambrass…

~

Reev watched as Agent Secunda approached the statue, and leaping upon its neck, grasped the bracelet with the purple gem and dislodged it from the arm and then the stone hand. On the statue's pedestal, before Reev could protest, she slid the bracelet upon her left arm, and as she did, power filled her, and the purple gem on the bracelet turned to a burning purple fire.

"*Mainyu,*" Agent Secunda said, and her eyes were white marbles. Foam and ectoplasmic fluid began to dribble down her mouth.

As the air in the room changed, from purity to impurity, Agent Secunda howled, and then began to cackle.

"They walked into our trap, the Telantines," Agent Secunda — or whatever possessed her — said. "They placed the bracelet we corrupted on their hands. Such silly fools, so simple, so dim-witted. We shall surely kill them to a man.

"Not against Qadirra shall the bracelets be used, but against

Telantines. All Telantines shall be killed… Telantis shall never be born."

Mainyu had been corrupted. The Seven Bracelets of Arstibara would not ensure Qadirra's fall. But Qadirra's fall was written.

"*Ab* and *Azar*," said Agent Secunda with a demented smile. "*Satar* and *Mah*. *Zam* and *Abrah*? *Zam* and *Abrah*?"

The demented smile turned to a despairing grimace.

"*Zam* and *Abrah*!"

~

Mainyu saw that *Zam* and *Abrah* had combined, as intended, into the Bracelet of Might called *Khvarenah*. But *Mainyu* was watching as the Telantine resisted her, as he wrested control of *Khvarenah* unto his own. The Bracelet of Might was his, now, and *Mainyu* could not stop it.

Mainyu despaired.

The Bracelet of Might would now grant the Telantine strength wherever he walked, all over Varda. Its power would not end beyond Potam's fertile soil.

~

Reev fled from the changed Agent Secunda, out of the shrine and into the cold desert night.

How could Qadirra fall now, Reev had wondered?

He thought — Heaven's Spear, and the point that had been marked on the magic screen, south of Qadirra.

Chapter Fifty-Three: She Said She Was Loved

Xan looked on as the air changed again, from impurity to purity and then back to impurity.

Artabanas looked about. He seemed mystified by the change.

And then fires appeared in the dining chamber, burning fires, fires to light the night, to cook and to feast. Globules of water appeared, and starlight seemed to shimmer even within the dining chamber, a light and a wonder show for all the diners to see.

"*Mainyu*," Artabanas said. "*Mainyu* has been recovered. The Qadirrans cast upon it a spell. Wise, were the Qadirrans. Beloved above all are they. They shall never mourn. Exalted shall they be, forever. The bracelets have been turned to their favor, and tonight, we shall feast again — with their gods."

~

"If you do this, I will free you," Samira said to the genie in the privacy of her room.

Das fixed his gaze on her with his bright yellow eyes, as his lip twisted, and he seemed to believe her this time. His body, rising from the candelabra, seemed radiant with hope, that this time his master spoke the truth. "An oath," said Das.

"If you do this," said Samira, "I vow on my blood, on my life, I will free you. I will let you strike me dead if I go back on my word."

Then Das was filled with sadness, sadness radiating from his eyes, at the malign task that had been assigned to him. Samira supposed genies had consciences they could violate, even if it would result in their freedom.

"I shall do it," said Das. "One last task for you, wicked Samira."

And Samira smiled as he departed, knowing her plans were coming to fruition.

~

Fortunato was down the hall, beside Wrinn, headed back to the room with the wine keg, which despite three overflowing cups each, had barely been touched. Ambrass followed them a step behind, her mind full of thoughts of marriage and courtship, of love — even in the Dark Land.

But as she strode, she had a horrible sense, a terrible feeling of danger.

She turned and saw a green face, and a bright green hand reaching for her.

Then, all she saw was red.

~

"Where is Ambrass?" said Wrinn.

"She's coming, I'm sure," Fortunato replied.

As he settled into his seat, and Wrinn poured himself another cup, Fortunato thought he should have his wits about him, that he shouldn't have another drop.

He wondered about the practicality of marriage in the Dark Land. But Fortunato would make it work. He and Ambrass would be together, from now until the day they died.

"Wrinn," Fortunato said as Wrinn took a sip, "you'd better put that down. Go find Xan and meet me in the palace yard. Asté's waiting."

Wrinn nodded and set the cup aside. And as he left, despite his high-minded speech, Fortunato began to sip, and drink the cup of his own. He hadn't poured himself cups as overflowing as Wrinn. He had room in his liver to spare.

~

In the dining chamber, Artabanas's men had hauled in statues of Qadirra's gods, of Tamtum the Destroyer and Utuk the Creator, Enzu the Illuminator and more. Not gods they seemed to Xan, but fiends with their flaring tongues and unsightly faces, beings with the heads of humans but the bodies of wild beasts and reptiles.

"Qadirra is beloved," said Artabanas. "And now she shall always be. Always beloved, above all. She shall never mourn.

"Her gods protect her, and her gods have returned. She shall reign above all other cities and above all other lands. The name of the *lugals* will perish from the earth."

Amid a room where fires and globules of water, spheres of starlight and moonlight were suspended, as kitchen staff began to cook more stews, Xan could not argue. It seemed true, that Qadirra would never be destroyed, that she would reign forever, that she would never mourn. She had never been divorced…

"Reign, Qadirra, the beloved!" Artabanas said. "Reign! And now, say, Your Reverence…?"

He eyed the priest of Tamtum, with the horned headdress and the mad eyes.

"Perhaps, we can hasten our wedding, and I and Ambrass can be married now."

"At once, Your Majesty," said the priest.

~

A woman had appeared before Fortunato, standing at the door. She wore a bright yellow gown, and there was a red gemstone necklace about her neck. As he stood, she began to prance with her feet, and dance sensually.

Fortunato thought she was beautiful. He gazed at her, perhaps in a way he should not.

The woman strode into the room, as she began to slip off her gown, laying bare her shoulders.

Fortunato was tempted to draw near.

~

Ambrass watched from her prison in the red gem, as the one she had called her love looked upon her tormentor, his eyes hardened with lust.

Heartbreak filled Ambrass at the betrayal, at the betrayal of the eyes and surely the heart.

Fortunato, he saw, was inching nearer to Samira.

Who was this man, she had thought she had known?

~

"Fortunato," said a man's voice.

Fortunato backed away from the woman who had been trying so hard to tempt him, but whom he had been about to push away.

He uttered curses at the woman as he turned and saw an elf, standing in the doorway in a purple cloak.

Fortunato made a show of pushing past the woman, then entered into the hallway.

The elf looked upon Fortunato with a grim smile. "From the elvenking, *namsita*. I bring ill tidings."

"And what tidings do you bear?" Fortunato said.

"The Six Servants of Seymus enlisted the help of a far greater foe than they, one which we could not contend with. He made quick work of our warriors, who were attempting to stop the worst from happening — the largest shard of *Serpentax* ever discovered, falling into the Six Servants' hands."

"And what will become of it now?" Fortunato said.

"Their weapons have been infused with the molten shard," the elf said. "Their weapons can now kill Reev, and put an end to the hopes of humanity and of elvenkind."

Fortunato's gut dropped.

"I do not know if the mission can now succeed," the elf said. "I do not know if we can prevent the Dark One's rule over Varda, and the enslavement of all mortals… but one thing I know, you must take your party, and move with all haste to your goal. To *Naron Da,* speed, as fast as your horses and your black wolf can take you.

"We will do our best to restrain the movements of the Six Servants of Seymus, and create doors where there were none, and gates where there are none to be found. Do not delay a moment, Fortunato. Leave everything behind."

Even Ambrass… and Fortunato despaired at the thought, but if the Dark One ruled, there would be no hope for him or her, anyway.

"I will ride," Fortunato said. "If you see a woman with long dark hair and a dazzling face, tell her I love her, and that I will see her soon…"

~

Reev had galloped at an Elvish horse's speed from the Aegis Shrine of Hyperborean Hindrance to a view of the city that the gods hated.

He could see where the blinking dot on the magic glass had led him, and in the sand, against an iron panel, was a red circular protrusion of an elastic material, and beside the red circular protrusion, a square black protrusion covered in holes.

Reev dismounted from Cobalt. He looked into the distance, and saw hundreds of men — Telantines, he could see, in the moonlight — sitting in chairs and gazing upon the city's walls.

He put his finger to the circular red protrusion, and pushed. There was the sound of hissing air, and a magic voice began to speak from the square black protrusion.

The magic voice spoke, and though Gastreel had never taught him the language, again he understood it perfectly.

"Engagement initiated. Coordinates found. Beginning Operation Heaven's Spear in thirty… twenty-nine…"

Cobalt reared up on his hind legs, as a desert wind blew, and the prideful city, Reev thought, was at the height of its pride.

~

"Qadirra, Qadirra!" shouted Artabanas. "So little did the wicked *lugals* think of you. But now we know, you shall reign forever."

And Xan saw through a door a woman emerge, one in a yellow gown and a red veil. He thought it was the King of Kings' former chief wife, Samira. She was lingering in view of the statues of the city's gods, and despite her humiliation, she seemed wrapped up in celebration, in the knowledge that the city would never fall.

Wrinn walked up to him, and as he did, Fortunato appeared through the door.

"Xan! Wrinn!" Fortunato said. "Let's go…"

"Qadirra shall never fall!" Artabanas shouted. "Qadirra, beloved above all, unto the ages of ages… She was always beloved, and she still is…"

~

"Twenty-one… twenty…"

The magic voice coming from the black box was echoing through the desert night. In their seats, the Telantines' joy seemed to be full.

Where was Fortunato, Reev wondered. He couldn't be behind the walls of the city, could he?

~

"Qadirra, beloved forever!" Artabanas shouted as Fortunato and Wrinn sped out of the palace, as a sense of urgency suddenly filled Fortunato, the thought that he should gallop away on Asté with all due speed.

"Qadirra, beloved forever!" Artabanas's voice was audible in the palace yard as Fortunato, then Wrinn, then Xan, mounted on Asté.

"Qadirra, beloved forever!" Artabanas's voice followed them, as the three, barely managing to cling together on her saddle, were carried away like a bolt of lightning, an Elvish horse galloping at her fastest pace, a blur beyond the palace gate, a darting jolt of light speeding down roads, to the gate.

~

"Eleven… ten…"
Where was Fortunato? Where was Fortunato?
Reev uttered a prayer for him, and for Xan and Wrinn.

~

Fortunato burst through the open gates, with Xan and Wrinn behind him, galloping into the night air, into the brisk coolness under a crescent moon. A hundred yards away, he turned back to look at Qadirra's walls, when there was fire, and smoke, and destruction.

~

Qadirra had exploded into a massive fireball, a column of flame rising up into the desert night. All of it was gone as the smoke settled, all save a crater in the ground. But Reev inclined his eyes upward, and saw a point of fire soaring through the night sky, toward the clouds, a brilliant flame coursing through the sky and above it, headed due northeast.

What was it? Reev thought it was Heaven's Spear.

~

Fallen is Qadirra, the haughty, the proud,
Who thought she was beloved but is not
"I will never mourn," she says.
"I was never divorced!"
But a certificate of divorce was given to her
She shall mourn, yea, and be destroyed,
Her land a haunt of ghosts and of serpent's children
From now until Varda is made new
Fallen is Qadirra, the proud, the divorced
Who thinks she is beloved but is not.

— from *The Telantine Codex*

~

As the Telantines in their chairs cheered, dark shapes were approaching — Fortunato, Xan, and Wrinn riding three-a-saddle, somehow, on Asté. As they got close, Fortunato dismounted, and as he dismounted, Tyra Jade came rushing up to her, in the night.

"Qadirra has been destroyed," Reev said.

"Yes, it has," Fortunato said, "but I have bad news."

~

Fortunato would not tell Reev the whole truth, the truth that would terrify him — the knowledge that the Six Servants possessed weapons that could kill him and end all humanity and elvenkind's mortal hopes. He would only tell him what he needed to hear.

"We must leave now," he said. "We have to move with all due speed. The Six Servants are on our tail, and whatever pace we intended, we have to double it."

Fortunato then turned back to the smoking crater that was Qadirra.

"Was Ambrass in there?" Wrinn said.

"No," Fortunato said. "She was not. I can sense her. I know she is still alive."

"Something else troubles you," Reev said from Cobalt.

Fortunato turned to Reev and looked into his eyes. His eyes had a strange light. "I made a vow to the gods," Fortunato said, "that it would be my sword that plunged into Artabanas's heart, that it would be I that took his life."

"Your sword did take his life," Reev said. "Your sword, the sword of your blood and your kinsmen. Your kind put an end to Artabanas and his kingdom that would never prosper."

And Fortunato, though mystified, believed what Reev said was true.

"Come on," Fortunato said, and leapt astride Tyra. "With all due speed... Xan, lead us to the Dark Land. Let's tread Seymus underfoot."

Xan, riding behind Wrinn, nodded a frantic assent. They galloped into the night, and Fortunato and Reev speed after him.

Qadirra is fallen, Reev thought. *Qadirra, the divorced...*

~

In the gem, Ambrass would walk on the red floor, with a red sky above her, and the landscape would not change. She was truly trapped within the red gemstone, the gemstone the sorceress Samira had cast her into.

She despaired at the thought of being captive on Samira's neck, from now until the end of her days. But she looked beyond the red gemstone, and thought she could see a crescent moon, and stars just barely visible against the redness. Had Samira gone outside?

A voice spoke, deafening over the red ground and the red landscape.

"Ambrass," the voice said, "I am a genie, but I have a heart. You are imprisoned in this ruby, but you have a way out. A riddle you must answer. To some are given impossible riddles that cannot be solved, and the imprisoned spend their whole lives trapped in a gem. But to you I will give one you know the answer to, though you shall resist what you know.

"Answer me this, Ambrass," said the genie, "and you shall escape from your prison. Who does your heart belong to?"

Who did her heart belong to, indeed?

Chapter Fifty-Four: Eyes Wide Open

The Dark One watched from his post on the Plains of Abollon as the four warriors galloped down the way. They were headed southeast, in the wake of the destruction they had just left.

The Dark One had winced at the destruction of Qadirra. But he would get his revenge, this he knew.

He could see them galloping, and their animals would be strained for all they had.

But the beasts that Lothan had forged for the Dark One's six riders did not rest, only hungered for carnage.

The Dark One filled Mephis, Gogg's steed, with hunger. And he told Gogg to move with all due speed, before the gates and doors the elves were already setting up would restrain him without recourse.

~

"Past the ruins of Qadirra," Xan said, "southeast, to the Sea of Coral, through the Wastes of Shahr."

"Past the crater of Qadirra," Wrinn answered.

But neither Xan nor Fortunato, and certainly not Reev, were in the mood for cunning quips.

As they sped along, and the horses had slowed from a breackneck gallop to a trot they could manage, Fortunato could see that the sun was rising over the hot plain, and they had put a great deal of distance behind them.

They had not slept, nor would they. The Six Servants were behind them, and at any time they could appear.

Was the cause lost? Fortunato had a terrible sinking feeling.

They had delayed in Qadirra. If they had allowed Qadirra to be rebuilt, and to reign over the kingdoms of the earth, would none of this have befallen them? Would the Six Servants be so far behind them, the newfound weapons would be of no use?

Fortunato could not afford to care.

It was noon, pushing to afternoon. There was a timber bridge against the waters of the Black Khazan. Through the hazy sunlight was a landscape of parched earth, brambles and thorn-bearing trees, a hostile place to human life, and one where, Fortunato guessed, there was little hope of finding water and food. They had road-bread, enough for many days, and some water in their waterskins. But Fortunato feared that in their mad flight from the Six Servants, they would make mistakes, and their journey would end in hunger and dehydration amid the desert sands.

He could not afford to care, but only to trust Xan's recollection, that he knew where he was going. He could only trust someone in whom there was little reason to trust, someone who had been a warlock — the Dark One's thrall — a little more than a year ago.

Fortunato would try his best to put his old grievances and his distrust aside. For the sake of Xan, and the party, and the success of the mission, he would try to ignore the feeling of his heart, that Xan was leading them to doom.

To darkness, Fortunato feared, Xan was leading them, the same darkness that had consumed his soul. But for now, they rode.

The animals were slowing to a stop, and they had ridden through the night, and into the day. As twilight threatened to settle in, Fortunato knew the animals were not invincible, that they needed rest, even amid such danger.

~

The Dark One watched as his Six Servants tread through the desert on their six steeds. Amid the sand and dust, they had drawn their dark iron blades, now infused with the poison of *Serpentax*.

The Dark One saw that they were not alone.

A band of elves was standing in their way, a band of about a thousand, some garbed in chainmail, others with bows and with spears, all dressed for battle.

What piteous fools they were.

An elf wielding a greatsword charged at Gogg, and Gogg pierced him with his sword's jagged edge. The elf fell to the ground, dying.

Other elves shot bows at the six barguests, but the arrows were like pins on pincushions against their skin, only angering them and causing them to fight, more furiously than before.

A barguest bowled through the elven lines, slaying a dozen with each slashing of his teeth, until there was a trail of bodies through the desert, and the sand and dust had turned to dark crimson.

Elves wailed, and lightbearers began to fire beams of light, but the Dark One shielded his Six Servants from mortal magic.

Gogg stormed through the army, then, and Mephis served only as mount as Gogg slashed with his dark iron sword and cut down swathes with each stroke.

The elves began to break in a panic, but then the Dark One saw that the elves had not been as great of fools as they thought, that there had been a purpose to their madness.

Lines had been drawn in the sand, lines with gates, stretching into the interminable horizon.

The restraints that the gods had placed on the Six Servants would make the Dark One's final victory difficult.

But the Dark One's victory would be achieved.

He watched as the Six Servants hissed and howled, amid the scattered bodies now going to death and worse. They could not venture past the line in the sand, the arbitrary gates crafted from impressions in the dust.

A little delay, a small frustration.

But the Dark One knew his victory was at hand.

~

Fortunato was awake before dawn, and he could see the animals had recovered enough to continue their journey. Tyra Jade was no longer panting like a wolf in her death throes. Cobalt and Asté, tied to the branches of a bramble tree, seemed even eager to begin the journey anew, amid the bleak landscape of the Wastes of Shahr.

As light began to spread and the day was almost here, through the dusty landscape Fortunato saw something that caused a bottomless well of fear to form in his heart.

Giants were walking about the landscape, giants the height of the spires of St. Sigmund's Cathedral back in Galiope. They had ash-gray hides and eyes like coals. Some were holding tree branches in their hands. One was clutching a boulder.

Xan seemed to sense Fortunato's fear. "The Gray Giants are more afraid of us than we are of them," Xan said.

To say that about a bear or a lion always seemed preposterous to Fortunato, humans with their un-clawed limbs and slight forms. But to say it about the Gray Giants almost seemed irreverent.

Yet it was true that the Gray Giants weren't approaching the road, and seemed to avoid it.

"We must put as much distance between us and the Six Servants as possible," Fortunato said. "Let's get going. We ride all day and into the night."

~

"Faster," the Dark One urged his Six Servants, "faster," as they passed down the road through Potam.

The crater that was Qadirra appeared and Gogg wailed in terror at the sight. He stopped Mephis's frenzied sprint, caught up in bottomless fear at what had been done to the city he had loved.

But the Dark One seized control of his emotions and urged him to fight on, that vengeance could be had, for a small price, if they only could continue. He reminded Gogg that he possessed a blade of dark iron, infused with *Serpentax*'s poison, and then at last seized control of Gogg and forced him to turn, and to continue his journey.

The four warriors had done a great deal of damage to their cause. Some would call it catastrophic. But the Dark One knew his victory was sure.

On they rushed, having been forced like puppets on the Dark One's string, past the crater of what was Qadirra.

He sensed Telantines, the beings that the Dark One hated above all, watching the Six Servants' fleeing forms as they raced down the path, under the sun and the blue sky.

~

"Faster!" Fortunato coaxed Tyra, "faster!"

His black wolf was struggling to keep up with Cobalt and Asté's breakneck gallop, as the four of them passed swiftly through the Wastes of Shahr. As Xan had indicated, the Gray Giants did not give chase, nor did they hunt after them with their clubs formed of tree trunks or their giant boulders they used as missile weapons.

The road wound its way through the Wastes of Shahr, and each stride took them closer to their goal, and further away — Fortunato hoped — from the Six Servants of Seymus as the Six Servants of Seymus continued their mad pursuit.

~

"Who does my heart belong to?" Ambrass said in her gemstone prison.

It couldn't have been the one who had looked upon her enemy with eyes of lust.

Perhaps, it was the one with whom she almost had two children, though her womb had proven infertile, a barren soil to grow.

"Gaius," she said.

"Wrong," said the genie's voice. "You have two more guesses, Ambrass, and then you'll be trapped in the ruby forever…"

Chapter Fifty-Five: For the House of the Tannin

The bracelets had ceased working with the doom of Qadirra, and in the wake of the fiery explosion that had consumed the desert, the Imperial Bay Company had fled.

Julian was wearing a bracelet of dull gold, with a green gem that looked like a huckster's fake emerald, and hadn't bothered to take it off, as the gypsies in their wagons came to the crater's edge.

"What's that, down there?" Julian heard his brother Anton called out.

And Julian looked down, and saw that at the bottom of the crater, something red was glinting.

Julian had had enough of objects gleaming in the distance. He knew whatever it was wouldn't avail him now.

But Anton seemed desperate to uncover the meaning of what lay amid Qadirra's doom.

~

At the bottom of the massive crater that had leveled the city was a gold necklace that had been unspoiled by the flame, on the gold necklace, a red gem. Julian thought of burying it in the dirt, or else discarding it and forgetting about it, but for the fact that this object had survived, unscathed, an explosion that had destroyed everything in its path.

There were few ways to explain how it had occurred but for the fact that the necklace was special. Julian took the necklace and placed it about his neck. He felt no power fill him.

But he thought he would keep the necklace, just in case.

~

"Ambrass must be dead," Anton said, standing at the rim of the crater.

But Julian hadn't given up hope. He had a feeling she was still alive, that she had escaped Qadirra and its destruction. But what proof did he have of that?

It was anyone's guess, whether she was dead or alive. But the thought she was broke Julian's heart.

As he stood on the rim of the crater, surveying Qadirra's destruction, he saw dark figures approaching from the north, thousands of them in number.

The horses they rode were hairless, colored a greenish-white, with mad eyes. They themselves had sharp features — humans or something like them, but most with hues to their skin of varying greenness. Some of those who approached had ears that came to slight points, and some were possessed of eyes of yellow.

Their swords, though, were well made, and keen edged.

The chief of them was approaching the gypsies on their wagons. "Gypsies," he said, "little better than *lugals*. Do you rejoice at Qadirra's fall?"

"I don't," Julian replied, because he thought that was the answer the strange man wanted. "I think my cousin may have died in the fire."

"A fire, that is what you call it," the man said. "The Telantines' domination, and you call it a fire. The Telantines wish to put us to ruin, that we may never rebuild the House of Tannin, and you call it a fire.

"It is more than a fire. It is an outrage that must be answered. It must never happen again..."

Julian looked at the strange man with a face he was sure showed suspicion and distrust.

"You are strong and young," the man said. "You shall be put to good work. You shall till the fields of Potam, or else mine the quarries, under the supervision of Yukarib.

"Yukarib… that's me. You shall suffer under me, gypsies, and the rocks you cut will rebuild the House of Tannin in Ash-Land. Yes… you shall be put to good use…"

The gypsies were outnumbered, and more of the strange men were approaching from the horizon beyond the crater. There were countless thousands of them, and their swords were sharp, and their shields were forged of a shining metal.

Yet even Yukarib seemed to know that Qadirra was destroyed, that it would never be rebuilt.

~

The strange men led Julian through the stinging sand, and the ruby necklace Julian wore gave him some strange kind of hope. He felt a presence radiating from it, calming him down as he feared the worst would happen to their people.

They followed the strange men on their wagons, the gathered gypsies, until they had reached the far east of Potam, where there was a rocky ridge, and shelves of rock that indicated the beginnings of a quarry.

Yukarib said the stones they cut would be used to rebuild the House of the Tannin. What was that?

Chapter Fifty-Six: Doors in the Desert

The Dark One watched as the Six Servants of Seymus rattled over the bridge and entered the Wastes of Shahr. He would not accept failure and he made sure the Six Servants knew it, filling them with fear of what he would do to them if they did not cut down the three warriors, and kill the young man they protected.

Gogg howled as the Dark One filled him with anger and fear of failure, as sands were whipped up by the barguest's quick sprint against the dry dusty landscape, amid thorny trees and brambles, under a sun that was burning him — but the Dark One would not tolerate complaint.

The Dark One knew what rode on this, how important this was, in the wake of the launch of Heaven's Spear, and the devastation of Ash-Land that had happened an hour later. He knew what peril there seemed to be, but he remained certain of their final victory, if they could only kill the boy turned young man, the one who bore the sigil of Telantis — the nation the Dark One hated — about his neck.

The sight of the young man attired as a Telantine warrior, his neck tattooed with lightning marks, filled the Dark One with a fury he could not control. And he filled the Six Servants with that same fury, and as he did, Gogg howled and hissed as Mephis carried him away, speeding faster than any Elvish horse or black wolf could take them.

Fury at the fall of Qadirra, the devastation of Ash-Land, and now it would seem to the Telantines that their final victory was at hand. But it was not so. For the boy, turned young man, would be killed, and the Dark One would reign over Varda in the flesh.

There was a low dull roar. Amid the six darting forms there was movement, the form of one of the Gray Giants.

They feared humans, but the Dark One's minions they did not. No, the Dark One's minions they hated, and treated as abominations. The Gray Giants would not let the Six Servants of Seymus be.

It was just as well.

One threw a boulder and the boulder struck Tharogogg, Gogg's lieutenant. The hard rock crushed him but his flesh was not of a mortal kind. Tharogogg rose, and drew his dark iron knife, as his wounded barguest scrambled from under the crater.

Tharogogg fixed his eyes on the Gray Giant who had struck him. He rushed, and then he sprinted, and then he seemed to fly, so fast did his legs carry him. He struck the Gray Giant's knee and the Gray Giant howled with inestimable pain. Tharogogg struck his other knee and using the knife-wound as a vault, climbed and heaved himself up to the Gray Giant's chest, stabbing him in the heart and then making an incision on the Gray Giant's throat.

The Gray Giant gurgled as it slid into death.

A Gray Giant struck at Gogg with his tree-trunk club but Gogg and Mephis, acting as one unit, dove underneath the blow, low to the ground. Gogg on Mephis climbed up onto the Gray Giant's body, as Mephis sank its claws into the Gray Giant's body and vaulted upwards, before Gogg was able to pitch back his dark iron sword, and stab the Gray Giant in the chest.

Blood spurted as the Gray Giant emitted a low howl, as it sank toward the ground and then to its knees.

The Gray Giants who had gathered to fight saw what would happen if they resisted the Six Servants of Seymus.

They fled into the sands and dust of the Wastes of Shahr, disappearing amid the dust-blown trees and brambles and bushes.

The Six Servants, having recovered, sprinted ahead on their six beasts. They were making up lost time. Soon, they would be upon the four warriors, and all hope for humanity and elvenkind would be finished.

~

Fortunato raced on down the road, riding upon Tyra Jade, as Cobalt and Asté sometimes trotted and then galloped through the Wastes of Shahr.

Fortunato hadn't seen the Six Servants, but that only made Fortunato more afraid, for fear they were not far away, but closing in on them. It was impossible to know how close they were, but it was a fact that the Six Servants were in relentless pursuit, for their victory and the victory of their master was now at hand.

It was up to Fortunato, Reev, Wrinn and Xan to thwart them. It was up to Fortunato, Reev, Wrinn and Xan to tread Seymus underfoot. And though the mission had never been so hopeless, Fortunato would cling to confidence, the thought of the dying spark of light that remained.

But he knew that whatever happened to the four of them, the ruin of Qadirra, and of Seymus and all his children, was sure.

Pushing, then, down a twist of the road, he called out after Xan, "How much farther?"

"A port by the Sea of Coral," Xan was narrating his experiences, "a dhow to Bezakirah. Then, another desert road."

It seemed an inevitability that the Six Servants of Seymus would catch up to them.

~

The Dark One watched as Gogg sniffed the air, and the Dark One sensed that Gogg had perceived the scent of the one they sought.

They were now not far from the four warriors of light, and the Dark One's victory had never been more certain, though he had been unable to stop the destruction of Qadirrra.

Amid a dust-blown waste, between gnarled trees and brambles, they raced through a landscape now bereft of Gray Giants. The Gray Giants had fled in the wake of Gogg and Tharogogg's work, and feared what happened to their two brethren happening to them.

He gave a fire of urgency to the Six Servants of Seymus, and drove them forward like dogs on a leash. He would not accept any complaints about exhaustion, not when their victory was so close at hand.

Their victory — and the Dark One would rule in his dark land, on his dark throne.

But there was something up ahead, amid the waste.

Elves, standing amid the sand and dust.

The Dark One raged at the sight, more lines drawn in the sand, a gate fashioned from cloth that the Six Servants by the powers of the gods could not cross. The Six Servants hissed on their barguests and would do their best to evade, to find a point where the line ended, where they would continue the pursuit.

The hundred elves standing by with swords and shields would be unable to stop the Six Servants from reaching their prey. The Dark One's victory was at hand.

He had known it.

Now, he felt it.

~

They had been on the road for four days through the Wastes of Shahr. Tyra was panting, and Cobalt and Asté were struggling, no longer able to gallop or even manage a trot.

They were pushing through sand-blown wastes, when on the horizon there was a sea, and the walls of a city.

"The port," said Xan. "San-El-Shahr."

Yet Fortunato looked back, and saw the Six Servants of Seymus in the distance.

"Gallop! Run! With all due speed!" Fortunato howled.

He raced to the gate, and saw it was closed, but that guards had been posted on it, wrapped in white headwraps.

"My liege! Open the gate! We are in danger," Fortunato said.

"What trouble do you bring?" said one of the guards.

"Open the gate," Reev said with a commanding boom, and the guards scrambled, and moments later, the gates began to grind open.

Amid stinging dust and sand, as the Six Servants turned from inky blots on the horizon to recognizable shapes, Reev, Wrinn, Fortunato, and Xan fled through the gates of San-El-Shahr.

Beyond buildings of mudbrick and plaster was a reddish-brown sea, stretching into the horizon.

As the gates closed, Reev could see the Six Servants rapidly approaching.

"To the docks!" howled Ivan Xandrast. "A dhow to Bezakirah…"

~

The gates were shut, and the Dark One could hear Gogg uttering silent curses. He could feel the four warriors of light slipping away, but their mission — he knew, was doomed.

The Dark One watched as Gogg strode up to the gate, the chief of the six riders on the six barguests, and he watched as the men on the gatehouse looked upon them with mixed fear and horror.

"Let us pass," Gogg hissed, and his hissing voice carried over the whipping desert wind, and the ambient sounds of the town of San-El-Shahr.

But the men on the gatehouse were clearly afraid of the Six Servants of Seymus. They were terrified at the sight of them, at the hellish gleam in the eyes of the six barguests.

"Let us pass," Gogg hissed again, "or else we shall cut out your heart."

"The gate shall be closed," said one of the men on the gatehouse. "The sultan Saif does not like outsiders."

"You just let in four outsiders," hissed Gogg.

But the man, bewildered at the sight of him, trembled, and feared letting him by.

In the palace of San-El-Shahr, the Dark One sent one of his children, the sultan's chief advisor, to the throne. Stirring in him urgency, he gave his child the words to speak.

"My lord," the advisor said amid the spare throne room, the unornamented wooden throne. "Six men approach the gate. They wish to give you aid. Their dark visages belie a more beneficent cause. A *lugal* is in town, wishing to thwart you."

"*Lugal!*" the sultan cried, his body and giant belly spilling over the wooden throne.

The Dark One thought his gluttony made him a more willing pawn.

"Let them in!" the sultan said.

The gates opened, but the Dark One was furious about being thwarted, about being told no, even once. And so he filled his Six Servants with mad fury, and allowed them to take out his fury on the town of San-El-Shahr.

There was a storm of fury on the streets, as any building with open doors became the sight of a massacre. The man on the gatehouse who had refused him, Gogg beheaded and stuck his head a post of the gate. Tharogogg was the most bloodthirsty of all, and had crossed into the open doors of the palace. The Dark One had not refused his request, and he watched as Tharogogg beheaded the sultan and then pierced the heart of the Dark One's child with a dark iron blade.

The fury had consumed San-El-Shahr, the one who had dared to hint at refusing the Dark One's request.

The fury had consumed them, and the Dark One — but in it, they had forgotten the mission.

A dhow was now skipping in the wind, across shore.

~

On a dhow, on the back of the wind, Fortunato, Reev, Xan and Wrinn sped across the waters of the Sea of Coral. The waters that stretched into the interminable distance, forming a red backdrop to the blue sky, were swiftly bearing them to their next stop, the town of Bezakirah.

Then, another desert road.

Reev felt helpless at the situation, for he felt it was inevitable that the Six Servants of Seymus would catch up to them.

The port of San-El-Shahr was now a vanishing dot in the distance.

The Six Servants couldn't swim, could they?

~

Stunned by the delay and the swift way the four warriors of light had thwarted him, the Dark One ordered his Six Servants to ride their barguests through the Sea of Coral. They could not traverse as fast as a dhow, but the barguests could swim, and follow the dhow, and when it broached shore, quickly catch up with them.

Gogg dared to grumble, and the Dark One inflicted him with a lash of pain.

Gogg then swiftly rode his barguest up to the docks, which were now dripping with the blood of dead sailors and pocked with corpses.

The barguest whined, but took a step in, then two. With a splash, it entered the open ocean, and began to swim, paddling with its paws.

~

"How far to Bezakirah?" Reev said, eyeing the horizon where the port had once been.

"Two days, if we're lucky," Xan said.

Reev still did not know if the Six Servants of Seymus could swim. But he knew they would be hunted from now until they reached *Naron Da.*

But once the party was back on land, Reev had a feeling they couldn't get far.

And so he prayed under his breath that somehow they would be rescued, that somehow the Six Servants wouldn't be able to find them and end the hope of Telantis's birth.

~

A day of paddling, and the barguests were near to drowning. Dawn was rising over the reddish-brown waters of the Sea of Coral, and the barguests whined that, to the struggles of swimming, would be added the daylight that they hated.

The waves were waxing or waning, but generally waxing, as the Six Servants of Seymus on their six barguests paddled through the open ocean. A day in, and they were losing ground against the dhow, but certain of their final victory.

Then bubbles appeared in the water.

The Dark One cried out from his post on the Plain of Abollon as the bubbling continued, and the waters began to toss and dive underneath the blue sky and burning sun.

The Dark One felt a pang of something — what was this

emotion? — as the bubbling built to a roaring sound, and through the waters emerged a beak, and then a head.

A monster had emerged from the waters, the size of a city.

He knew what the elves called it, *Lormon Narsannad.*

No sooner had its massive head and its giant black eyes opened then its arms pierced the surface of the hot waters, one then ten, then a hundred, giant arms that could fell a ship with one stroke, all lined with suckers.

Gogg hissed, then bellowed. He struck an arm and severed it, and the *Lormon Narssanad* wailed.

An arm took Mittoth in the back of the head and almost sent him into the water, but Mittoth gripped the arm and pulled, then severed it with his jagged knife.

Gogg sped ahead through the water, riding on his barguest who threatened to drown, were it not for his body that could never drown, but was designed for Hell's airless climes.

Gogg's barguest, Mephis, struck with his teeth, sinking his razor-sharp fangs into one of the *Lormon Narssanad's* arms, before Gogg took up his sword, and severed three arms with one blow.

Tharogogg was piercing through the waters on his barguest, driving his barguest to exhaustion and madness, as the *Lormon Narssanad* fought with all his might, trying to prevent the Dark One's inevitable victory.

The *Lormon Narsannad* was a storm of wriggling tentacles, striking with arms and trying to pull the Six Servants of Seymus toward its beak.

But Gogg sensed this, and fought harder, slicing, three, four, five, tentacles with one stroke.

As Gogg did battle, Sokkoth drove forward on his steed, Sokkoth the terror of Abollon. As he rode, his barguest fumed and howled with a blood-curtling howl, as its paws paddled and drove him ever closer to the *Lormon Narsannad's* massive head.

The wriggling of his arms was now more than a storm, a

thousand battering blows each moment, a battering such as no *lugal* ship could ever endure. But the Six Servants of Seymus did not have the same kind of flesh as mortals, but a different kind, and the *Lormon Narssanad* would have to be possessed of greater powers than that, to end the Dark One's hopes.

Gogg was now getting closer, despite the storm of arms writhing in the middle of the sea. Under a burning sun, as the winds whipped the waves, the *Lormon Narsannad* opened its beak, and out poured a stream of ink that would liquify an entire city.

Gogg fell back, writhing in the ink, but Sokkoth made his move.

Sokkoth's barguest had paddled up to the *Lormon Narssanad*'s head. Sokkoth pitched back his dark iron knife and pierced the *Lormon* Narssanad's beak.

A roar that could end all hopes in a mortal that heard it echoed across the sea. But Sokkoth struck again and again.

The storm of arms was weakening, and now there were fewer of them to be seen.

Writhing in the midst of the Sea of Coral, the Dark One could see the *Lormon Narsannad* beginning to sink under the water's surface. Yet he dared not retreat, for the Dark One's victory was his loss.

Another blow, and another, from Sokkoth's knife, and the *Lormon Narssanad* was gushing blue blood.

The red sea around the *Lormon Narsannad* was quickly changing to purple, as Sokkoth's merciless blows continued pummeling him.

The storm of arms was slowing, and they were falling in much weaker strokes. Sokkoth pierced the *Lormon Narssanad* in the eye, and the beast began to sink under the waters, as the arms ended their motion, and eventually ceased.

The Six Servants of Seymsu had slain the *Lormon Narssanad,* but the Dark One would not gloat in his victory. He filled the Six Servants with fury and passion, and urged them to swim all the harder for shore.

~

Two days on the back of a swift wind, and the dhow was approaching shore. Reev's feeling of fear had not at all ceased. He thought there was little hope of victory. But he knew the prophecies, and what was promised. He would cling to that.

He turned his head to look back into the sea, and he felt he could sense the Dark One's minions behind them. They could swim, or else their beasts could… Reev was certain of it, now.

He drew Doomblade, and it helped to ease some of his fear.

His fear, though, followed him, as the dhow approached a pier, and Bezakirah was in the horizon.

~

In the red gem, Ambrass puzzled over the question that had been posed to her. Who did her heart belong to?

Through a veil of tears, she knew, and was certain, it was not the man who had looked upon her enemy with eyes of lust. So who could it be, if not Gaius?

She thought of all the loves who had passed her by. One she remembered, stunningly handsome, a complexion like winter snows and hair like the space between the stars. That one, the one she thought of, had a witty tongue that knew how to work magic. And their passionate love had consumed her.

"Who does my heart belong to?" Ambrass repeated the genie's question.

She tried to think of the name of the one she had pondered. After much straining, she recalled.

"Nocturne," Ambrass said.

"You are wrong," said a voice. "And you know you are wrong. You deny the truth of what is written on your heart.

"One final guess remains, Ambrass, or else you'll be trapped in the ruby forever."

Beyond the gemstone she could see the world beyond it, through a red veil. She was being worn by someone, but she didn't think it was Samira. No, she could see hands carrying a pick, cutting against a block of stone.

Chapter Fifty-Seven: Her Heart

The strange men, Julian had learned, called themselves "men of Ash-Land." And the gods they worshipped they called the Tannin. Julian as he struck with his pick at the stone of the quarry prayed silently that their god Kama would save him and his people, that somehow they would be rescued.

But the men of Ash-Land were well-armed, with sharp swords of tempered steel and fine breastplates that would not easily fall to Julian's recurve dagger, which had long been confiscated from him.

And so Julian thought he would work as they had demanded, on the brutal sun, hoping at all times, and at all hours, that the gypsies would be rescued.

Under the brutal sun, under brutal conditions, and fed a brutal diet of bread and water, it didn't seem entirely wise, and Julian wondered if he had failed his people, that they should have fought off the men of Ash-Land in a final charge.

The men of Ash-Land had a mind for profit, but the gypsies' wagons lay in view, untouched. Julian wondered if the men of Ash-Land would sell the wagons and then the gypsies would have no hope of leaving and finding Vharat.

As the journey had progressed, Julian wondered if Vharat was real. He wondered if there really was such a place, where wine was on the leaves of the tree like dew and honey was gained not from bees, but from strumming your finger on the tree's bark.

He wondered if there was another place, besides Vharat, that the gypsies belonged to, one where they would immediately feel welcome. Perhaps, there was such a place they had passed by on their journey, one where the hostility would melt away, and they would be welcomed.

But now, he supposed, swinging his pick in the quarry, all hope of that was long gone. Vharat, and another homeland, had vanished into the desert sun, as the gypsies labored under the men of Ash-Land, under the supervision of Yukarib.

They had cut ten blocks today, and hauled them onto carts. Yukarib said they would be transported by ox-cart and then by boat to the Ash-Land, wherever it was.

And whenever Julian looked at the blocks, he had an inexplicable sense that what he was doing was wrong, that the gods did not approve.

And yet he continued to cut with his pick, removing the stone from the limestone quarry.

The ruby necklace he wore somehow comforted him. A warmth radiated from it, and though he knew his cousin Ambrass was long gone, he could feel her presence even now.

~

Who did her heart belong to? Ambrass had only one more guess.

As she gazed out from her ruby prison, which she now realized her cousin Julian was wearing, she knew more was riding on this than just her.

Who did her heart belong to? Did she dare allow the truth to spill out, or would her heart cling to bitterness?

Who did her heart belong to?

She thought of bright eyes, and a smile that sent her heart racing. She thought of the battlements of Galiope under the moon, on a summer night.

Chapter Fifty-Eight: Hope and A Hero

Bezakirah, the City of Deep Waters

A signpost was outside the city gates.

"We must stock up on food," Fortunato said.

"We don't have any time," Xan howled.

"Will we starve, then, in the desert?" Fortunato said. "We must stock up on food… that's an order."

Xan was beside himself as they strode through the city gates, which were open, and as they pushed through, the faces in Bezakirah that were not covered in veils scowled at them openly, and seemed to look on Reev in his Telantine garb, with his loin cloth and his Telantine lightning mark tattoos, with an especially grave hate.

~

Some Bezakirans spat at them as they entered the market, as Fortunato dared to speak the Imperial tongue. But eventually they found someone selling road-bread, and Fortunato handed him two gold libra, enough to fill their entire pack.

"A *lugal* enters the City of Deep Waters, and is not ashamed!" howled a woman in a veil as she passed them by. "The City of Deep Waters where the House of Moezin has at long last triumphed. Praises be to their name…"

The four warriors of light did not disguise themselves amid the bazaar, as they ventured from the road-bread seller to the well, where they began to fill their waterskins to bursting, under the scorching desert sun.

Reev continued looking through the streets, beyond the hostile faces, for fear the Six Servants of Seymus would storm in on their barguests. Reev thought the Bezakirans would treat the Six Servants of Seymus on their six barguests better than four *lugals*. He was not willing, though, to put that to the test.

Their waterskins had been filled.

There seemed to be little hope.

"Come!" Fortunato said. "Let's go, and run with all due speed. For the dawn, my friends…"

"For the dawn!" the three shouted after him.

"And the treading of Seymus underfoot," Reev added.

They mounted their steeds, Fortunato Tyra, Wrinn and Xan Asté, and Reev Cobalt. As Bezakirans spat at them, and their angry faces threatened to spill into violence, and a riot, the four warriors of light galloped out of Bezakirah's north gate, through dry dust and scrub-land, and sand that was building to hillocks, and then to mounds.

~

With ample food and ample water, they followed Xan's lead. Under the burning sun they traveled, as the heat of the day built, and sand stung their eyes.

Under the scorching sun, they traveled from dawn until dusk, and well into the night, resting for only a few hours each day. The fifth day after they set out from Bezakirah, the animals were winded, and all members of the party were faced with exhaustion. There was a bridge crossing the waters of a river, as Xan took another turn, another turn down another road.

The hillocks of sand had turned to mounds, and as they pressed on, the mounds were turning to hills.

Hills, then, and still they traversed, as Reev feared a landscape that Cobalt could not hope to navigate.

As hills built to dunes, and dunes built to a sea of sand, stretching to the horizon, Reev could hear Xan's helpless cries began to escape his lips.

"This can't be," he said. "This can't be… It was here."

"It was where, Xan?" Fortunato snapped. "What was where?"

"There was a road," Xan said. "But the desert has claimed it. The desert has grown."

Reev cried out and dismounted from Cobalt. Xan followed, then Wrinn. When Fortunato hopped off Tyra Jade, they were all on foot.

"What do you mean, the desert has claimed it?" Fortunato said.

"When I was here ten years ago," Xan said, "there was a road — a path through the dunes. But the desert claimed the road. Now there is just sand — *sand!*"

He kicked at the ground in view of the towering dunes, the shifting mountains of sand that stretched into horizon, a yellow monster that threatened to end all their hopes. Under a burning sun, Reev prayed, as his amulet glistened, and he turned, and he saw they were not alone.

The Six Servants of Seymus were approaching in the distance on their barguests.

Reev turned and eyed the dunes, and knew that even without the threat of the Six Servants, the horses would not avail them in this new desert.

"*Cobalt! Asté! Ananda pan!*" he shouted.

He had told them to go home. And though they hesitated, and looked back wistfully, they seemed to know what Reev knew, that they had completed their life's work, and now it was time to rest.

With a prancing of hooves they fled northwest, beginning the long journey home to the Elf Land's pastures.

And the Six Servants were approaching. They had drawn their

dark iron blades.

Their dark iron blades had a different look to Reev, now. Instead of blackish-gray, they had a greenish hue.

Fortunato strode out to face them.

~

Fortunato thought there was no hope, but for what the prophecies said, that the Dark One would be trodden underfoot. Fortunato thought there was no hope, and perhaps his journey would end here, but he would fight until the end. He would give the fight against Seymus his all, as he had — all his life.

And so he drew Danenhir in view of the approaching six phantoms, mounted on hell-beasts. He allowed Danenhir to glisten in the scorching light of the desert.

And though the Six Servants had drawn their swords, they did not quickly cut them down. They were enjoying and savoring this moment, the moment of their final victory.

Fortunato would not bare his fear to them. He would face them boldly.

"Fortunato of Ríva," said Gogg.

Gogg's voice was like a winter wind in the Dragonteeth Mountains at midnight, one that threatened to grasp Fortunato with an icy hand, but for the hate that Fortunato felt in his heart.

"Your cause is ended," said Gogg.

"So it seems," Fortunato said.

The Six Servants of Seymus were surely smiling behind their iron masks.

Behind Fortunato, the three other warriors of light were paralyzed in fear, not least Reev.

"Whom shall I kill first?" Gogg said. "Perhaps, the Sage…"

But Fortunato moved protectively in Reev's direction. "I have another idea, Gogg," Fortunato said, "one I do not believe you will be able to resist. A deal of sorts."

"A deal?" The rising tone of Gogg's voice indicated his delight.

"A duel," Fortunato said, "to the death. If I win, you and your five associates perish from Varda, and relinquish all your powers within it. And if you win, you may have my soul."

Reev cried out behind him in pain, that such a wager had been made.

But Gogg was silent. He was not refusing. He said, "Not just your soul, but also the one that you love."

Fortunato despaired at the thought of dragging Ambrass into this. But he had dedicated his life to the defeat of Seymus. All he would risk, and all he would give, to deal to the Dark One his defeat.

"Very well, Fortunato of Ríva," Gogg said. "With our master as witness…"

"With the gods as witness," Fortunato corrected him. "Vow, by the gods, that you will uphold your end of the deal."

"By the gods," Gogg strained to say, and his hissing voice seemed weaker, "I vow…"

But he stepped off his barguest, and brandished his poison blade. He took a ghostly step toward Fortunato.

And Fortunato said, "I shall bear the garb of a demon-slayer."

He removed his shirt, then let his belt fall loose. His trousers dropped, and he was in his undergarment. Then, he tore off his undergarment, and he was in the nude.

The Eloesian actors, if they knew, would be proud.

~

The Dark One fumed silently at Gogg's calculation.

How badly did he lust for a Telantine's soul.

So great was Gogg's desire, the Dark One had decided not to

quell it.

But a mortal man could not defeat a Servant of Seymus.

Fortunato had made a massive miscalculation, and now the Dark One's victory would be even sweeter.

~

Reev watched Gogg took a step toward Fortunato, and as Fortunato took a pace back.

Gogg struck with his sword, and his blade pierced the tip of Fortunato's shoulder.

Fortunato did not cry out in pain, but stepped backward, then twirled as Gogg drew near.

Danenhir met dark iron blade, and Gogg's sword nearly shattered it.

Fortunato, his body bare to the sun, appeared as a hero of Imperial legend, clothed only in what the gods had given him.

Gogg slashed with his blade and Fortunato dove under. He pierced and Fortunato dodged, just barely in the nick of time. He slashed with his blade and Fortunato was nearly beheaded, when Fortunato stabbed with Danenhir, and the blade pierced the edge of Gogg's cloak, and there was a hiss, a fuming of ghostly vapor.

As Reev uttered silent prayers, the battle continued, phantom against mortal man. Gogg pilloried him with a frenzy of blows, and slashed Fortunato across the chest, opening a wound from his shoulder to his groin. The wound did not bleed, but seemed to blacken and burn as soon as the wound was made. And Fortunato seemed to have been weakened, his slashes and stabs less vigorous than before.

Wrinn, Xan, and Reev were spectators as Fortunato tried to regain his strength, as he slashed and then he stabbed, mostly swiping the air with Gogg's perfect dodges, but occasionally cutting bits of Gogg's cloak or cutting his ghostly body, which resulted in a hissing of air, and the turning of ectoplasm to vapor.

And as Reev turned to the five phantoms looking on, he couldn't help but feel that they were watching in fear, now, and not in delight, that though Fortunato had received poison wounds and was sure to die, that they were worried, now, in a way they had not been before.

Gogg pierced Fortunato with his poison blade in the thigh, and Fortunato cried out and fell a step back.

"Your love shall not like her new home in Abollon," Gogg hissed.

Fortunato barely managed to bat away Gogg's sudden strike.

And Reev called out to him, "Fortunato, the birth of Telantis is in your hands…"

Fortunato seemed to swallow his pain, and despite his agony, he gained control. When he eyed Gogg, he was looking at the chief of the Six Servants in a new way, not with pain or fear, but only pure anger and resolve.

A burst of blows from Fortunato was met by a storm of parries by Gogg, and Gogg stabbed Fortunato again, this time in the foot.

Fortunato's body, bare to the sun, was now pocked with wounds in every place, wounds that would surely kill him. Fortunato was beginning to stagger in the sun.

"Fortunato," Reev said, "remember your blood…"

Fortunato gazed into Gogg's eyes, and the anger in his visage was like nothing Reev had seen in anyone or anything.

Not a burst of blows did Fortunato deliver, but a storm of the apocalypse, and Gogg at last was pierced straight through.

Gogg hissed as air escaped his body, and ectoplasm burst from his black robe. He seemed to shrivel and buckle in the sunlight, and then at last fell to his knees.

Fortunato pitched back Danenhir, and pierced Gogg straight through the face, straight through his iron mask.

~

The Dark One screamed as the impossible happened, as a blow from a mortal weapon slew his greatest servant.

The Plains of Abollon echoed with his scream of despair, and the cries of the damned joined him in agony.

He screamed as Gogg's body dissipated into the light of the sun.

He screamed, and for the first time in his existence, he thought defeat was possible.

~

Gogg's body had turned to ectoplasm and water, and a black cloak now lay inert on the sand, beside an iron mask.

Fortunato then staggered, then fell to his knees. He was close to death.

The five remaining Servants of Seymus drew their knives and daggers, as if to kill Fortunato.

But Gogg had made a vow.

"You gave me your word!" Fortunato shouted.

And something in the air changed, and the Six Servants looked about.

"You gave me your word!" Fortunato shouted. "You will perish from Varda, and your powers will be relinquished. These wounds you dealt me will be relinquished! You gave me your word!"

One of the five Servants' body seemed to bend, like a limb crammed through a narrow space.

"You gave me your word!" Fortunato shouted.

And there was a hissing sound, and a pop, as one of the five Servants' masks fell to the ground, now twisted and contorted.

"You gave me your word!" Fortunato shouted, as the burn-marks of Gogg's wounds lost their green color, and turned to mere scars.

All then was pandemonium, masks popping and twisting as they hitting the ground, ghostly bodies turning to pools of ectoplasm and liquid in the sand.

"You gave me your word," Fortunato said, once more, but now the Six Servants of Seymus were defeated. They were gone.

Reev turned to Fortunato, and was tempted to look upon him reverently.

But worship was for the gods.

Xan, though, had a darkness in his eyes as he surveyed the pools of ectoplasm, the twisted iron masks that had contorted unto death, the poison blades that would never be used again against mortalkind.

"He survived a dark iron wound," Xan said. "He slew the Six Servants of Seymus, which no mortal man can do. Fortunato — it is he. He is the Dark One's Hand!"

Fortunato, naked in the desert sun, looked at Xan with an expression of bottomless disgust. "I save the party," he said, "I rescue the mission from ruin. And this is the thanks I get."

Reev would not argue with that.

"I have done my part," Fortunato said, "and this is how you thank me. Find your own way to *Naron Da*, then…"

He staggered off, into the dunes, and Tyra Jade's dark form followed him.

And whereas Reev had looked upon Fortunato with something that bordered on reverence, he eyed Xan with bottomless contempt.

"I have rescued you from the Dark One's Hand," Xan said. "And now, I will show you the way."

"You will do no such thing," Reev said. "You will depart from us at once, you thrall of Seymus."

And Xan seemed to give no disagreement, and he staggered off into the distance.

Reev and Wrinn were alone.

They would find a way, somehow. But they did not know the way.

And so Reev eyed the towering dunes of sand, and walked into the desert, into what could be his death. He could hear Wrinn's trudging feet, a step behind.

~

"Who does your heart belong to?" said the genie in the ruby.

And Ambrass knew it in her heart, the answer she would not hide. She knew his face, the smile that sent her heart racing.

"Fortunato of Ríva," Ambrass said.

And cracks appeared in the red ruby horizon, the gem prison breaking open.

"You are free," the genie said, "but you will be rewarded for your trouble. You will be granted one wish, in accordance with what is possible for genie-kind."

"Take I, and my people, where we belong," Ambrass said, thinking of Vharat, and its wine on the leaves of trees like dew, and its honey flowing down the trees' sap.

There was a shattering sound as the ruby prison burst.

Ambrass opened her eyes, and did not see trees. She was in a room with wooden floors and plaster walls, a room that was homey — and immediately familiar.

She saw the bed she used to sleep in.

It was terribly cold, the dead of winter.

She heard a voice — "Ambrass? Is that you?"

It was the voice of Glenda, the innkeeper.

She was at the Dragonpaw Inn.

She was in Galiope.

~

There was no hope, Reev thought, as he staggered through the desert sands, under the burning sun, under the clear blue sky. He was starved for water, and hungry, and as soon as he reached the top of a dune, there were thousands more stretching into the distance.

A sea of dunes, stretching into the horizon, and there was no water, just the sound of Wrinn struggling to breathe.

As he began to ascend a dune, he strained to breathe, having lost all hope of reaching *Naron Da*. He realized that he and Wrinn would die here in this desert, for lack of water, for lack of hope.

He strode through the sand, having lost hope. No hope there was — he felt it. He sensed it.

"There is no hope," he said, as the heat and lack of water, the scorching sun and the sand burning his feet, at last caused him to faint.

~

He felt himself stir awake, under the burning sun. He looked up and saw he was not alone.

He saw feet, and a gold robe, an elven woman fair and beautiful, with hair of burnt gold and fiery green eyes.

It was the Lady of Danyen in her fair guise, the guise she wanted mortals to see.

"Hope abounds for the Telantines," she said, "and you will crush Seymus under your feet."

THE END

Continued in Book Eight, *Order From Chaos*...

Glossary

Times and Dates

Vardic Calendar	Julian Calendar Equivalent
Albos	January
Kaldsil	February
Primrane	March
Tidusca	April
Brenua	May
Aurelios	June
Odens	July
Sextil	August
Harona	September
Brightleaf	October
Anthanos	November
Candlebright	December

Currency

Aesa: A copper coin, worth an eighth of a denara.

Denara: A silver coin, worth about a day's wages for a typical laborer.

Libra: A gold coin, worth twenty-five denara.

Talent: A unit of measurement in gold, worth eighty-four hundred denara.

Southron phrases

Lugal: An Imperial, or more broadly a northerner. A loan-word from Naamer.

Namsita: From the Naamer, "Hello" or "Well wishes."

Hul: An anguiped. A loan-word from Naamer.

Shakrathite phrases
Adwanim: "Sacrilege."

Elven phrases
Cobalt! Asté! Ananda pan!: "Cobalt! Asté! (You all) go home!"

Ab: A magic bracelet with power over water. It has a blue gem.

Abrah: A magic bracelet with power over cloud and storm. It has a yellow gem.

Aegis shrine: A shrine used to extend and continue ancient Qadirran witchcraft to hinder the power of the Telantines.

Aegis Shrine of Borean Hindrance: A shrine used to extend Qadirran witchcraft over the land of Potam, against the power of the Telantines of Borea.

Aegis Shrine of Hyperborean Hindrance: A shrine used to extend Qadirran witchcraft over the city of Qadirra, against the power of the Telantines of Hyperborea.

Anguiped: A hostile non-human species native to a region called Ash-Land. They can, however, interbreed with humans.

Athra: The Fharese god of fire. Magi, who are sorcerers of fire magic, are his priests.

Arstibara: A genie sheikh of ancient days. He crafted seven magic bracelets purposed for Qadirra's destruction.

Arah: A month in the lunisolar Qadirran calendar, corresponding to Candlebright or Albos.

Azar: A magic bracelet with power over fire. It has a red gem.

Baradon: A forgotten city of ancient history, located northeast of the Desert of Hamma.

Caliga: An Imperial military boot with metal studs on the soles.

Cataphract: A warrior of Fharas, cloaked head to toe in armor. Their horses are also fully enclosed in armor.

Cathay: A kingdom of the far east, ruled by a man called the

Dragon Emperor.

Cathayan: A native of Cathay.

Consulary Armies of the Imperial Bay Company, the: The armies of the Imperial Bay Company, a powerful consortium of merchants, operating with the consent of the Imperial Council.

Consulary legate: The equivalent of the leader of a legion in the armies of the Imperial Bay Company.

Consulary soldier: A member of the army of the Imperial Bay Company.

Engineer: A creator of non-magical wonders.

Eloesian: A native of Eloesus.

Eloesus: The easternmost province of the Empire, famed for its rich history, philosophy and former power. It was once a disunited region of warring city-states.

Enzu: The Qadirran god of the moon, depicted as a humanoid with the head of a jackal.

Fharese: A native of the vanished kingdom of Fharas.

Fharas: An ancient kingdom which once reigned over the Southern World.

Galiope: A large city of the Northern World, called by those that love it the Queen of the North.

Gallia: A region east of Zarubain and west of Kardir, a place of mixed forest and farmland. Its greatest city is Galiope.

Genie: A magical spirit, normally invisible to mortals. Those who trap them can turn them into servants.

Great Fharas: A revanchist state in Potam, with its capital in the rebuilt ruins of Qadirra.

Haroon spice: An illegal drug, banned in the Empire. It causes euphoria but its side effects include weight loss and crimson-colored eyes.

Imperial Bay Company: A powerful consortium of merchants controlling much of trade throughout the Empire.

Ink-of-Tyrrhenos: A black liquid made from the ink of a squid of the Imperial Sea, used in cosmetics.

Kama: The god of the gypsies.

Kobolds: Half-elf, half-rokahn creations of the Dark One's lieutenant, Lothan.

Kukri-knife: A kind of short-sword, a slashing weapon common to the Pashupat Plateau.

Legate: The commander of an Imperial legion.

Mah: A magic bracelet with powers over the moon. It has a black gem.

Magus: A member of the Order of Magi.

Magi: A group of magically gifted priests, once widespread throughout the Southern World, with powers over fire. Their attire was purple robes and white turbans.

Mainyu: A magic bracelet with powers over mind. It has a purple gem.

Mountain guide: One of a tribe of mountaineers and mountain-dwelling folk in the south of the Sky Mountains, in the Pashupat Plateau.

Naamer: An ancient people who once lived in what is now the Desert of Hamma. They left behind many ruins in the midst of the desert which tomb raiders seek after.

Pashupat: A native of the Pashupat plateau.

Pashupat Plateau: A high plateau south of the Sky Mountains, abutting the desert.

Potam: A region between the Black Khazan and the Blue Khazan in the Southern World.

Qadirra: A city originally founded by the Naamer as Kadingirki, located in the hot plain of Potam. Abandoned ruins as recently as ten years ago, the descendant of the Fharese king retreated here and rebuilt it. Deposits of liquid tar surround Qadirra.

Recurve dagger: A sharp dagger common to the Southern World.

Rock Hills: A region south of Khazidea, bordering the High Plain.

Rokahn: Humanoid creatures known to dwell in the Dragonteeth, considered creatures of shadow. When their population swells, they will often raid the lowlands for food. Breeds include kehrad, toltar, and the standard species simply known as rokahn.

Satar: A magic bracelet with powers over the stars. It has a white gem.

Scimitar: A curved slashing sword of Fharese origins, common to the Southern World.

Serpentax: The Dark One's sword.

Seshán: Once an ancient city in the Southern World. Now ruins, it is a tourist trap that draws Imperial visitors.

Seven Bracelets of Arstibara: Magic bracelets fashioned by the genie sheik Arstibara, purposed for Qadirra's destruction.

Shahan: A small city in the west of the Southern World.

Shush: A large province of the Southern World, dominated by rainforest and mountains.

Southron: A native of the Southern World.

Southern World: A vast region south of the Empire. It has wildly varying geographical features but is generally hot. Most of the Southern World is arid, but steaming rainforests cover other sections.

Tamtum: A Qadirran god of chaos, portrayed as a dragon.

Thénai: A large city in the east of the Empire.

Shem-El-Shah: The chief town of the Zahrim Basin.

Udara: A group of warring cities in the center of the Southern World.

Utuk: A Qadirran god of creation, portrayed as a bearded man.

Women's apartments: A wing of a southron palace where women live.

Zam: A magic bracelet with powers over earth. It has a brown gem.

Zahrim Basin: An arid basin in the south of the Southern World.

Zarubain: A large kingdom of the north, west of Galiope. Its legal ruler is the king of Zarubain, who dwells in the capital city of Zarubad; outlying regions are governed by dukes (duchies), counts (counties) and barons (baronies).

APPENDIX 7: THE BRACELETS OF ARSTIBARA

The genie sheikh Arstibara fashioned seven bracelets to wage war on the wicked men of Qadirra. Ancient Qadirran witchcraft disallows their use between the Black Khazan and the Blue Khazan Rivers, i.e. the borders of Potam or modern Great Fharas. They work within about a hundred mile radius of Great Fharas, their power weakening with distance. Their purpose is to destroy Qadirra permanently.

1. *Mainyu:* This bracelet gives its wielder power over mind. The sheikh bracelet, it has no opposition.
2. *Ab:* This bracelet gives its wielder power over water. It can produce waterspouts, flooding, and the feared carnivorous waves. It is opposed to Azar.
3. *Mah:* This bracelet gives its wielder powers of lunar magic. It gives the powers of lunar light and lunar gravity. It is opposed to Satar.
4. *Azar:* This bracelet gives its wielder power over fire. It can produce columns and balls of fire. It is opposed to Ab.
5. *Zam:* This bracelet gives its wielder power over earth. It can produce earthquakes. It is opposed to Abrah.
6. *Satar:* This bracelet gives its wielder powers of star-magic. It can produce meteors and dazzling starlight. It is opposed to Mah.
7. *Abrah:* This bracelet gives its wielder powers of cloud and storm. It can create rain and lightning. It is opposed to Zam.

About the Author

Cursed at birth with a wild imagination, Andrew Cooper spent his youth dreaming of worlds more exciting than Earth.

He is a graduate of the Odyssey Writing Workshop. His stories have appeared in Morpheus Tales, Fear and Trembling, Residential Aliens and Mindflights, among others.

He is also a graduate of the Creative Writing program at Western Michigan University.

Visit **www.aj-cooper.com** to sign up for the newsletter and stay up-to-date on new releases.

Find him on **x/Twitter** @ajcooperwriter.